60

FARRAR
STRAUS
GIROUX

After This

Alice McDermott

After This

Farrar, Straus and Giroux
New York

·

Farrar, Straus and Giroux
19 Union Square West, New York 10003

Copyright © 2006 by Alice McDermott
Printed in the United States of America

ISBN-13: 978-0-7394-8133-2

Designed by Abby Kagan

For Mildred

After This

I

LEAVING THE CHURCH, she felt the wind rise, felt the pinprick of pebble and grit against her stockings and her cheeks—the slivered shards of mad sunlight in her eyes. She paused, still on the granite steps, touched the brim of her hat and the flying hem of her skirt—felt the wind rush up her cuffs and rattle her sleeves.

And all before her, the lunch-hour crowd bent under the April sun and into the bitter April wind, jackets flapping and eyes squinting, or else skirts pressed to the backs of legs and jacket hems pressed to bottoms. And trailing them, outrunning them, skittering along the gutter and the sidewalk and the low gray steps of the church, banging into ankles and knees and one another, scraps of paper, newspapers, candy wrappers, what else?—office memos? shopping lists? The paper detritus that she had somewhere read, or had heard it said, trails armies, or was it (she had seen a photograph) the scraps of letters and wrappers and snapshots that blow across battlefields after all but the dead have fled?

She squinted against the sunlight on taxi hoods and bus windows, heard the rushing now of air and of taxis, wheezing buses, and underneath it all something banging—a loosened street sign, a trapped can, a distant hammer—rhythmic and methodical. The march of time.

And then George approaching, his hand stuck to his hat and the hat bent into the onslaught. She went down the steps just in front of him, drawn more by forward momentum than by any desire to meet up with, or to avoid, her brother's latest best pal.

The cold wind made it difficult to breathe, as if it could snatch your next breath before you had time to swallow it, and she bent her head, too, hand to her hat, submerged in wind and beginning to imagine herself slowly losing ground with each step forward, slowly beginning to stall, and then to sail backward—a quick scramble to regain ground and then another sailing backward. In church she had prayed for contentment. She was thirty, with no husband in sight. A good job, an aging father, a bachelor brother, a few nice friends. At least, she had asked—so humbly, so earnestly, so seriously—let me be content.

And now a slapstick windstorm fit for Harold Lloyd or Buster Keaton.

It was either God's reply or just April again, in the wind tunnel that was midtown Manhattan. The scent of it, the Easter scent of April in the city, all around her, in the cold air itself as well as on the shoulders of the crowd; the smell of sunlight and dirt, something warming at the heart of it all.

And then she felt his hand on her shoulder and he shouted, "Mary Rose," which bound him forever to her brother and her father and her life at home since nowhere else did she tolerate the double name. His head was still lowered, his hand still on his hat—he might have been waiting for the right opportunity to doff it—and he peered around at her from under its brim as if from under the rock of another life.

And she, her hand on the back of her own hat, did the same.

"Hello, George," she said. She could feel the crunch of city grit between her back teeth.

"Some wind," he said. He had one eye closed against it, the other was watery.

"You're telling me," she said.

They walked together to the corner and as they stepped off the curb, he suddenly reached up and took her raised elbow—the one that led to the hand she held against her hat—and kept it between his fingers as they crossed. She thought he must look like a man attached to a subway strap. At the next corner, he did the same; a gesture that was either brotherly or proprietary, but awkward either way, as if one of them were blind or doddering, or as if both were involved in some odd, raised-elbow folk dance. At Forty-sixth, the light was against them and the wind paused enough for her to take her hand off her hat while they waited with the crowd.

She turned to him—was he going to speak? His eyes were teary from the wind, red-rimmed and bloodshot. His nose was running and there were tears on his windblown cheeks. She clicked open the purse that hung on her arm and found her handkerchief, but he refused it, reaching into his overcoat for his own. He mopped his face and blew his nose before the crowd got them moving again and as they got to the curb, she placed her left hand on her hat so he could reach her elbow at a more convenient angle—which he did, guiding her across the street as if she were a novice pedestrian, and this time, perhaps, putting a little more pressure behind the fingertips that held her.

"Where are you headed, George?" she asked him. He shouted something unintelligible into the wind.

"Have you eaten yet?" she asked, because it was only polite. And then the wind paused completely, as it will in April, a sudden silence and maybe even the hint of warmth from the sun, so that he replied with odd gentleness, "Yeah, I had my lunch."

They were at the door of the restaurant. The wind was picking up again. "Would you like some coffee?" she asked.

He shook his head and she could not deny her own relief. "I'm out of time," he said. And then added, "What about dinner?"

"Lamb chops," she told him. "You coming over?" Anticipating already a stop at the butcher's to pick up two or three more.

He shook his head. There was another tear streaming down his windblown cheek and as he replied she lifted the handkerchief in her hand and wiped it away, feeling the not unpleasant pull of his beard against the thin cotton.

He said, "I mean, what about us having dinner?"

The wind puffed up again and they both put their hands to their hats. "Where?" she said, rudely, she realized later. But it was like having a passing stranger suddenly turn to sing you an aria. Anyone would have a second or two of not quite knowing what was really going on.

"Out," he told her. He was a broad-faced man who looked good in hats. Who looked better now than he did at home, where he had been thus far only the unremarkable source of her brother Jimmy's unpredictable enthusiasms. "At a restaurant," he said. And then to make himself clearer, "The two of us."

"Tonight?" she said, and then they both turned away for a moment from the peppered wind. When they turned back, he said, "Why not?" but without conviction, confirming for them both that this was a sudden impulse that most likely would not last out the afternoon. "What if I come by at seven?" he said.

She paused, squinting, not for the chance to see him better but for him to see her. "I'll have to cook those lamb chops anyway," she said. "Or else Jimmy and my father will be gnawing the table legs by the time I get home."

He smiled a little, unable to disguise what she was sure was a bit of confusion about his own impulse. He said again, "I'll come by at seven," and then turned back into the wind.

She pushed open the door to the restaurant. More lunchtime bustle, mostly women in hats with their coats thrown over the backs of chairs, the satiny linings and the fur collars and cuffs, the perfume and the elegant curves of the women's backs as they leaned forward across the small tables, all giving the hint of a boudoir to the busy place. She found a seat at the counter, wiggled her way into it. Saw the man beside her who was finishing a cigarette give her a quick up and down from over his shoulder and then turn back to flick an ash onto the remains of his sandwich. She imagined returning his dismissive stare, and then maybe even letting her eyes linger distastefully on the crust of bread and the bitten dill pickle and the cigarette debris on his plate. She could slide the ashtray that was right there between them a little closer to his elbow—hint, hint. Emboldened, perhaps—was she?—by the fact that she'd just been asked out on a date.

She ordered a sandwich from the waitress, whose pretty youth was still evident in the doughy folds of her weary and aging face, and a cup of tea. And then she held her hands over the steaming water for a few seconds. Thin hands, long fingers, with a kind of transparency to the chapped skin. Her mother's gold ring, inset with a silver Miraculous Medal, on her right hand. The man beside her rubbed his cigarette into the plate, then stood, swinging away from her on the stool and causing a slight ripple through the customers all along the other side of him. He took his overcoat from the hat rack and put it on standing just behind her, and then leaned across his empty stool, brushing her arm, to leave a few coins under his plate.

"Overcoats in April," he said. "Some crazy weather."

She turned to him, out of politeness, the habit of it. "I've never seen such wind," she said.

He was handsome enough—dark eyes and a nice chin, though his hair was thinning. He wore a dark overcoat and a dark suit, a white shirt and a tie, and there was the worn shine of a brass belt buckle as he reached for his wallet. "Reminds me of some days we had overseas," he said, taking a bill from his billfold.

She frowned, reflexively. "Where were you?"

He shook his head, smiled at her. Something in his manner seemed to indicate that they knew each other, that they'd had such conversations before. "In another life," he said and snapped the bill and slapped the wallet and returned it to his pocket with a wink that said, But all that's behind us now, isn't it? He was thin and his stomach was taut and his starched white shirt was smooth against his chest and belly. The brass belt buckle, marked with decorative lines, a circled initial at its center, was worn to a warm gold. "Once more into the breach," he said, turning up his collar. "Wish me luck."

For an odd second, she thought he might lean down and kiss her cheek.

"Good luck," she said. Over her shoulder, she watched him walk away. A slight limp, a favoring, perhaps, of his left leg. A flaw that would, she knew, diminish him in some women's eyes. Even if he'd been wounded in the war, there would be, she knew, for some women, the diminished appeal of a man who had suffered something over which he'd had no control. Who had suffered disappointment.

She turned back to her sandwich. And here, of all things, was desire again. (She could have put the palm of her hand to the front of his white shirt.) Here was her chicken sandwich and her tea and the waitress with a hard life in her eyes and a pretty face disappearing into pale flesh asking if there's anything else for now, dear. Here was the boudoir air of respectable Schrafft's with its marble counters and pretty lamps and lunchtime bustle (ten minutes until she should be back at her desk), perfume and smoke, with the war over and another life begun and mad April whipping through the streets again. And here she was at thirty, just out of church (a candle lit every lunch hour, still, although the war was over), and yearning now with every inch of herself to put her hand to the worn buckle at a stranger's waist, a palm to his smooth belly. A man she'd never see again. Good luck.

She sipped her tea. Once, ten years ago, at a Sunday-afternoon party in some apartment that she remembered now as being labyrinthine, although it probably had only four bedrooms, as opposed to the place she shared with her brother and her father that had two, Mike Shea had seized her by the wrist and pulled her into a dim room and plastered his mouth against hers before she could catch her breath. She had known him since high school, he was part of the crowd she went with then, and he had kissed her once or twice before—she remembered specifically the train station at Fishkill, on a snowy night when they were all coming back from a sledding party—but this was passionate and desperate, he was very drunk, and rough enough to make her push him off if he had not, in the first moment she had come up for air, gently taken off his glasses and placed them on a doilied dresser beside them, and then, in what seemed the same movement, reached behind her to lock the door. It was the odd, drunken gentleness of it, not to mention the snapping hint of danger from the lock, that changed her mind. And after two or three rebukes when he tried to get at the buttons that ran up the back of her dress, she thought, Why not, and although her acquiescence seemed to slow him down a bit, as if he was uncertain of the next step, she was enjoying herself enough by then to undo the last button without prompting and then to pull her bare shoulder and arm up out of the dress—first one then the other—and to pull dress and slip (she didn't wear a bra, no need) down to her waist in a single gesture. And then—was it just the pleasure of the material against her bare flesh, his shirt front, her wool?—she slowly pushed dress and slip and garter belt and stockings down over her narrow hips until they fell to her feet. And then she stepped out of her shoes. ("Even the shoes?" the priest had whispered in the confessional the following Saturday, as if it was more than he could bear, or imagine—as if, she thought later, he was ready to send her to perdition or ask her for a date.)

The banging at the door was his excuse to turn away—some people had their coats in there—and while he stood with his back to her she dressed again and unlocked the door and walked out. She smiled at the taunts and jeers of her friends and when someone asked, "Where's Mike?" she said, "I think I killed him," which got a great laugh.

Mike Shea became a medic during the war and was now married, working for Pfizer. To this day he can't look at her straight. To this day she can't quite convince herself that the sin was as grave as it seemed. (She thought, in fact, of telling the priest as he whispered his furious admonitions that she weighed barely a hundred pounds and was as thin as a boy and if he would adjust his imagination accordingly and see the buds of her breasts and her flat stomach and the bony points of her hips, he would understand that even buck naked, her body was not made for mortal sin.)

She can't quite convince herself, these ten years later, that anything at all like it will happen to her again.

She finished her sandwich, gave an extra quarter to the waitress, who also wore no wedding band, and headed back into the breach.

IN THE LOBBY of her building, people fresh out of the wind were huffing and puffing like swimmers just crawled up on shore. She rode the elevator with a group of them and then ducked into the ladies' room before she headed for her desk, ten minutes over her hour.

Pauline was there already, at the desk just across the aisle, facing her typewriter but with her hands in her lap and her shoulders slumped under the good wool of her handmade dress, her big, freshly powdered face watchful and, no doubt, full of news. "Nice lunch?" Pauline asked, batting her eyes at the clock and flicking her tongue over her teeth, as if to indicate she had finished her own some time ago.

"Nice," Mary said and bowed her head. She felt some guilt: she had not, this lunch hour, invited Pauline along.

She uncovered her own typewriter, feeling Pauline's eyes on her. Although their desks both faced the front of the room, their typewriters were off to the side so that Pauline's eyes on her—on her back when she turned to type, on her profile when she turned to her desk—had become by now a condition of her employment.

"I didn't see you leave," Pauline said. "I just got a sandwich and brought it back here."

"Sorry," Mary said. "I had some errands to run."

Pauline eyed her. It would be Pauline's way to say, No you didn't. It would be Pauline's way to refuse the decorum of the fib, to embrace the painful honesty. It would be her way to say, You just didn't feel like having lunch with me. Which would have been true, of course. And no less embarrassing, regrettable, awkward, no less vigorously denied, because it was true.

But Pauline had another conversation to pursue. She lifted her hands and put them over the top of her typewriter, she scooted her chair as close as it could get, a familiar routine, so that her breasts were pressed against the keys. She mouthed something, a name— Mr. Someone-or-Other—and rolled her eyes and cocked her head toward the front of the room. "Adele," she mouthed. Mary looked up, she couldn't help it, toward the desk where Adele sat, her back to them, her dirty blond hair draped perfectly over her lovely shoulders. "Rita," another girl from the office, "saw them both," Pauline whispered. "At lunch." She paused, her eyes joyous, her lips pursed, her cheeks drawn in, as if the piece of news were butter-scotch in her mouth. "Adele was crying," she added, only mouthing the words, or only speaking them with a breathless wheeze in place of where the words might have been. "Crying." She pantomimed, dragging her own manicured finger down her cheek.

Pauline had a large face, a strong jaw, and blue eyes forever darting, gesturing, scanning the room, scanning the faces and the backs of passersby—salesmen, bosses, other girls from the secre-tarial pool—taking everything in with one set of eyes, avid and hungry, and then turning another set, triumphant, well satisfied, to Mary, leaning over her typewriter to report what she'd seen, a bit of gossip, a bit of outrage, a bit of indecorous truth (did you see the shine on his coat, the bad toupee, the yellowed tooth, the pimple, the belly she's getting?), all of it the same to Pauline, all delightful to savor, all evidence to be used. Evidence of what, Mary some-times wondered—of the decadence and the decay, the homeliness, the paucity of good intentions that plagued the world? Evidence that no one else's life, despite whatever false appearances, was any better than her own.

"I knew something was going on there," Pauline said returning to her stage whisper. And then, louder still, "Something rotten in Denmark," just as another girl from the pool walked between them, turning attentively to the sound of Pauline's voice. Pauline raised her eyes to her. "Oh yes, rotten indeed," she said and gave the girl a "tell you later" smile.

Mary lifted her own steno book. Only about six pages old, it still had its cool, slim heft and straight cardboard covers. By the end of the month, its pages would be bloated with the pencil strokes of her shorthand, its back would be cracked and its edges softened. And then she would begin another. The march of time.

Pauline's eyes were still on her, even as Mary found her place and set the open book upright on her desk. The goal, Sister Clare had taught them in school, was shorthand so neat and so legible that anyone can pick up your steno book and type your letters for you. So neat and so legible, she had said, smiling at them from within her wimple, that if you elope on your lunch hour, another secretary can finish your letters for you that afternoon.

She looked over her shoulder, glancing at Pauline, even smiling a little, but Pauline only tilted her head again toward Adele's back. Mary nodded. This was the kind of moral dilemma Pauline often got her into. Mr. Someone-or-Other, Pauline had mouthed. Adele at lunch with him, crying. But Mr. Who? She turned to her typewriter, Pauline's eyes still on her. She would like to ask "Who?"— but to do so, in that same mouthing whisper Pauline had used, would be to enter too fully into Pauline's tale, Pauline's bitter triumph, and, in some way, into Pauline's unhappy life.

But Mr. Who?

This was the dilemma Pauline put her in: as much as she would like to know the story, the gossip, the whole tale, she hoped not to hear that desperate breathlessness in her own voice. As much as she wanted to know whatever it was that was worth knowing about the secrets and complications and (yes, even) failings and foibles of the people in the office—and she had to admit the few days that Pauline ever missed work were always long and dull—she did not, with equal longing, wish to be a part of the whispering spinster chorus at the edge of other, more interesting lives. She did not want to be one of the gray-haired harridans, one of those brittle and bitter middle-aged virgins who can never be sure that the world is indeed as full of deceit and ill will as they claim, or whether it's their own tainted version of things that creates the ill will and deceit in the first place. She did not want a life drained of kindness and compassion and humor. It was as much as she had prayed for an hour ago in church, now that the war was over and she no longer prayed for the boys. She had prayed for if not a better life than this daily, lonely one, a better way to be content with it. And then the sudden windstorm, the stream of strangers either bent into it or leaning back to resist it, tears running down all their faces in this valley of tears. George putting his hand on her shoulder. God's answer.

Never kid a kidder.

"Maybe," she said to Pauline, not looking at her, just turning her head a bit to speak to her from across the aisle and over her shoulder. Not whispering either. "Maybe it was just the wind."

It was the lack of a reply, clack of typewriters within the silence, that made her finally raise her eyes to Pauline's face, which was blank, her jaw thrust forward beneath the neat pink lipstick.

"The wind," Mary said again. "It was making everyone tear up."

Pauline examined her face for a few seconds more, her jaw set. And then she smiled a little, not kindly, raising her eyebrows and slowly shaking her big head. "You are naïve," she said, as if confirming something she had already spent a good deal of time discussing, elsewhere. "You really are."

Mary shrugged. "I suppose. But that wind was making everyone tear up."

Pauline continued to smile, shaking her head, and Mary, turning back to her work, smiled too. She had escaped the spinster chorus only to join the naïve. And here was the other part of the moral dilemma Pauline embodied. Would it have killed her to play along? To have told Pauline, Oh my! You're kidding! What a scandal! If gossip gave Pauline pleasure why deny her? Surely there was little enough pleasure for Pauline outside of work. A mother she'd nursed through cancer, a brother she was estranged from because of a terrible wife, a small apartment and a cheap landlord and an unending series of contacts with people—a grocer, a butcher, a waitress, a salesclerk, a bus driver—who did not meet her expectations.

Feed my lambs, Jesus said. What was the cost of a little kindness toward someone who found her pleasure in being unkind? What was the good, as Sister Clare at school used to say, in loving only the lovable?

Oh my, you're kidding, what a scandal! Would it have killed her to play along?

She whispered a quick mea culpa, resolved to be less naïve, and then let herself settle into her work, the pleasure of the speed of her fingers and the neat, dark strokes of her own shorthand, her confident spelling and punctuation, her sense of purpose and community as the busy sound of her own typewriter joined with the busy sounds of the typewriters beneath the hands of all the women in the room. This much she was sure of: if she kept busy, kept her mind to the task at hand, let herself sink into the busy industry of her job, her shoulders straight and her ankles crossed beneath her chair, her desk neat—blotter, stapler, paper clips, dictionary, the surface dusted with a tissue every morning and every afternoon—if she simply worked, worked well, efficiently, competently, then time would pass. Time would march on. Not merely the afternoon hours but the weeks and months. The lunch hour would come and then five o'clock would come and then the evening would come, and then the weekend again, and then another. Christmas would come and mad April again and lovely summer and fall. The war would begin and the war would continue and the war would end and time would pass with all that behind us now, another life (she would have put her palm to the worn gold on his belt), and all that was ahead would pass, and none of it, looking back, would seem to have been very much time at all, even though looking ahead it had seemed endless. If she kept her back straight and her ankles crossed beneath her chair and her hands over the keys, if her fingers struck them quickly and rhythmically and the sound of all their industry filled the room, and if she remembered to take some pleasure in it, the sound, the industry, the feel of Pauline's eyes on her back, even after Pauline herself had gotten up to take dictation in one of the offices, if she found some pleasure in the changing light as the afternoon moved forward, in the fading perfumes of the other girls as they passed her desk, in the good smell of the paper, the carbon, the old building itself, then time would pass and when she stood to cover her typewriter and to run another tissue over the surface of her desk, to smile apologetically at Pauline already in her hat and coat and waiting like the schoolgirl she surely must once have been for the stroke of five (adding, in her hissed stage whisper, "This isn't the first time they've been seen together like that"), she could tell herself another day gone and not so bad at that and what else to do when you're a single girl of thirty still at home, the war over and no prospects in sight, your body not meant for mortal sin or a man's attention or childbearing, either, it would seem, what to do but accept it and go on—a walk to the subway, the air chilled even further without the sun but the wind not nearly so bad as it was, and the ten-stop ride among the crowd of other office workers, and then the walk home, spears of crocus and daffodil rising out of the hard dirt around the caged trees and along the brick foundations, not so bad.

She unwrapped the lamb chops from their white butcher paper and peeled a few potatoes and opened a can of peas. Her father came in with the newspaper under his arm and then swatted her on the hip with it as he went to the table to sit down. And then Jimmy came in still wearing his overcoat to say, "What's this? What's this?" And then told their father with his hands on his hips that George was taking "our miss here" out to dinner. And her father lowered the paper and smiled at her—his round, florid face and his sparse white hair which he no longer bothered to slick down with water or tonic, being mostly housebound and hardly out of his slippers all week long—and only began to pout a little, Jimmy too, when she set the plate of lamb chops and the mint jelly and the mashed potatoes and peas in their bowls on the table and then pulled off her apron and said, "I'm just going to take a shower."

"Be sure to put it back," Jimmy said and winked at her father, but she was barely out of the small kitchen before the two men faced each other across the table, across the empty place where she usually sat between them, and glimpsed the possibility of a change in their routine.

George took her arm again, walking across the sidewalk to his car. He opened the car door for her and once she was inside, he leaned down to smile through the glass. And once inside himself, he took the wheel and told her without prompting that they were going to a steak house downtown that a friend had recommended. His hands on the steering wheel were short and clean and it slowly dawned on her that his fingernails were buffed, perhaps even manicured. She looked at his ear, under the brim of his hat. Sometime since this afternoon, he'd stopped for a haircut, too. The thought flattered her, even made her shy as he talked about this pal of his who knew from steak houses and fish markets, a connoisseur of mushrooms and artichokes who actually ordered cheese for dessert, his tastes were so refined. He took his eyes from the road for a minute to look at her, smiling again, laughing as he spoke, being charming even as she, smiling back at him, found herself growing demure.

In the restaurant, he told her everything about himself that he had already told them over dinners at home—a Midwest childhood, a kidney condition that kept him out of the service, a stint at the Navy Yard before the job at the brewery. She merely nodded, trying to look attentive but actually studying his face, which was pleasant enough, studying his table manners, which were passable but in need of certain refinements—he buttered the back of his entire roll and put the half-bitten piece on the edge of his dinner plate.

In the car coming home he kept his hand on the seat between them. She wished out loud for the weekend and then told him a little about Pauline, and the story of Adele and Mr. Someone-or-Other. He nodded, his eyes on the road. She wasn't sure he followed, or had any interest. She wondered if he thought this was girlish gossip that she was foolishly telling him, if he had missed her point that girlish gossip was what she had sought to avoid. The uncertainty that had clouded his face this afternoon in the moment after he'd asked her out to dinner was now a tangible presence in the car as they approached her building and the time for some kind of conclusion to this odd impulse of his had finally come.

"Thanks so much for this," she said as he pulled to the curb. She put the strap of her pocketbook over her arm, put her hand on the door handle. "You really didn't have to."

He seemed to rouse himself from a growing disengagement. "I wanted to," he said. "It was nice to have a chance to get to know you better," he added, although she could not imagine a single thing he might have learned. He leaned toward her, slowly raising his hand to his hat and then doffing it quickly, as if taken by surprise, when she leaned forward to meet him. And this, she thought, of course, was what the whole evening had been for, the delightful feel of his rough cheek against her fingertips, his hand and lips and warm breath. The lingering taste of coffee in his mouth. Something awkward and lovely (a drumming on the roof, was it rain?) and absurd about Jimmy's pal George moving his arm around her waist, pressing his hat into her back, and her fingers finding the newly trimmed border of his hair. All that trying to be charming and trying to be demure and hoping to look attentive and to speak well and wondering how this strange impulse of his will come to a conclusion put aside now that they had agreed, finally, that this, after all, was simply what they'd wanted. The warmth of it, the moment's respite.

Jimmy was in the living room, in his undershirt, reading the *Daily News* beside a single lamp. He lowered the paper and began to fold it neatly as soon as she came in, but asked only where she had eaten before he said good night. She went into the kitchen and was surprised to find the dishes, including the serving bowls, washed and drying in the dish rack and the remaining lamb chop, a scoop of mashed potatoes, and a handful of peas on a plate in the icebox, another turned over it. She wondered at their logic: Had they thought she'd be too nervous to eat with George? Or that she'd just nibble, hoping to appear dainty, like Scarlett O'Hara at Twelve Oaks? She decided they simply didn't know what to do with her portion: something ungenerous about eating it themselves, something unkind about throwing it away. She wiped down the kitchen table and the counter and swept the floor, and then ran into Jimmy in the hallway, now in T-shirt and pajama bottoms, as he came out of the bathroom. He held the glass of water he would put by his bedside, on the nightstand between his bed and their father's.

"Sleep tight," he whispered, and then surprised her by putting his arms around her, the glass at her back. "Our Mary Rose," he said, and kissed her head, as if he were bidding her a fond farewell.

She laughed. There could be worse lives than this lonely one. There could be life married to someone like George.

In her own room, she pulled back the covers, took the rosary beads from under her pillow, and got into bed. Joyful, Sorrowful, Glorious Mysteries. She chose the Joyful for this night—another day gone, not so bad, a date no less—but in her weariness forgot where she had begun and followed the Visitation with Jesus being lost in the Temple and then Mary's assumption into heaven, wondering all the while just who—Mr. Who?—had wiped the tear from Adele's eye.

The next afternoon she lit her candle and said her prayer, and then playfully linked arms with poor Pauline who always waited at the back of the church, no longer on speaking terms with Catholicism. It was a lovely afternoon, a bright afternoon in spring that even Pauline was taking some pleasure in (there were her good new shoes in a rich burgundy, a fresh Danish she'd had this morning at coffee break, a blouse she had made last night from a remnant of green silk and placed on Mary's desk this morning, because, she'd said, it would only fit someone without much of a chest). There wasn't a tear to be seen on the faces of the men and women in the street as the two of them walked down to Schrafft's. Only him, again, leaning by the door, suit jacket and fedora, the sunlight striking gold, the leg he had favored bent back and pressed against the building. He was smoking a cigarette. He was the handsomest man on the block. He was waiting for her.

She felt Pauline beside her, stiffening against his greeting. She thought, giving him her name, how there was a trace of sorrow in every joy. She thought, as he held the door, smiling at her, *Poor George.*

The day before Mary and John Keane were married, Pauline

tripped on the sidewalk outside her building (the landlord was somehow to blame) and broke her wrist. When she appears in photographs of that day, her dark suit is slashed by a white sling, and under her stylish turban, her big powdered face is dignified, carved in ivory, only a certain determination about the jaw and the mouth betraying a reluctant smile.

THE RUSH HOUR that Friday night began with a wet snow. Sitting at her typewriter in her lambskin coat and hat, Pauline saw the first fat flakes pass like small shadows across the office window and expressed her disapproval of nature itself with a loud clucking of the tongue. Impatiently, she leaned down to pull her folded rain boots from the bottom of the desk drawer. Throughout the typing pool all the girls began to do the same.

An hour later, crossing the lobby of their apartment building, Mary Keane felt her own transparent booties squeak and slip on the linoleum floor, which was so streaked with mud and melting snow you'd think the steady stream of residents tramping home had crossed ditches and fields, not merely the four blocks of wet sidewalk between here and the subway. She carried her umbrella and a white bakery box now dappled with gray—a pair of apple turnovers for tomorrow's breakfast.

The elevator was open and inside it a young man in a dark overcoat was holding the bucking door with his forearm.

Double-stepping, still uncertain of her traction, she hurried to reach it. "Gee, thanks," she said, although, after a lifetime in her old walk-up, she still preferred to take the stairs. He dropped his arm as soon as she had stepped inside and some impatience in his posture conveyed the idea that he would have dropped his arm at that precise moment had she stepped inside or not.

"Floor?" he said, turning only his profile toward her. He wore a dark fedora and had a roman nose.

"Five," she said. And then added, "Thanks again."

Gloveless, he pressed a long pale finger into the elevator button that was a faded shade of ivory, seemed even to grind it in a bit, and then, stepping back, placed the hand into the pocket of his oversize coat.

They both stared into the lobby's baleful yellow light. Tamed, the doors now remained impassively open. Through them, she saw another pair of residents—another young couple—swing into the lobby, laughing and shaking wet snow from their shoulders and hats. He pressed the button again, with his thumb this time, banging it a bit as if to make a stronger point. The elevator suddenly shook itself, coming to, and the doors slowly closed before the newcomers could look up from their clothes to cry, Wait.

Alone together in the little box that smelled of his wet wool and her wet fur and the various beginnings of other people's dinners, he glanced at her and then politely doffed his hat, placing it over his heart as if for the national anthem. He raised his eyes to the numbers above the door.

"Some weather," she said. He merely, barely, nodded. "Who knew it would snow?" she said.

Now he shook his head, shrugging a little, a wordless, No one knew.

He was pale as salt. Although along his jaw there was, beneath the pale skin, the outline of a black beard. His hair was cut short, but it was clear that left to its own devices it would curve, and then curl. He was not tall, but the fingers that held his hat against his overcoat were exceptionally long and thin. She saw how they moved one at a time against the dark brown felt, pressing themselves against the fabric almost imperceptibly, like a pulse under the skin. The way a child's fingers might move in sleep.

At the third floor, the elevator stopped haltingly, bouncing them both on the balls of their feet. The doors slid open to show the familiar green walls, the chipped ledge and decorative mirror that marked each floor. A smell of frying onions.

They both looked out at the empty hallway and then she turned to him to say, "No one," as if this were indeed a small mystery.

He stabbed the button once again. He had a thin face behind the large nose, and pretty, dark brown eyes with heavy lashes. He was younger than she, not even thirty, but he would have to be far younger still before she could say what it was that came into her mind to say: A girl would kill to have those eyelashes.

The door closed again and again the elevator shook itself and slowly rose. She tried to think of some small talk. (Because it was simply what you did. You made small talk, you commiserated.)

Her eyes fell on his hands again, so white against the dark felt of his hat. She watched them moving, involuntarily, rhythmically, one at a time and in no apparent order, and thought briefly of a friend of her brother's who had come back from overseas with what they'd called Saint Vitus' dance. But was this kid even old enough to have been in the war?

Suddenly she said, "Are you the piano player, upstairs?" For that was how she and John had come to refer to him, The piano player, upstairs.

He turned his nose to her again, warily now. "I play," he said.

She nodded. "We hear you," she told him. "My husband and I, we listen," she said. Every evening from seven fifteen until nine and Saturday mornings eight to eleven, which she preferred, since they woke to it. "You play beautifully," she told him, although the music was obscurely classical and, because there were no lyrics, unmemorable to her.

But the compliment was like a drop of water on the dry wool of his face. His cheeks seemed to soften, color, even swell.

"I hope it doesn't disturb you," he said.

She held out her hand, the thin string of the bakery box looped around her wrist. "Not at all," she said, although three or four times now she had hung on her husband's arm to keep him from banging the broom handle against the ceiling. "We enjoy it," she said. And then, at a loss for a more substantial compliment, she added, "You must have some beautiful piano."

They had reached her floor and once again he put his forearm against the door to hold it for her. "A Steinway," he said, his tongue poked behind his lips as if to suppress a boastful smile.

Stepping out of the elevator she said, "Oh, sure. The factory over in Long Island City."

"A baby grand," he added with such sudden animation that she thought for a moment he might follow her into the hallway to say more. But the doors were once again butting against his arm.

"No kidding?" She smiled at him. He was very young. "How'd you even get it up here?"

He gave his smile the go-ahead, moving to put his shoulder, too, against the elevator door. "It was already there," he said. "Someone left it behind. They didn't want it. The super said they couldn't even rent the apartment for a few weeks because it takes up the whole bedroom and nobody wanted to pay to take it out. Can you believe it? A Steinway."

"Lucky that you play," she said. She would have put her gloved hand to his cheek, patted it gently to temper his sweet and sudden enthusiasm, were it not for the way the thumping doors were sending rebukes from the poor souls waiting downstairs. She put out her hand again, the bakery box rocking against her wrist. "That would have been something to see," meaning getting a baby grand piano from Long Island City to the tiny sixth-floor bedroom just above theirs.

Little wonder, then, that the next morning when she woke to the heavy run of scales that began his three hours of practice, she saw in her mind's eye Laurel and Hardy waving their hats beneath a dangling baby grand, saw them catching their fingers in piano lids or pressing their cheeks against the broad rump of a Steinway as they carried it, nimbly wavering, up a long flight of stairs. Saw in her mind's eye that delicious moment when Stan—a version of the piano player himself, when you thought about it—smiled the sweet self-satisfied smile that always preceded the double take, the panic, the inevitable disaster. (Down, down, down the keyboard he went and down, down, down in her mind's eye went the poor piano.)

Images that stayed with her even as John woke and sighed and cursed a little under his breath before he lifted the hand she had already placed on his belly and took her into his arms.

And there was comedy in this too, in the musical accompaniment—the scales that drew them to their first, stale-mouthed kiss followed by the inept and repetitive beginnings of some vaguely familiar but as yet unrecognizable piece as they shyly (still) got out of their pajamas. And then ineptitude giving way, on all their parts, to a certain confidence, even grace.

Did he hear it, she wondered as she glimpsed her husband's face through half-closed eyes and saw what was quickly becoming a familiar look: a kind of determined concentration, a grimace to the lips, and a far-off gaze to his eyes that marked a consummation that she was beginning to suspect turned him in on himself far more than it would ever turn him out toward her. She imagined it was akin to the look the piano player upstairs wore as he worked the keys, that kind of crazy-eyed focus on the task that could obliterate all distractions, even the very instrument under his hands. Does he even hear the music, she thought, arching toward him as he labored above her. Does he even see my face?

This was something she had never anticipated before she was married, the painful, physical struggle he seemed to wage with himself in the course of their joining. She had thought it would all be whispered endearments, only pleasantly breathless. She was surprised to learn that there was labor in it, pain and struggle as well as sweetness.

There was still more music to listen to after they had fallen apart. She thought she was beginning to recognize some refrain, or maybe he was just going over the same notes. With her eyes to the ceiling she said, "It's a baby grand."

Her husband turned his head on the pillow. He might have been startled to find her there. He frowned, and then hesitated, and then whispered, disbelieving, "You can tell already?"

There was one window in the corner of the bedroom, its sill worn to velvet, looking like velvet even in the weak, winter morning sun that came from beneath the wooden blinds and marked the new day. Another day. She grew giddy with laughter, convinced as she was, and would remain, that there was portent in his misunderstanding, that their child's life had indeed begun at that hour. Their baby grand, first of four.

II

EITHER THE WIND kept them all away or the entire population took to heart the notion that the beaches were closed after Labor Day. In the deserted parking lot, on a Sunday morning that was only, after all, in mid-September, the wind moved a thin scrim of sand across the bleached asphalt, brushed it along the ground in wide, crossing arcs that thinned and ebbed in much the same way the beige sea foam thinned and ebbed at the edge of the beach that was just beyond the trees.

The wind took the sound of the slammed car doors, the slammed trunk, and sailed it off like a black scrap, over their heads, back toward the long highway and the crowded towns and the churches on shaded avenues choked with parked cars. It took their voices, too, but more gently. The parking lot was empty and so there was no need to cry out after the children as they ran ahead.

"Not a soul," Mary Keane said to her husband, the wind lifting her words, tossing them gently back over her shoulder, the way it moved the colorful tails of the scarf she had tied under her chin. In her arms she had bundled a wool blanket and a tufted pillow and a stuffed bear, and her husband stepped in front of her to take everything from her arms at once, leaving only the bulge of her belly under the green canvas car coat.

"They're all in church," he said and saw the flush of guilt, or of wind, on her broad cheeks. The wind lifted his own thinning hair—those long strands he combed back over his crown—made it stand, briefly, on end.

Something done right—at least so far—this suggestion of his, whispered to the ceiling this morning, his hand on her thigh. That they skip Mass just this once and head to the beach.

Some weeks ago, a tropical wave had slipped off the African coast, as if (he'd thought, reading the account) the continent itself had shuddered, and moved into the waters of the south seas, stirring the ocean and the air and the various inhabitants of small islands and southern shorelines, until finally it woke him this morning at dawn with the sound of the wind in the eaves, with some memory or dream of the Ardennes, and a hankering to see what the shudder of a continent did to the waters off Jones Beach.

Across the ceiling of his bedroom, the dawn had appeared to be made up of reflected light, light that moved with the rise and fall of the wind as if it were light reflecting off water—although the house was ten miles from any shore, smack in the substantial heart of his own spit of island, and even the neighborhood backyard pools had been drained and dismantled.

Beneath this watery light the room itself was in steady shadow. His wife was beside him, buried in pillows. He was fifty-one and would be a new father again by the end of the year. This morning, woken by the wind, he had put his thumb to each fingertip, counting decades.

The children ran ahead. A white trail of sand cut through the scrub pine and the yellowing beach grass, rising across the dunes and then dropping down again to the wide white beach that then itself dropped down again, sharply, a kind of cliff, a kind of collapse—the way the children felt their breaths collapse, coming to its edge, to the terrific thunderclap of the ocean.

The sand here, at their feet as they looked down from the dry cliff, was dark gray, the color of a thundercloud. The children bowed, putting down their toys (plastic machine guns, a football, a shoe box filled with green army men and small, camouflaged jeeps), unlaced their sneakers, and jumped down, arms raised, heels digging into the falling sand of the seawall.

Not a soul.

At the foot of the dunes, John Keane dropped the wool blanket and the tufted pillow and the teddy bear, unhooked the quilted hamper from his shoulder and his wife's hand from the crook of his arm. He felt the wind raise the sand and fling it, stinging, into his cheek, saw his wife pull the folded edge of her scarf over the side of her face, turning away from him and the blowing sand.

He picked up the wool blanket and moved it farther inside the dunes, to a shallow valley where even the sound of the moving air seemed suddenly to retreat. He spread the blanket, walked out again to lift the tufted pillow and the bear and the plaid quilted hamper, then returned a third time to give her his arm.

She stood, holding the edge of her colorful scarf over her cheek, shading her eyes with the other. Her face made harsh and unlovely by the sand and the wind and the deep line between her eyes.

"Sit back here," he said. "You'll be out of the wind."

Under her chin, the bright red-and-blue tails of her scarf rose, writhed, paddled the air. "I can't see them," she said.

He looked toward the ocean, the forlorn image of the abandoned sneakers and toys—the shoe box had already lost its lid—at the edge of the known world where the sand disappeared and there was only water and sky.

"I'll tell them to come up," he said and knew she would not move—some vestigial habit of her race or of her sex, this frowning vigil at the edge of the sea—until he had returned them to her sight.

He crossed the wide breadth of beach, hearing their voices coming to him on the wind before he saw them at the shoreline. The two boys were stamping at the creamy edges of the waves—making small explosions of water and wet sand—his daughter down on her haunches, examining something, a mussel or a crab or just the mysterious, bubbling holes that opened and closed like mouths under the retreating waves.

Beyond them, the ocean was high, whitecapped, agitated. There were disks of black and gray as well as gold among the rushing swells. In the panhandle, in the Carolinas, metal blinds had been drawn, iron awnings brought down on the white houses that were bunkers now, among the palm trees and the flamingos. But here the sky was mostly blue and clear, except for a few white, rushing clouds just above the horizon.

Some vestige of his race or of his sex made him think, whenever he looked out across the ocean: As it was before me and as it will be long after I'm gone. For the second time today, he touched his thumb to his fingertips. He could make it to the 1980s or 1990s, perhaps even to the next century, when the new baby would be grown, maybe with children of his or her own. But even with the best of luck, it would not be equal to the time he'd already spent.

He called to them. "Come up," he said against the wind. "Your mother wants you up."

The wall of sand the sea had made, the cliff, the collapse, seemed smaller now with their father standing on top of it, his hair raised in the wind. They scaled it quickly, in wide strides, their arms pumping.

He put his hand out to his daughter, pulled her up easily over the edge. And then bent to gather the shoes and toys, swinging the canvas straps of the two toy machine guns over his shoulder (surprised to find that some mistaken memory had caused him—momentarily—to be surprised to find they had no weight). Jacob, the oldest, ran to retrieve the cardboard lid while Michael, his brother, lifted the shoe box, shifting the contents—green army men, toy bayonets, machine gun, camouflaged jeeps—taking roll.

With his thumbs hooked over the lid, the boy carried the box up the beach, behind his father and brother and sister, feeling the drag of sand but feeling, too, that with a small effort he could overtake them.

Their mother stood at the base of the dunes, her hands seeming to cup her broad face as she waited for them.

"Back here," their father said. "We'll be out of the wind." And once more gave his wife his arm. The children ran before them, the boys running up and down the sides of the dunes, sand slipping, as if they had no choice in the matter, as if the world itself were tilting, the little girl imagining shipwrecked and island-lost, and only her father's cleverness (there were guns slung over his shoulder) to keep them safe and warm.

The plaid blanket was already spread in a gap between the dunes, the tufted pillow on it, the lunch hamper, and the teddy bear who had not been lost, not drowned in the wreck, after all. She threw her arms around it, an extravagant reunion. "If it weren't for me," her mother said dryly, smiling, "you would have left him behind in the car."

Too soon to eat, they agreed, and her husband gallantly gave her his hand again as she lowered herself to the blanket, first onto her knees and then, carefully, onto the pillow. Straightening himself, he palmed the football like a younger man and called the boys to follow him out to the beach.

She leaned back on her palms, the wool prickly against her skin and already dusted with sand.

There was the now oddly distant knock of the waves against themselves and the softer yet similar sound of the football meeting their hands. There was her husband's voice, Go out, now, Keep your eye on it, Good, and the voices of the boys, mostly complaining: My turn, Hey, Interference. The ball a kind of shadow passing before her, between them, across the sun itself or so it seemed.

Annie, her daughter, had claimed the corner of the blanket, sitting perversely, her mother thought, with her back to the ocean and to her father and the boys on the windy beach. The worn bear (cherished now that she had recalled its existence) on her lap. She was not speaking, but her lips moved and her eyes were clearly engaged in a conversation of some sort—she frowned, she shook her head—and despite the echo of the ocean falling down on itself, the slap of the football in their hands, and their voices, carried on the wind, it was this conversation as it played like light across her daughter's features (she raised her eyes, made them smile) that absorbed the mother's attention.

Mary Keane watched her daughter and felt as well the punch and turn of the baby not yet born and saw the similarity of the mystery of them both—the baby unseen, moving an elbow or a foot, the means to an end all its own, unfathomable; her daughter with the unseen life playing like reflected light over her face, her lips moving in a conversation forever unheard.

She slipped her hand under her belly, shifted her weight on the pillow, and looked up to see the boys returning, windblown, kicking up sand. Her husband behind them, boyish, too, with the red flush across his cheeks and the thinning hair scattered every which way across his head. The baby rolled, roiled, beneath her ribs and the beach grass shuddered in the wind. He sat beside her heavily, while the two boys fell on the shoe box full of soldiers, carrying it off to the foot of another dune—for this had been their plan all along, to restage Okinawa or Omaha Beach, continuing the war game they had begun last night in their room, across the sheets and blankets and pillows of their twin beds, in one of those hours of grace when they had not quarreled and their parents had not called to them to

put out the light. They had named each member of their platoon—
Murphy, Idaho, Sarge, Smitty—ambushed some Germans, and collected commendations from Patton himself. This morning when
their father had come into their room to say, "We're heading for the
beach," the dissolution of the plans they'd made to continue the
push toward Berlin right after Mass was quickly compensated for by
the possibility of dune and sand—Okinawa, Omaha Beach, North
Africa and Rommel.

It was their father who had put the football in the trunk.

Now they scattered their men across the sand and among the
bending stalks of sea grass. Their sister heard the changed pitch of
their voices, the harsh and breathy pitch they used when they were
speaking for someone else in an imaginary game. She rose to join
them. The bear was still in her arms but once again forgotten.

"Can I play?" she asked finally, understanding, even at six, that
the timidity of the question invited a single reply.

"No." Looking to each other, not to her.

She watched them. The orders they barked were low and intimate, running under the sound of the wind.

"Can I have a man?" she asked.

"No," again, but now their parents on the blanket together
looked toward them.

"Boys," their father said, a warning. And a single green soldier
was plucked from the shoe box of reservists and replacements and
tossed her way, through the air. She picked him up from the sand.
The mold had shaped his features precisely, a strong jaw and a
sharp nose, the little combat helmet and a sash of ammunition
across his chest. Unlike the men her brothers preferred, this one had
no rifle pressed to its shoulder, no hand grenade about to be thrown,
but stood instead with his arms extended from his sides, palms out.
His head was slightly raised, as if whatever he confronted was still
at some distance, and was larger than just another man.

His name was Steve. Steve Stevens. And he was a scout, sent ahead. Alone.

She moved him through the sand, up over the boulders and hills that were the arms and legs of the bear.

John Keane, leaning over his knees, watched the children carefully, seeing that they behaved and then, reassured, allowed himself to lie back on the blanket. The sky was blue. They were nicely out of the wind. He placed his fingertips on his wife's back, just lightly. The football had reminded him that he was not (he would have said) entirely pleased with the behavior of his two sons. It upset some notion he had of order, of rightness, that Jacob, the older, was the smaller of the two, the lesser athlete, the lesser student. It made something unkind, even cruel, about Michael's efforts to outdo him. Michael's triumphs over his older brother—and the self-satisfaction they brought him—came too easily. Jacob's defeats seemed too indicative of a certain kind of future.

He kept his fingers on his wife's back and placed his forearm over his eyes. The wind was just above them. It seemed to skim the tops of the surrounding dunes, bending the grass. But here the sun on his knees and on his forearm felt warm.

His love for his children bore down on his heart with the weight of three heavy stones. There were all his unnamed fears for them, and hopes for them. There was all he was powerless to change, including who they were—one too mild, one too easily tempted to be cruel, and the little girl (it was the weight of a heavy stone against his heart) a mystery to him, impossible to say what she, through her life, would need. And soon one more.

He hoped the fourth would be another boy—although he would never say so to his wife. What he had in mind most especially was a daughter's wedding day and the pall an absent father casts on the scene, that sad tincture of mortality that mixes with the bright day when the bride appears at the door of the church on the arm of an uncle (as his own niece had done) or an older brother—it would be Jacob, of course.

No equal ghost appears at the ceremony, as far as he can recall, when it is the groom's father who is missing.

Enough reason, he thought, for a man his age to wish for another boy. But it would be another stone, nonetheless.

He could hear the two of them now, softly crying orders to their men, even as they interrupted themselves to provide machine-gun fire and exploding hand grenades, the sound of the ocean and the wind and the occasional cry of gulls lending a certain authenticity to the scene with their steady indifference.

Then his wife's voice, startlingly close and yet oddly distant, specked with disks of black and gray as well as gold. "Pick him up and put him on the blanket," she said to their daughter. "He's full of sand."

And then she stirred, moving beneath the lightly placed fingertips of her husband's hand. The baby moving as well, roiling like a wave under her skin, pressing an elbow into her ribs, a heel against her hip.

"Thank you," she said to her daughter and took the forgotten bear and shook it and brushed the sand from its worn fur and then set it carefully beside her, against her hip as if to offer it comfort, as if it were itself some spurned youngest child. The baby turned again even as Mary Keane glimpsed the drama of Steve Stevens (he had gone down on his belly behind a stalk of grass as Adolf Hitler drove by) on her daughter's small face.

"Is anyone hungry yet?" she asked, and only Annie, who was never hungry yet, said No without raising her eyes. The boys, who had heard her, she knew they had heard her, ignored the question. Michael was crawling up the side of the dune, his plastic machine gun raised. Jacob—how like him—was watching his brother's progress warily, his arms encircling his small platoon of green men, protecting them from the sliding sand. They both had heard her.

She looked over her shoulder at her husband. His forearm was thrown across his eyes, his mouth was slightly open. His fingertips, lightly, were on her back.

She leaned down to the bear, or leaned as much as the hump and heft of her belly would allow. "Are you hungry?" she asked it. Her daughter, compelled as equally by whimsy as by drama, suddenly straightened up and turned to her mother. "He's not answering, either," Mary Keane told her daughter, and they both smiled.

"I guess no one's hungry," Annie said gently, and here the mother glimpsed some future commiseration between them, some future understanding they would certainly share of what passed between women while the men in the world were distracted, unheeding, unconscious.

She shifted again, leaning her weight onto one thigh and then the other as the baby offered its own counterbalance. She moved her hands inside her coat and grasped her belly, the way she might hold a child's face between her hands to silence tears, or to ask, What is it, what's wrong?

She stroked her sides, the loose knit of the cotton sweater she had confiscated from her husband's closet ten years ago, when she was pregnant with Michael and could bear only cotton or silk against her skin. She felt the baby ripple under her fingers. She felt a heel—surely it was a heel here on her left side—press against her skin and then dart away, going under, before she could quite gauge its shape.

It was possible it had something to do with the ocean, all this activity. Something to do with the salt scent of it on the air and on the wind. The tug of some ancient memory—didn't they say life began in the sea—or maybe some dawning hope that the what-do-you-call-it, the fluid the baby now floated in (which someone had told her was also precisely as salty as the ocean), was a tributary, not merely a pool.

She ran her palms over her taut belly, soothing the poor thing, even as a swift kick under her ribs nearly took her breath away. Or maybe, she thought, it was the hurricane down south, agitating water everywhere—in oceans and bays, dog bowls and cisterns, in the bellies of pregnant women all up and down the coast.

Mary Keane smiled and looked around because the thought amused her, although she knew that in another minute she would not be able to retrace it clearly enough to retell.

Michael had slipped beyond the crest of the dune. Jacob was lying flat out now, on his stomach, his little men all before him, and Annie had followed her single soldier up the dune to a grassy patch where the wind whipped her dark hair and the blowing sand made her squint, even as her lips kept moving—now a conversation between her little army man and a headless creature formed by the two fingers of her right hand. But Michael was out of sight.

She waited. Were it not for the ballast of her big belly, she would casually stand, stretch a bit, casually stretch her neck until she got a glimpse of him. Casually because her husband said she worried too much, fretted too much, and would eventually infect their boys with her fearfulness—had, perhaps, already, in Jacob's case, infected them with her fearfulness. So she waited, trusting, but feeling, too, the pins-and-needles prick of blown sand on her cheek and her forearm (was the wind changing?) until, sure enough, there was the top of his head, the tip of his plastic machine gun, just over the next dune.

She resisted calling to him, telling him to come closer. Her husband was asleep beside her. She could hear the way he pursed his lips with each breath, something like the soft sound of the football against their palms (although it was softer still), something like the thud of the ocean as it punctuated the rise and fall of the wind. He deserved the rest, poor man. They were alone on the beach. They were perfectly safe.

Michael's head crested the dune again. Then his shoulders, the rump of his blue jeans, the short barrel of his machine gun. He was crawling on his belly along the top of the dune, crushing the sea grass, filling his shirt and the pockets of his pants with sand. She would have to remember to shake him out before he got into the car.

Down the path through the dunes she could see the pale expanse of beach and then the place where it gave way to sky. She leaned forward a little, toward it, resting the bulk of the baby on the edge of her thighs. It was possible that the sky was darker, out there, to the east. It was possible that they would catch some part of the southern storm. She had an image of her unborn child, its head up under her heart, its ear pressed to the wall of her flesh, treading water with the flutter of its small legs, listening. It would hear the echo of the waves, the whistle of the wind, the rise and fall of its father's breath as his lips opened and touched closed.

Mary Keane was more than certain (she would have said) that this was her last pregnancy. These the last weeks she would live with the toss and tumble of a child in her belly, with the unseen future a real presence inside her; the unseen future actual flesh and blood inside her, not, as it was for the rest of the population and would be for her again once this child was born, merely imagination or hope or plan—the man Jacob would become, and Michael, the woman (commiserating with her mother while the men were turned away) who would be Annie. What was moving under her hands, pressing and turning under the taut skin, was the future itself, already formed, pressing an ear to the wall of her flesh.

With a cry, Michael leaped down the dune above his brother, charged, fell, rolled, collided with Jacob's back and Jacob's carefully arranged soldiers, kicking up sand. He leaped up again and with his machine gun drawn mowed down sister—who was already crying, her fists to her eyes—brother, green army men, mother, father, and then whatever other advancing hordes came at him from the sea.

John Keane was off the blanket in an instant, crying, "Michael!" Jacob was stretched out on the sand, his legs straight before him, crying, plaintively, "Michael!" Annie was heading toward her mother, wailing, her fists—one of them still clutching Steve Stevens—to her eyes. There was sand across her nose and in her hair. John Keane took Michael by the arm and shook him. The boy looked up at his father as if he were an utter stranger, materialized out of the salt air. Mary untied her scarf and, pulling her daughter's fists from her eyes, gently brushed it over her face. Jacob, resignedly, perhaps, was lifting his flattened men, smoothing an area of sand to his left, setting them upright again.

"What is wrong with you?" their father was saying. "Why can't you behave?"

Michael—it was not fear on his face, only a kind of disbelief, as if this tall, red-faced, shouting man had materialized out of the wind—looked up to say, "Just playing. I was just playing." But his father shook his arm with the litany of his transgressions: "Hurt your brother, hurt your sister, ruined the day." He finally tossed aside the boy's arm as if it were something to be thrown away. "Why don't you use your head?" he asked him. "Why can't you behave?" And felt the pain of his own anger, in his chest, in his shoulder. He moved his hand to his neck, moved his shoulder. It was the arm he'd used to throw the football. He looked to his wife. Annie was now collapsed on the blanket beside her, pressed into her side because she could not sit on her lap, the bright scarf, now spotted with her tears, wrapped in her fingers. Mary Keane was fumbling in the pocket of her car coat for a tissue. She found one, held it to the girl's nose. Leaned a little to say something into her ear. The girl nodded. Mary reached for the stuffed bear that still leaned against her hip, lifted it, and placed it in her daughter's arms.

A s suddenly as the peace of the morning had turned to bedlam, peace returned. John Keane looked around, his hand on his neck, his love for these children three heavy stones against his thumping heart. Jacob was once more bent over his men. Michael, his machine gun hung over his back, was sitting Indian-style just a few feet away, pulling apart a stalk of sea grass, watching the ocean, not crying, his father was relieved to see, but, he suspected, not chastened either. He rubbed his neck. Swung his arm out, shaking it a little. It was the arm he had given to Catherine, his niece, his brother Frank's only child, at the door of the church on the day she was married. "Maybe we should eat," he said. And then, raising his voice only enough to be heard over the wind, "Boys. Come over and eat."

But the wind had indeed changed and as the five of them gathered on the blanket they could feel it prick their faces and their arms. Mary Keane, with Annie still leaning heavily against her and the baby like an iron beach ball in her lap, leaned toward the quilted hamper, unzipped it, and then paused, a single wax-paper-wrapped sandwich in her hand. "Our food will be full of sand," she said, "with this wind." And her husband said, "Well, they are sandwiches," and winked at Michael, who seemed suddenly to recognize his father again.

"Maybe," Mary said, "we'd better eat in the car."

Slowly everything was gathered and they made their way out to the beach once more and then over the path that returned them to the parking lot. They placed the blankets and the pillow and the toys into the trunk, depositing as they did a residue of sand that would be there throughout the winter. Standing above the knot the three of them had formed before the open back door of the car—a debate about who would go first and who would get the middle— their mother said, her hand on her belly, "Just get in," and they did, sliding across the soft fabric of the backseat. Annie was in the middle because Michael moved so quickly and Jacob had put a definite pair of fingers to her shoulder to make her follow him.

Mary Keane eased herself into the front seat. The size of her belly made her legs feel short, as though they could barely reach the floor under the dashboard. Her husband closed the door on her, gently, with both hands, as if he were covering her with a blanket. He crossed in front of the car, his hair on end and the pale scalp at the back of his head exposed. He now looked every bit his age, she thought. As he grew older, it seemed to her that she was not losing sight of his younger self but coming to recognize instead another man altogether, one she was just beginning to find familiar. He opened the door, slid the quilted hamper onto the seat between them, and then got in behind the wheel. He pulled the door closed and the wind became just the slightest rush of air against the rolled-up windows. There was suddenly a pleasant warmth. Their voices, suddenly, seemed rich and sure now that they could speak quietly, now that their words were no longer scattered by the buffeting wind.

Mary, one knee bent up onto the seat—her legs seemed only inches long, her feet in their small loafers appeared no larger than her daughter's—handed sandwiches into the backseat while her husband poured lemonade from a glass jar into small paper cups.

"Careful now," he said each time he slowly moved the cup over the back of his seat, bending his arm like a crane, awkwardly, because it was the same arm he had used to throw the football and it still seemed to echo with the strain. "Ladies first," he said and felt his daughter take the cup from him with both hands. "Careful now." There was coffee in the plaid thermos and, when he had screwed the lid onto the glass jar and placed it back into the quilted hamper, he poured some for his wife and some for himself. She had packed two china teacups, wrapped in paper towels. She would not drink from anything else. He exchanged a cup for one of the sandwiches. The whole thing was a balancing act: cup and sandwich, napkin and wax paper—careful now—the three children in the back (the fourth would have to be up here, in the front seat between them, the hamper on his wife's lap, or at her feet), his wife and her belly perched beside him, the wind shut out and their voices suddenly gentle and clear. A sweetened cup of coffee, a ham-and-cheese— the bread a little dry but the meat thick and tender. The wind shut out. It was a balancing act, to hold off quarrel and worry, the com- ing years, the coming months, even tomorrow morning for just whatever time it took to finish a sandwich, to drink the coffee while it was still hot. Careful now.

All around them, the parking lot was deserted, only a scrim of sand moving across the bleached asphalt. Mary Keane stretched her legs and touched her side. "This baby is doing somersaults," she said and Jacob laughed softly, imagining it. Beside him, his sister put the crust of her sandwich to the line of brown thread that was the bear's mouth. Beside her, Michael looked through the rolled-up window, across the long and empty parking lot to the dark green pines that seemed to be raising their arms to the wind, shaking spindly fists. His own hands were full, sandwich and paper cup, but the small ivory knob on the silver handle was a temptation. Just a few turns and he could fill the car with the sound of the rushing wind. The hair was mussed across the back of his father's head, the familiar gleam of his white scalp peering through. His father leaned forward to put the china teacup on the dashboard and then, leaning back, placed his hand over his shoulder, kneading the material of his shirt, raising the shoulder toward his neck, like a pitcher on the mound. "Are you all right?" their mother asked, all their voices grown soft and gentle now that they were out of the wind.

"An ache is all," their father said.

The wind seemed to come up from under the car, it pressed against the window, muffled, shut out, although they all still felt the sting of it on their cheeks. Michael placed the paper cup, almost empty, between the knees of his jeans and moved his fingers to the ivory knob. His hands were pale, the fingers plump and squared-off, the nails flat and broad, just like his father's.

He tested the give of the handle with his fingertips. He imagined paper napkins and paper cups, wax paper, cheese, wafers of white bread lifted by the wind, swirled about the car.

Their father took his hand from his shoulder. The wind rattled the windows, careful now.

"Listen to that," their mother said. "It's really picking up."

Above the pines, the sky had turned a deeper blue. In another minute, there would be rain.

"We just might feel the brunt of this hurricane after all," their father said.

Mary Keane saw how the news made Michael pause, and then change his mind about rolling down the window. He lifted the paper cup from between his knees, took a drink of it. Annie said, "Really?" but it was Jacob who said, "Maybe we should go home," a crimp of fear in his voice. Her fault. She saw her husband flex his jaw. He did not love his oldest child as he should. There was gray at his temples and a roughened thickness at his throat. His face was not the face of the man she had married, but resembled, instead, some of the men she had worked for when she was single, or a doctor who had cared for her own father in his last days. Closer now, in appearance, to any number of fifty-year-old men she had known than he was to the young stranger he had once been.

"There's nothing to be afraid of," he said, and raised his eyes to the rearview mirror. There was the ache in his heart, and now over his shoulder and down his arm, as he caught the reflection of the boy's pale cheek and full girlish lips, his dry mouth hanging open in fearful expectation of what?—the sky growing black, the wind moaning, the scrim of sand that blew across the empty lot forming itself into tooth and mouth and open jaw. "What are you afraid of?" More derisively than he'd meant it.

"Let's at least have our dessert before we go," Mary said, soothing. A balancing act. "I have plums," she said, leaning over her stomach, over the baby's feet that were now—little acrobat—pressing themselves up against her breasts. She leaned over the curve of its back and spine as they pressed themselves into her stomach and bladder, leaned over the head that was now pressing itself down toward the worn upholstery of the old car, sensing, perhaps, that its watery world was a tributary after all, not a pool. She leaned into the quilted hamper where she had plums and grapes and sugar cookies shaped like laurel wreaths.

In a few minutes, the rain began. The children spit the plum pits into their paper cups and handed them across the seat to their mother. John Keane pressed his chest to the steering wheel as he put the key in the ignition, taking a deep breath as he did, hoping the change of movement would ease the growing pain. The windshield wipers were like a new beat in the day's rhythm. Mary Keane wrapped the two coffee cups in paper towels. Her husband put his arm across the back of the seat. "Everybody set to go?" he said. He had been too harsh with Michael, too derisive of Jacob, and who knew what his daughter needed, looking up at him, the bear in her arms. "I'm ready," she said, primly, the first to respond. The apple of his eye.

"Let's just go," Jacob added, fighting tears. His face was once more turned to the window. "Let's get home," unable to keep the crimp of fear out of his voice. Michael leaned forward, looking toward him across his sister's lap, and his mother saw that his lips were pursed with either the sour aftertaste of the plum or the sharp phrase of an insult, a tease. She watched him until he sat back again, thinking better of it. He understood, even then, that he could repeat word for word something his father had already said about some weakness in his brother and still be reprimanded for it as severely as if he alone had let the cat out of the bag.

THAT EVENING, just after midnight, John Keane was drawn downstairs by a pounding at his door that might have been theatrical, something falsely urgent and echoing about it. Something familiar and rehearsed, too, in his own manner as he asked Mary, "Who could that be?" and then slowly pushed the blankets aside and found his slippers. The rain was a steady rush against the roof and the windows. The light in the empty living room was just enough to see by, to distinguish the black shape of the couch and the chairs, the tables and lamps, the television set and hi-fi and decorative mirror that caught and reflected the oddly gauzy, deep blue light that came through the front window, cast off by the storm. A puddle of darkness in the center of the floor was the board game the boys had left there. In the short hallway, which lacked any light whatsoever, he could feel under his slippers a remnant of sand on the linoleum. The football and the box of soldiers were beside the door, invisible. "Coming," he cried when the rapping began again, on the heels of a distant roll of thunder, and in the instant before he reached for the doorknob, he felt with utter certainty, as if all of this were indeed merely something revisited, rehearsed, recalled, that he would not return—not to the living room behind him or the narrow stairs or the small rooms where his wife and his children slept.

This was the culmination, then, this odd darkness, this familiar dream, of the day that had begun with the tugging of the wind at his eaves; this was the simple and terrible meaning, after all, of the pain in his arm, the weight on his heart. Here now and at last, and too soon—as it had come to his brother's heart too soon—the utter darkness, the black street, wind rain and sea and some glimpse, in his final fall, of the damp room (odor of salt, odor of peat) where in another darkness he had been conceived. An instant so close—in its familiarity, in its blackness, in the cry of the wind—to everything he had been told as a child would attend his last moment (he would hear the banshee, he would open the door, he would see the black coach, wet with rain), that he felt both amused and terrified.

Still, he pulled firmly at the door, knowing how it swelled and stuck in wet weather. He might have wished to see their faces once more.

The face that met him was under a fireman's helmet, lit by a flashlight held low and expertly angled. The light caught the silver needles of rain, in the air, off the rim of the black hat. It showed him a mouth and a chin and the broad shoulders under the wet rain gear without blinding him or turning the man himself into a grotesque.

"I only wanted to warn you," the man said. He moved the flashlight across his body, to the shrubs beside the steps and then to the grass and then to the weeping willow at the edge of the yard, beside the house. The streetlights were out. Following the moving beam of white light, John Keane saw the grass of his small lawn stir like a rising wave and the roots of the tree—thin as an arm, bent here and there like an elbow—breaking through. The fireman moved the light until it caught the base of the tree where a wider swath of dirt was opening like a mouth, an unhinged jaw filled with broken roots and dirt, and then it closed up again, as if with a breath. "We were driving by and saw it," the fireman said. "That tree's gonna fall. It'll probably fall straight back, but you might want to get your family downstairs. Keep them to this side of the house."

He felt the wind and the rain on his bare ankles, against the hems of his thin pajama pants. He looked beyond the young fireman. In the street, there was no sign of the fire truck or car that had brought him. No coach, either. "Yes," he said, thinking himself foolish, in his thin pajamas. "Thank you."

"There are trees down all over," the man added. He raised his chin and in the darkness his eyes seemed as black and wet as his coat. He couldn't have been more than twenty-five or thirty. "Take care of your family," he said, and turned, using his flashlight to get himself down the three steps that led to the door. Squinting against the rain, John Keane watched him cross the path to the sidewalk, the circle of white light leading him, first to the right and then across the street where he might have disappeared altogether, leaving only the pale beam of his flashlight and a flashing reflection of two streaks of silver on his back, and then, as he apparently rounded the opposite corner, not even that.

The wind was howling in long gusts, driving the rain straight across his face, against his slippers and pants legs. He listened for some sound of an idling motor, strained his eyes against the wind and the rain to see some indication—a stain of red light or blue light, perhaps—of the truck or car that must be waiting for the fireman on the next block. But there was nothing he could see, or hear above the sound of the wind and the rain and the shaking leaves. Across the street the blue storm light briefly caught the blind windows of his neighbors' homes.

He stepped back and closed the door. His fingers, too, where they had gripped it, were wet. He dried them on his pajamas, then groped for the closet door and found the flashlight he kept on the shelf there. The living room was as it had been. He turned to the

stairs, aware, now, of the sound of the willow branches brushing
the opposite wall of the house. It would indeed fall straight, from
the front yard to the back, parallel to the house, and for the next few
days his children, all the neighborhood children, would crawl over
its trunk and up into its branches, like Lilliputians over a long-
haired Gulliver, until Mr. Persichetti down the street arrived with a
newly purchased chain saw and a borrowed truck, offering his ser-
vices. Mr. Persichetti was a night nurse at the state hospital, inspired
by the storm's destruction (he would say) to make better use of his
days. The loss of the tree, then—the lovely willow that had made
them, ten years ago, choose this house above any of the others—
was all of the inalterable change that the long day had portended.

In their room, the boys, who had been awoken by the pounding
at the door, watched silently as the beam of their father's light
moved slowly up the stairs. For Jacob, the slow pace of the rising
beam was a comfort; there could be no immediate danger if his father walked so steadily up the stairs. Michael felt only disappointment at his father's quiet return. But then their father stood in the
doorway, the light pooled at his feet, and told them, whispering,
that they'd better get up and come downstairs. He whispered the
same to their mother, who was already standing beside her bed, ty-
ing her robe at the narrowest place left to her, high up on her belly
and just under her breasts. He lifted their sister from her bed and
carried her downstairs over his shoulder. Even in the peripheral
light (Michael had asked to carry the flashlight but his mother had
taken it instead, and Jacob's hand), it was clear that she was only
pretending to still be asleep—her eyelids fluttered, there was the
smallest shape of a smile. Herding them all toward the basement,
their father paused at the dining-room window, pulled back the curtain and shone the beam through the window and out into the darkness until it caught the yawning base of the doomed tree.

After only a quick glimpse, a glimpse that was like a gulp of foul air, Jacob pulled at his mother's hand to draw her to safety. But Michael lingered, and even Annie squirmed out of her father's arms to stand by the window, her two hands on the painted sill. The roots reared out of the black ground, the trunk leaned and then straightened, the long branches swung this way and that. Their mother patted Jacob's hand to soothe him. On their way through the kitchen she took a bottle of milk from the refrigerator and the remaining paper cups from their picnic. They followed their father's flashlight down the wooden steps. It was a tunnel of light and it seemed to draw all the surrounding shadows to its edge. Only Michael walked alone although, at one point, as they made their way down the stairs, he touched his fingers to the back of Jacob's neck and made him jump. They sat together on the old couch that was just the other side of the toy-train table. Their mother between the two boys to avoid trouble, Annie on her father's lap. The washing machine and the sink and the long string of the clothesline where she hung clothes in bad weather were just behind them, each illuminated, however dimly, by the blue light of the storm at the narrow windows. Around their own circle of light, their mother said, "Let's say an Angel of God," the bodies of her two boys pressed against her. "Angel of God," they said, following her voice. "My guardian dear, to whom God's love, commits me here, ever this night, be at my side, to light and guard, to rule and guide. Amen."

And then the thrashing of the wind against the house and then what might have been a volley of pistol shots, and then a sound like something slowly spilling from a great height. Jacob pulled his knees up into his arms and whimpered. Annie, dramatically, put her arms around her father's neck. "There went the tree," he said.

In the small circle of the flashlight, their mother poured milk into the paper cups and carefully handed them to the children.

WHEN JOHN AND MARY KEANE said "during the war," their children imagined the world gone black and white, imagined a hand passing like a dark cloud over the earth, blotting out the sun for what might only have been the duration of a single night, or the length of a storm. Long before any of them was born, after all, their parents, the world itself, had emerged from that shadow.

During the war, their father said, we sometimes slept in people's cellars. France, Belgium, into Germany. (The milk in the paper cups smelled like candles, like the small votives they lit in church.) Sometimes the houses were deserted, even partially destroyed. Sometimes it seemed the families must still be upstairs. There were old bicycles in some, or baby carriages. A steamer trunk, once, filled with broken dishes. A jar of pickled cauliflower.

Once, three or four of them had taken shelter for the night, in the cellar of an abandoned farmhouse—it was maybe late '44 or early '45—and when the sun came up (not a sun, really, as he recalled it, only darkness turning to pale gray) they realized a new guy, a replacement, had joined them during the night. He just appeared among them, as if he had sprung from the dirt floor while they slept. No more than nineteen or twenty. Anxious and poorly trained, the way all the replacements were at that stage of the war. "Who the fuck are you?" one of the guys said. (Although telling the tale to his children—around the single flashlight—John Keane said, "Who the blankety-blank . . .") "Jacob," the boy said. "Jake. From Philadelphia." Then he shook everybody's hand, like he was joining a poker game. Another Jacob.

Michael turned to his brother whose eyes were large and dark at the edge of the light. He had hoped until now that his father's story pertained to him.

The two of them walked out of the cellar together, into the cold. Jake seemed to think that John Keane, perhaps because of his age, was of some superior rank, and it was possible that the kid was looking for some advantage, sticking with him. Or it may have been only that the other men, superstitious about replacements, had given him a wide berth. It was a gray dawn, an overcast day, only the beginning of the worst of it. There would have been the sound of boots breaking frost—tramp, tramp, tramp. A smell of diesel fuel, which was pervasive. Creak of army boots and canvas cartridge belts. Maybe wood smoke somewhere. Jacob was dark-eyed and pale. He had a young man's beard, only potential, the hint of black whiskers along his jaw looking like something black pressed under a thick pane of smoked glass. At one point he pulled off a glove with his teeth and left it dangling from his mouth as he, what?—opened a K ration? lit a cigarette? The condemned man's last. His bare hand was as white as bone, as small as a child's.

At one point during that cold day John Keane had said to the kid, the other Jacob, "We're a regular Gallagher and Shean," and the kid had surprised him by knowing more choruses than even his brother Frank did, humming them softly under his breath, carrying the tune.

Oh, Mr. Gallagher, oh Mr. Gallagher, if you're a friend of mine you'll loan me a couple of bucks. I'm so broke, I'm nearly bent and I haven't got a cent. I'm so clean you'd think that I'd been washed in Lux.

Oh, Mr. Shean, oh Mr. Shean (how did it go? Frank would

know), *to tell the truth I haven't got a bean. Cost of living's gone so high, why it's cheaper now to die.*

Absolutely, Mr. Gallagher.

Positively, Mr. Shean.

He'd said to the kid (he'd shaken him off late that afternoon, in a frozen rain, and only learned he'd been hit after nightfall, when they were pressed into foxholes, the taste of dirt and smoke like blood in their mouths), What can I do for you? Not out loud, but in his mind, like a prayer. Plenty of others had been killed, but this one had sprung up out of the dirt floor, fresh faced and too young. He'd spent less than twenty-four hours at his war. This other Jacob. What can I do for you, John Keane had said in that foxhole in the Ardennes, in the winter of '44 or '45, the worst yet to come—more death and the bitter snow, shrapnel, three toes of his own lost to the cold. What can I do for you? He'd said it like a prayer, it was a prayer, believing the kid heard him because (he told his children) all of us are immortal or no one is. You prayed to the dead or you let them go silent. What can I do for you? he had said, in his mind, like a prayer, and later their mother, in her hospital bed, their firstborn in her arms, grimaced and said, "That's a Jewish name."

Michael grinned, turning to his brother whose mouth hung open, dark as his eyes behind his raised knees.

But their father had told her, "It's just something I'd like to do."

In the small circle of flashlight, with the sound of the storm already seeming to fade—as if the tree's fall (or perhaps her husband's story) had abated something—Mary Keane pressed her two sons against her sides. It was pleasant, to be in the basement like this, with her family, in the middle of the night. She looked across Jacob's dark hair to her husband, who still had Annie's thin arms wrapped around his neck. She doubted, thinking back, that she had said, straight off, That's a Jewish name—or perhaps she did not doubt it as much as regret it, since it had become, in the intervening years, Jacob's name alone, the name of her own boy, the Jacob from the war having become, in the intervening years, poor kid, mostly forgotten.

Much as she had forgotten, already, what it was that had brought him to mind tonight, that other Jacob. Was it the storm itself? The banging at the door? The young fireman, appearing like a guardian angel to warn them that the lights were out and trees were falling all over the neighborhood?

She wondered briefly if her husband should have told the children this particular war story at all. Michael would surely use it against his brother. There was always the possibility of bad dreams.

If he had wanted to tell the children the story he might simply have said that he and the boy had sung vaudeville tunes together, in the middle of a war. Gallagher and Shean. Mutt and Jeff. Catholic and Jew. Fresh-faced replacement and aging veteran, tramping through the cold, singing. He could have left it at that. He could have left out the fact that one had but a few hours to live, while the other had another life entirely still before him. This one.

With her arms around her sons and the new baby curled against her rib cage, her husband and her daughter a mere arm's length away, and the storm turning from them even as the sun was surely approaching, Mary Keane considered the wisdom of leaving certain, difficult things unsaid. She considered the wisdom of the Blessed Mother who, as the Christmas gospel told it, pondered everything in her heart.

Gently, she collected the children's cups. With her silence alone she held off, for a moment longer, the suggestion that the worst was over, the tree had fallen, the storm was passing, and time, as she was given to saying, was marching on: school tomorrow, work for their father, laundry, shopping, meals. For just a moment more, she let them linger.

THE TINY SPIDERS that lived in the higher branches of the downed tree (which now meant the branches that lay on the other side of the crushed fence that separated front yard from back) were bright red. At the end of the day, even the careful children had the marks of them, bloody starbursts on their palms. And the smell of the green wood, the tender leaves and pliant branches, on their skin and in their clothes. Mr. Persichetti, standing at the top of the three steps, the borrowed truck with the new chain saw just behind him, saw Tony, his own son, moving among the fallen branches as if through a jungle. Tony wore a plastic combat helmet and carried a toy pistol. He was thirteen, three years older than the oldest Keane boy, and Mr. Persichetti wondered if he wasn't too old for such playacting. He resolved, even before Mrs. Keane had agreed to let him do the job, that he'd get the boy to help out tomorrow afternoon, hauling the thin branches and the smaller slices of tree trunk.

He was asking twenty dollars—not an exorbitant amount. Some of the women in the neighborhood merely spoke to him from behind their storm doors, but Mrs. Keane opened hers and invited him in. He stood in the small vestibule. She wore a maternity dress with a bow at the neckline and bedroom slippers. She seemed pale and somewhat puffy, not what you'd call a good-looking woman from the start, but she had a direct and friendly manner that encouraged him to say he had been inspired by the storm to make better use of his free days. He'd been on construction crews in the army. South Pacific. He knew how to handle a chain saw and clear away trees. He'd always thought that if he was ever going to get any kind of sideline going, he wanted it to be something that got him out in the fresh air. Listening to the wind on the night of the hurricane, he'd heard the crack and snap of a falling tree and it had brought the whole thing back to him, the fields he'd cleared, the forests hauled away. One thing led to another, he said. A new chain saw, a buddy with a truck. A place in Commack where he could dump the wood. The vestibule was identical to the one in his own house, although his wife was dark-eyed and thin-faced, younger than Mrs. Keane but well finished with childbearing. Twenty dollars wasn't a lot to ask but she, like the other women who were not so friendly, said she would have to check with her husband first.

She followed him out to the front step. It was a beautiful day, the kind that always followed such a storm. The September sky a perfect blue and the odor of dried rain still in the air. The green odor of the fallen tree as well. Mrs. Keane and Mr. Persichetti both looked toward it. The grass had been torn by the exposed roots, but the tree itself seemed beautiful in repose. They could see through the branches the children who played there, some brightly colored, others mere shadows amid the leaves. Her boys and the Persichetti boy and a dozen neighborhood children among them.

"It will be a shame to take it away," Mrs. Keane said, as if she'd already agreed to let him do the job. "We're the most popular place in the neighborhood." She put her hand under her belly, the way pregnant women do, holding up the weight. Mr. Persichetti watched his son slide along the downed trunk of the tree, his silver cowboy pistol drawn. There were strings of willow leaves, still strung on their wiry branches, wrapped around his helmet.

Impulsively, Mr. Persichetti called out his son's name, foiling an ambush (at the sound of the man's voice, Michael Keane's head appeared on the other side of the upended roots). He said it was time to go. The response was all in the boy's shoulders and arms—a slow sinking. Two more boys, also in helmets, emerged from the leaves, their indignation at being called from the game tempered only by the sight of Tony's father on the steps in his work pants and T-shirt. He was a broad, short man with muscular arms. "It's early," his son called back, squinting. And it was the squinting, the openmouthed squinting and the hint of contradiction in his son's voice that turned what had been mere impulse on his father's part into command. It was early, another two hours before dinner, and there was certainly no need for him to drive Tony home—he hadn't driven him here—but still he said, "Get in the truck," and bent his powerful arm. He was a night nurse at Creedmoor, the state hospital, and what he had seen there, the patients he had hauled and handled—the vibration of mad voices he had felt through bodies pressed into his arms, held against his cheek and his chest—made him quick to raise his hand to his own lucky child, smart as a whip and perfectly formed.

Tony bent his head to remove the borrowed helmet. Mournfully, he handed the helmet and the pistol to Jacob. His father went down the steps and joined him at the curb. He guided Tony to the truck with his hand on the back of his son's neck.

("Shoot him in the foot," Mr. Persichetti would tell Mr. Keane, years later, when Tony had already returned from the war and Jacob had drawn a bad number. "Break his legs before you let him go.")

The truck turned and headed down the street. The boys shook off the disruption and went back to their game. Mary Keane, returning to the house, her hand under her heavy belly, the baby, as far as she could tell, sound asleep within, wondered why it was that the Persichettis had only the two, Tony and little Susan, who was

Annie's age. She felt with some certainty that it would have been to Tony's advantage if they'd had at least one other son. (She had in mind the man's strong hand on the back of the boy's neck.) It benefited a child, she thought, to be forgotten once in a while. Lost in the shuffle (she would have said), benignly neglected. It reminded them they were not the center of the universe simply because they were loved by their parents. How many children, when you came right down to it (she would have said), were not loved by their parents? Never mind if the love was skillful or adept.

She picked up Jacob's school jacket and the box of toy soldiers that had been left on the floor of the hall, but the effort sent a pain up her back—like a crack through plaster—and drained the blood from her head. She leaned heavily against the front door, put her hand on the doorknob and although her husband had said nothing of his vision of the black coach wet with rain, she caught a glimpse of it herself in that second between the moment she closed her eyes and the next one when she began a Hail Mary. The amniotic fluid was like something sun-warmed against her leg. It quickly soaked her terry-cloth slipper and then pooled on the linoleum at her feet. Her heel skidded in it a little as she slowly let go of the doorknob and carefully—a reluctant skater on a pond—got herself across the hallway, onto the living-room carpet, and across the living room, a slug's trail of dark water behind her, and onto the couch. She still held Jacob's coat in her hand and she threw it over the cushions before she eased herself down, praying all the while the formal prayer that held off both hope and dread, as well as any speculation about what to do next. She must have said a dozen of them—it only occurred to her after about the seventh or eighth that she should have been counting them off on her fingers—when the first cramp seized her and then she threw the prayers aside as if they had been vain attempts to speak in her high-school French. Oh look, she said. Don't let this happen. Come on. Be reasonable.

Long before the fireman pounded at the door (or was it an angel, or a banshee, or the ghost of the other Jacob?), she had listened to the rise and fall of the wind outside. Long before her husband had woken and asked her, Who could that be? she had seen—in the silent anticipation between each long gust, in the fear that rose as the sound grew more terrible each time, as if edging toward something unbearable—the parallel between the rise and fall of the storm and the rhythm of labor. Now, as the labor began, it was the storm she recalled. The thrash of wind and trees and the quiet terror that had kept her flat in her bed, wide awake, anticipating disaster but unable to rise to avert it—or to shake her husband, to call for help. There was only silence now, in the small living room. There was a baby doll and a stack of comic books in one of the chairs, a Wiffle ball beneath it. The boys' board game with its scattered pieces was still on the rug, and there was a pale layer of dust over the hi-fi and the end tables. She wondered if the pregnancy had turned her slothful or if the room was always in some state of disorder and she was only, momentarily, seeing it clearly. Vaguely, she could hear the voices of the children in the side yard, climbing through the downed tree. It seemed to her (the pain rising again, third time) that they were not so much calling words as shining small silver lights into her ears. The gentle flash of a child's voice— was it Jacob?—appearing here and there through the more general silence and the nausea of the clutching pain.

The phone was in the kitchen, and when she got herself up she would call her husband first, in his office. And then the operator to send an ambulance. And then one of the neighbors to come and watch the children. And then Pauline, who had promised to stay with the children when the time came, although time was supposed to have been still another month away and Pauline would sigh at the inconvenience, the altered plans. And this poor baby, so eager to be born, would emerge from the womb with unhappy Pauline ready to recount, on birthdays, at the birth of other children, at any of the innumerable occasions in her life when she was once again forced to abandon her plans, how she had just powdered her nose and put on her hat when the phone call came.

The fourth contraction seized her and suddenly she was perspiring. She heard herself cry out and then she heard the children's voices like sparks struck from her own. And then heard a man call "Hello," the single word across what seemed a great distance. Calmly, because the pain was once again subsiding (she recalled the rhythm of the hurricane), she turned her head toward the vestibule. It was simply what you did: you made conversation in elevators, complimented small children in strollers, looked up from your magazine to greet the stranger who took the seat beside you on a bus. You said, with simple friendliness, That's a lovely hat, or Isn't it cold?—because it was another way of saying here we are, all of us, more or less in the same boat. It was the habit of friendliness, a lifetime of it. Mary Keane smiled. Her dress and her son's jacket and the slipcover on the couch beneath her were soaked and the next contraction was already gathering strength in the small of her back. Mary Keane smiled politely as Mr. Persichetti poked his head around the door to the vestibule and said, "Hello."

He took her hand and then her pulse. He put his broad palm on her forehead and then took her hand again as her face flushed and she drew her legs up against the pain. He had returned to say the Krafts down the street had an apple tree split in two that he was planning to remove at noon tomorrow (Mr. Kraft was a teacher and since the schools were closed he was there to answer his door and to engage Mr. Persichetti on the spot). He'd come back to say he could easily toss both the willow and the apple tree into his truck, and so charge her only fifteen.

He called the operator from the phone in the kitchen and then left a message for Mr. Keane at his office. As luck would have it, the first kitchen drawer he pulled open was full of dish towels and he grabbed the lot of them. The next held the kitchen scissors and bakery string and even—she might have planned this—a turkey baster, all of which he gathered up, just in case. He wet one of the dishcloths with cool water at the sink, and then returned to her. She was not the housekeeper his own wife was—there were crumbs on the kitchen table and stained teacups in the sink—but there was a sweetness in the way she asked when he leaned over her if she could just take hold of his arm.

Mr. Persichetti called his patients God's mistakes. He pressed his arms around them when the need arose and sometimes felt their wailing voices in his own flesh, in his chest, against his cheek. What was in their eyes, or, more precisely, what was not, he thought of as some failure on the part of God to fully animate what He had, perhaps too blithely, made. He thought of God then, God the Father anyway (for Jesus, of course, was a different case), as somewhat cavalier in His creations. Not indifferent—Jesus was proof of that, as was Mr. Persichetti himself, who might have worked construction with his powerful arms but had instead used the GI Bill to become a nurse—only swift and bustling and unheeding, like nature itself. Like the storm. When Mrs. Keane whispered, between contractions, that the baby was coming at least six weeks too soon, he shook his head and clucked his tongue, lifting the wet dish towel from her forehead and refolding it and then touching it gently to her cheeks. The dampness, and the perspiration, had darkened her hair and the pain had brought some color to her face. There was all about her a not unpleasant odor of oatmeal or wheat. He knelt beside the couch. When he leaned away, his T-shirt was wet with the amniotic fluid that had soaked her dress and the cushion beneath her. Her knees were already raised, her pale legs bare, and he asked, gently, if she would like him to check what was going on. She nodded and when the contraction had passed, added, "Modesty is always the first thing to go."

He folded back the hem of her housedress. Peeled the wet underpants from her skin and moved them down over her pale knees and her small feet and then dropped them on the floor. He could hear the voices of the children playing in the tree outside. He gently pushed her thighs apart and saw immediately that the baby had already begun to crown. Her skin was paler than his wife's was, even in midwinter. He gave her his hand to get her through the next contraction, keeping his arm steady as she squeezed. He spread the fingers of the other over her taut belly. Mr. Persichetti wore a silver Saint Christopher's medal around his neck and kept a Sacred Heart scapular in his pocket, but when Mary Keane asked him, catching her breath, "Who's the patron saint of women in labor?" he shrugged. He told her he only knew Saint Dymphna was the patron of the insane.

He'd had the story from an Irish priest assigned to Creedmoor. "A sad case himself," Mr. Persichetti said, and gently pulled the damp hem of her dress back over her thighs. For a moment he found himself incapable of remembering Mr. Keane's face, although they'd been neighbors for perhaps ten years. Nor could he remember another conversation he'd had with this woman stretched before him now on her living-room couch, her hair damp and her eyes a kind of gray, or green. He took her hand as if she were his child, or his own wife.

"Apparently," he said, "this Saint Dymphna was the daughter of an Irish chieftain, a pagan. But she had a beautiful Christian mother." Gray eyes or green, he thought they were the one thing that might have made her pretty when she was young. "So the mother dies." He paused only briefly. "When the girl's about fourteen. And the chieftain goes crazy and tells his servants to go out and find another beautiful woman who resembled his dead wife so he can marry her."

He paused again to touch her white lips with the wet towel. "They should be here soon," he said softly, interrupting himself. There was a bit of mad laughter from the children outside. The sun through the lace curtains at the front window had placed a small spotlight on the arm of the sofa, just above her head. He could see by the color in her cheeks that another contraction was on the rise.

"The servants were evil," he said, recalling the tale the way the whiskey priest they sent to Creedmoor told it, sitting with Mr. Persichetti at the nurse's station late into the night, those watery blue eyes forever bloodshot and sleepless. "They told the crazy chieftain that he should marry his beautiful daughter instead. Which he tried to do." ("If you get my meaning," the priest had said.) "But Dymphna ran off to Belgium." He saw her grimace and purse her lips, her face seemed to swell with color. "Her crazy father followed her," he said, tightening his own grip on her hand. "I guess he cut off her head."

Mrs. Keane said, "Oh my," but the contraction took hold and at the end of it she sobbed, "Mother of God," which he supposed was the answer he should have given her in the first place.

Jesus and Mary, most of the saints, even the alcoholic priest who could calm an agitated patient with just the laying on of his swollen hands, Mr. Persichetti himself, plagued by pity—indications all that the Creator was not indifferent to the suffering He engendered, in His bustling, in His haste, but also that there would be no end to His mistakes. Mr. Persichetti knew that six weeks before its time and with a good thirty-minute ride to the hospital once the ambulance came (would it ever come?), the baby would most likely not survive, would be born with flesh and plenty of blood but underdeveloped lungs and insufficient breath. He heard the children calling to one another outside, Tony among them once again since his father was taking so long inside the house and (stinging injustice) had been wrong to drag him away in the first place, two hours before dinner. (Although Tony had quickly discovered that the earlier war game could not be recaptured; that in the twenty minutes he'd been gone, it had lost its life, lost its charm.)

Mr. Persichetti knew there were children growing in nearly every house in this neighborhood, in every borough and every town. Thousands more were being born today, being conceived—women with their knees raised all over the world. Mrs. Keane herself already had three. If one of these, if a hundred of them, a thousand, came too soon or failed to thrive or were born incomplete somehow, born blue or ill made or with reason's taut string already snapped, it was of little matter in the long history of God's bustling. There was the Mother of God to turn to in prayer. There were the angels and the saints. There were the people like himself, plagued by pity the way other men were driven by ambition or greed, who would wade through the blood and the stool, the torn hair and ravaged flesh, the mad cries, to take the broken, raving thing—God's mistake—into his arms.

When the next contraction had passed, he gently pushed the dish towels (printed with teapots, printed with kittens) under Mrs. Keane's white thighs, pulling away Jacob's soaked jacket. He put one hand on top of her belly. "Isn't it lucky that you're here?" she whispered, holding on to his strong arm. And then, a little later, "Isn't it good the hurricane caused the tree to fall and so you came by?"

And Mr. Persichetti said it was good indeed, although he knew the baby might not survive.

"The storm came," she said, catching her breath, "and then a fireman came to the door in the middle of the storm, out of nowhere, and told us about the tree falling, and then you came by." She grimaced and paused, squeezing his hand. "And came back," she said as the contraction passed. "Because—who was it?" she said.

"The Krafts," he told her, "down the street."

"The Krafts lost a tree as well," she said, shifting uncomfortably. "Lucky for me."

And then she breathed another "Mother of God."

His T-shirt was soaked all across the middle. There was now the salty scent of her perspiration, and his, and the scent of blood. Her bare knee touched the side of his face. He saw the baby's dark scalp, streaks of hair. She cried out and he was aware, too, of the sound of the ambulance somewhere. He raised the volume of his own voice, a string of reassurances against his own fear that the baby would not survive. Skull and forehead and closed eyes streaked with blood. He reached for the turkey baster, cleared the mouth even as he tugged, gently, at the head in his hands. The shoulders and arms and the surprising burst of the pale blue umbilical cord, thick and writhing, and then the baby was in his hands—"A little girl," he told her—and the medics, the ambulance guys were in the room behind him, around him, a knee against his back as someone said, "Step aside," and leaned down to take the little thing from him. The baby's mouth opened and two fists went up in fury. And then it cried, but so thinly.

But of course, he couldn't step. He discovered that he was kneeling at her side. He merely sat back on his bottom and then crawled a bit, avoiding their shoes. Someone was opening a medical bag and a stretcher was coming through the front door. He blessed himself and then said, "I'm in medicine, an RN," lest they think him a fool. Then he leaned his back against a chair.

As they were hustling her and the child out the door (where the children from the tree had already gathered) he said to one of the medics, "Six weeks premature." The guy shook his head. He had a crew cut and a broad face and his white coat buttoned across the

shoulder. "That baby's full-term," he said. "Seven pounds at least."
Mr. Persichetti shrugged, rather nonchalantly, among men once
more. "She said she had six more weeks."

And the man shrugged, too, as if to confirm how well they both
understood, being in the profession, that it was all a small matter,
this coming into life and going out, merely part of the routine. "She
can't count," he said bluntly.

And then he laughed. He paused in the tiny hallway, put his elbow to Mr. Persichetti's strong arm. "My wife always knows exactly," he said. There was a bit of tobacco on his wet lip. "But that's
probably because she only lets me do it twice a year, Valentine's and
my birthday, so it's not hard to figure." He stepped out the door and
then turned to say, "I got two kids born in November, two in June.
No kidding."

The children gathered along the driveway briefly looked away
from the ambulance as the man went down the steps, shouting back
to Mr. Persichetti. "This guy," he said, pointing at the house, "is a
lucky man, if she don't know if it's been nine months or seven."
Mr. Persichetti raised a hand, agreeing, nodding and laughing, but
also saying under his breath, Get going, get going. He would not
rest easily until he was sure she was in a doctor's care. Then he noticed her boys. They were standing side by side at the edge of the
driveway, their plastic guns still in their hands and their faces pale
and forlorn beneath the toy helmets, his own Tony, God bless him,
with a comforting arm around each.

CAREFULLY, dipping carefully—the broad backside in the good wool skirt—Pauline reached into the car and took the infant from Mary Keane's arms. There was the pink receiving blanket, the long white shawl, the lace bib of her homecoming dress. Pauline stepped back, onto the grass that lined the driveway, the baby in her arms.

Mary said, "Where's her bonnet?" and then searched the floor, looking for it. Her husband was coming around the car to help her get out. Pauline held the baby in her arms, dipped her large, powdered face closer to its own, her eyes taking in, there on the grass at the side of the driveway, the cashmere shawl (her own gift, from Saks), the receiving blanket, the tiny body, the little face. Slowly, Pauline raised her left hand and cupped it over the child's skull to keep her warm. The sun was high but there was a clean chill in the air. The smell of autumn, and of the sawdust left behind from the fallen tree. She held the baby against her chest and raised her elbow to bring the small sleeping face nearer her own.

"Here it is," Mary said, lifting the bonnet from the floor.

Inside, the children were waiting around the dining-room table with their homemade cards and the frosted birthday cake their father had brought from the bakery this morning. Inside, Pauline's overnight bag was packed and waiting in the vestibule. As Mary, carrying the new baby, preceded her into the house, Pauline slipped her jacket from the hall closet and lifted the bag, even as the three children gathered around their mother. She simply walked out again, through the front door. She went down the steps. She raised her hand without turning when they called after her. She raised her hand without turning as John Keane followed her down the steps to say, "At least let me give you a lift to the bus stop."

"Go back to your new family," she said without turning. "This is a precious moment. There shouldn't be any strangers at this homecoming." Meaning it, every word of it, but not turning to see how thoroughly her sudden departure had disrupted the homecoming anyway, how the children had looked away from their mother and the new baby to stare after her, how John Keane had looked back to his wife, their new daughter in her arms, to shrug, to show her his annoyance. The woman drove him crazy.

Without turning, Pauline walked with her bag the three blocks to the bus stop, then changed at Jamaica for the bus home.

At her building, she struggled with the six days of mail shoved every which way into her box (she'd had no time, when the call came, to leave her mailbox key with her neighbor), bills and advertising circulars and bank statements and a mailman who would probably keep pushing mail into her box even if she was gone for six months, dead for a year—only one of the phalanx of indifferent strangers she faced every day.

Upstairs in her apartment she unpacked her bag—two housedresses in polished cotton and a floral housecoat, another good skirt and sweater and the underwear, girdle, and stockings she'd have to wash out in the sink this evening. In the bottom of the bag, beneath her makeup case and her slippers, the card Jacob had drawn for her—a vase with six spindly flowers: a purple tulip, what seemed to be a red rose, and four simple daisies (she guessed that the success with the tulip had inspired the rose and the failure of the rose had led to the safer daisies). Inside the folded piece of blue construction paper he had written only, in careful cursive, From Jacob.

Although she preferred Michael, whose distrust of anything placid echoed her own, she put the card on her dresser.

Moving into her small kitchen, Pauline went through the refrigerator, tossing out the milk and the sliced ham she had not had time to dispose of last week, when the call came that the baby had arrived early and they were on their way to the hospital. A minute later and they would have missed her, she told John Keane, when the call came. She had just powdered her nose and put on her hat.

She rode the elevator down again to shop briefly—it was Sunday and the stores closed early—for what she needed: milk and eggs and bread and margarine. She told the lady at the deli where she ordered her ham that it had not been a vacation by any means: three children to look after and a much neglected house to clean. The lady at the counter—Maria, in housecoat and worn slippers and swollen ankles—called her some good friend to do all that and Pauline said, "Oh, but the baby is beautiful," a kind of reprimand, as if it had been Maria herself who had complained so ungenerously about the dirty house.

The grocery bag was light enough but still her back ached and her legs were tired. She had slept fitfully all week in little Annie's bedroom, wall to wall with stuffed animals that the child never played with and that Pauline would have donated to an orphanage, had the choice been hers. And the little girl had cried herself to sleep in her brother's bedroom every night, lonesome for her mother. And that little Italian man in the side yard two days in a row, with his chain saw and his hatchet, clearing the fallen tree. Standing too close to her, Pauline felt certain, when he came into the kitchen for a glass of water.

The sparse trees along her block were showing signs of red and gold but there was also the smell of dog droppings and bus fumes and sun-warmed garbage in the air, which you didn't have out on Long Island. And the Empire State Building across the river was useless, a painted backdrop at this hour on a Sunday, its offices empty, its very reason for being temporarily drained. Her company's own building, her empty office within, not three blocks away. Home again, she changed into another housecoat, the red velvet one she had made for herself last Christmas, the covered buttons she'd found at A&S a satisfying perfect match. She boiled an egg for dinner. Mixed a Manhattan to sip with Walter Cronkite. She answered the phone only the second time it rang, Mary calling to say I wish you hadn't run off (but not meaning it) and that the house has never been so clean (no kidding) and what did you put in your mashed potatoes that made the kids love them so (a little sugar and a little garlic salt, but Pauline wouldn't tell).

Darkness had come down on the city by then, the lights in all the buildings had come up. With the phone still to her ear, Pauline dipped her head to notice through her own blinds that the couple across the street was having takeout Chinese again, in their kitchen. They were most likely newlyweds, only in the apartment for a few months. Pauline knew it did not bode well that the young bride never cooked.

"And you cleaned up that slipcover so beautifully," Mary Keane said.

The little Italian man had pulled the slipcover off the couch, bundled it together with the tea towels and the jacket and brought it all to the washing machine in the basement, but Pauline had done the scrubbing and the bleaching and the dyeing. Pauline had restored order after the ordeal of the birth. She had swallowed her revulsion—what a mess it had made—restored order, made things right for the homecoming.

"And how's my angel?" Pauline asked.

"At the moment," Mary said, "she is sound asleep on Jacob's lap."

Her own hunger to hold the baby again struck her as just that, a hunger—the ache of hollow longing, an awareness, as if for the first time in her life, of her own arms being empty.

"I wanted to give you some time with your new family," Pauline said, and meant it—although she couldn't say, too, that she had not meant to disrupt the homecoming with her own dramatic departure. Nor could she deny that she'd wanted both: the thoroughly self-effacing departure and the attention such generous self-effacement surely earned her. She'd wanted to give the family their time together, but she'd wanted as well a more vigorous pursuit, after all she'd done. It wouldn't have taken much, after all, for John Keane to have wrestled the overnight case from her hand.

"Kiss her for me," she said and hung up the phone and faced the most terrible hours of any week, made worse now by the days she had spent in the busy household: the hours after sunset on a Sunday night, all her own usefulness temporarily extinguished, and the terror that good clothes, perfect stitches, the pursuit of just the right buttons usually kept at bay edging closer to the surface of things—the yellow light on the polished table, the black night through the slatted blinds, someone laughing at her out in the street. In another few years this terror would catch her by the throat, but tonight she would have another Manhattan with Ed Sullivan. Rinse out her clothes and brush down tomorrow's suit and iron a blouse. Put on her nightgown and get into bed. There were worse things than this tinny loneliness, these last hours of a Sunday evening. Nice as he'd tried to be—he'd come home from the hospital each evening to put the children to bed, and thanked her profusely each morning for the coffee and toast she put before him, he'd gotten the children ready for church without waking her this morning—she would not want to be married to balding John Keane for all the tea in China. She'd heard him singing to himself in the bathroom, for instance, flat as a tire. Heard him clipping his toenails one night before he went to bed.

She recognized the simple pleasure of her own room and her own pillow and no child weeping for her mother across the hall, the boys whispering words of comfort but not thinking to call on Pauline for help.

In the morning there was the rattle of traffic and the wheeze of buses, the rising voice of the radio, the whistle of a teakettle. The slatted sunlight, as it did this time of year, moved across her bed and her quilted housecoat and her dresser and onto the construction-paper card that Jacob had made so that later when Clare (who last night had slept soundly in her brother's arms) lifted it to read the simple message, she would not be able to say if the front of the card had once been gray or blue, only that her brother had used a ball-point pen and had pressed so firmly into the soft paper that she could feel the shape of the letters in relief on the back.

DURING THE WAR, their mother lit a candle for the boys on her lunch hour, at St. Agnes or up at St. Patrick's, and of course Pauline knew she did this without anyone ever having to tell her so, and although Pauline was estranged from the church—it had to do with something some nun had said—she nevertheless began to tag along. And how could you pray with any sincerity if you were preoccupied with the thought of avoiding lunch with the lonely and annoying girl who was impatiently waiting for your prayers to be over?

If you love me, Jesus said, feed my lambs.

They were at the dining-room table, eating the frosted cake their father had bought at the bakery to celebrate the baby's homecoming.

During the war, Pauline's mother passed away and there were really only a handful of people at the funeral—four of them girls from the office. Pauline sat alone on one side of the church and her brother and his family on the other. None of the dates Pauline had, many of which their mother herself had arranged, led anywhere at all.

It's easy, their mother said, to love the lovable. There's no virtue in that.

They were using the good china and the embroidered table

linen. Milk had been poured into cocktail glasses. The woman at the bakery had written "Welcome Home, Clare" on the white cake. Annie had cried herself to sleep every night that her mother was gone, in full misery the first night, in anticipation, on all subsequent nights, of her brothers' sweet solicitation as they climbed onto the cot with her and said kindly in the dark, without teasing, that their mother would be home soon, with a new sister for her to play with, and she shouldn't cry.

Michael had thought himself indifferent to the new arrangements—Pauline, not his mother, there to greet him with her big, powdered face when he got home from school (and making him hang up his jacket and pick up his games), Pauline there at the dinner table with them, urging them to take more of everything they didn't want and laughing only (but with real delight) when he said his teacher didn't have a mustache but a nunstache, Pauline sitting behind him in the living room as he did his homework on his lap with the television on, asking every minute or so, "Doesn't the TV distract you, doesn't the TV keep you from concentrating?" He'd thought himself indifferent to it all until his mother came through the front door, the new baby in her arms, and he knew for the first time that he'd hated every minute of Pauline's reign. As had Jacob, although Jacob had known this to be true throughout the ordeal.

It wasn't that they'd found Pauline unlovable. The entire world of adult strangers was more or less unlovable, with their huge earlobes and their smoky breaths, their yellow teeth, their intrusions. It was only that the house was empty without their mother in it. Recognizable still in all its familiarity: the vestibule where they dropped their book bags and (at Pauline's insistence) hung up their coats, the living room where the slipcover was newly dark, the cluttered dining room, the Formica counters in the kitchen, the Dutch Boy cookie jar, the worn carpet on the stairs, the sunlight through the windows of their bedroom which seemed always, from the time they woke until darkness fell, the sunlight of four thirty in the afternoon, all of it familiar but seen, for the first time, as it might look when it was empty, with none of them there. This both puzzled them (because all three of them were indeed there, and Pauline was there, and by nine o'clock each night when visiting hours at the hospital were over, their father was there) and filled them with despair, which was what made them tell their mother, once she had returned, the baby in her arms, that they hated Pauline. That they hoped they would never again be left in her care.

It wasn't true, they hadn't hated her at all (Jacob had struggled with the choice between "From" and "Love" on the card he drew for her; Michael had laughed heartily himself when Pauline said that Mr. MacLeod next door, who looked like he dyed his hair with Orange Crush, should lay off that piano and find someplace else to tinkle; Annie now had three different vials of perfume samples tucked in her sock drawer, courtesy of Pauline), but it was an explanation that lingered, a conviction they would share for the rest of their lives.

"You choose likable people to be your friends," their mother said. She sat back from the table, the baby in her arms, and moved the prongs of her fork, the good silver, through the white icing. "And you have to love your family whether they're likable or not." She brought the icing to her lips. "But the people you have to feel sorry for are the ones without family. Unlikable people without family or friends. Who's going to care about them?"

Gripped by their new conviction, the three children shook their heads. "Just don't ever leave us with her again," they said, emphatically, crying it out, not because it was what they truly felt but because it was the only, boisterous way they could demonstrate (other than this birthday party in the dining room, on a Sunday afternoon, with the good silver and the good china and the embroidered tablecloth) their joy at her return.

Their mother, the baby in her arms, held up the small silver fork—it was her wedding silver. In the midst of joy there was, there would always be, the injunction to remember the sorrowful. "You must be kind," their mother said. "I know it's not easy. Pauline's not easy. But what would happen to her if there was no one willing to be kind?"

Later, recalling the homecoming, Annie would tell Michael that like the infant in a fairy tale, Clare's fate, her future, at that moment, must have been sealed. Long after all of them had scattered, Jacob, Michael, Annie, their mother and father, scattered—as their parents would have said—to the four winds, Clare would have Pauline, still a royal pain in the ass, in her care.

III

MAN IS IMMORTAL, John Keane thought, or he is not. And if he is, there's the whole question of whom you pray to. If he's not, then prayer is wishful thinking.

You either pray to the dead or you don't.

But the real question before them this winter evening, the six men on the building committee, the pastor, the two priests, the architect, the accountant, and the dead, beloved pope who still smiled at them in oil from the end of the rectory dining room, was far simpler: Could they break ground in the spring?

Like something out of a parable (The Good Servant? The Twelve Talents?) each of the six men had brought to the table this evening the stack of pledges they had garnered over the past six weeks from the people of the parish who had not responded voluntarily to the pastor's initial appeal for funds. Two weeks into the New Year, when, they figured, the financial burden of Christmas might have just begun to ease, the six men had divided the more or less eight square miles of St. Gabriel's parish into six sectors. After some rigorous debate, it had been decided that the men would not solicit from their own recalcitrant neighbors. (There was the matter of financial privacy, the threat of hard feelings among men whose children played together, whose wives might see each other every day.) John Keane had the names of thirty-three parishioners on his list, all of them more or less strangers—although he recognized many of the faces from church when they came to their doors to let him in. There was the phone call first: on behalf of Father Mc-Shane, I'd like to come by some evening to discuss the new church and gym. Then the appointment itself, usually scheduled between seven and eight so as not to interrupt anyone's dinner. They were for the most part strangers, but kicking the snow off his heels or brushing the rain from his hat, he never once felt that he was stepping into their homes for the first time. They brought him to their dining-room tables, or to the kitchen. There were children in pajamas on the staircase or stretched across the living-room floor, or biting pencils over homework on whatever table their parents weren't going to use. There were dogs, usually, pushed behind basement doors or banished to the garage. The smell of whatever had been made for dinner still in the air—garlic in the Italian homes and green pepper in the Polish, something fried among the Germans, broiled meat with the Irish. They offered him coffee or tea, sometimes sherry or a beer. The wives, for the most part, hung up his coat and put down the plate of cookies and then disappeared— or lingered only long enough to admire the architect's drawing on the front of the pledge packet. (Only the more observant asked, "Where's Krause's store?" Only the more prescient shook their heads skeptically when he said Krause had agreed to sell his property to the church.) He'd hear them walking around upstairs as he made his pitch to the man of the house, heard the vague repetition of spelling words or dates or catechism lessons as the men's conversations moved, inevitably, away from the financing of the new church and gym to the war, what service, what theater, what division, what years.

John Keane was older than most of the men by a decade. None of them asked him to call them by their first names, nor did he. The formality—he wore a suit and a topcoat to every call—seemed appropriate for the transaction he was there to discuss. The wives appeared again only when he rose to leave. They stood beside their husbands as the men shook hands. He would return in a week to pick up the sealed envelope, for Father McShane's eyes only. They were aiming for one hundred percent participation. In the mimeographed letter inside the packet Father McShane had asked only for "prayerful discernment" regarding what each family could afford to contribute. The men were impossible to read, but the wives' eyes told him everything—they were eager or wary or resigned, those of them who still loved their husbands, or their lives. Others showed him the battle already brewing, or, far worse, an amused conviction that Mr. Keane had not seen through them, through their guise of good parents, good Catholics, of domestic harmony or financial stability. In every case, he had the sense when he left the house that he had at least given the family by his presence alone the gift of a single, hushed hour of quiet civility, good behavior. It was, perhaps, as close as he would ever come to feeling like a priest.

Now the pledges had been counted (not, it turned out, exclusively by Father McShane but by Father Melrose and Father Hecht, his assistants, as well, and by Mr. Marrs, an accountant, whose respect for privacy—Father McShane had assured them all—was as inviolate as any confessor's), and through the power of prayer and (Father McShane said) good old-fashioned shoe leather, the initial goal had been more than met. But, he added (nerves or indigestion or simple displeasure caused him to precede all difficult announcements with a swallowed burp), there was an obstacle. Mr. Krause would not sell.

The architect's design for the new gym and eighth-grade classrooms was a marvel of symmetry. There was the simple brick square of the old school building's left side, updated by a wide glass door, then the new entrance to the new gym, a single-story swoop of steel and glass, then another, new brick square to balance the old.

A series of low white marble steps led from the gym's modern entrance to a green lawn (Saint Gabriel himself, in white stone, at the center of it) that was bracketed by two curving white paths that led directly to the sidewalk and the street. Mr. Krause's property, which consisted of a backyard, a small detached garage, and an eighty-year-old clapboard house out of which he had run a delicatessen for thirty-five years, began at the gym's modern entrance and ran to the edge of the sidewalk. A year ago, when Father McShane first approached him, Mr. Krause had agreed that he was more than ready to sell. His was one of the last houses left along what had become a mostly commercial boulevard, and the last bit of frontage on a block that was equally divided between St. Gabriel's Church and School on the one end and a small strip of stores on the other. A descendant of the Germans who had first farmed this land and established this village in the wilds of Long Island just east of Queens, Mr. Krause knew that the postwar sweep of homes and families had already obliterated most of the old traces of the last century, and that his little farmhouse was one of these. It was only a matter of time, he said.

He had been looking, as it happened, into moving the deli to a storefront in a new mall in the next town.

But buried in Father McShane's pitch to pay Mr. Krause a handsome price for his house and his land was the bad seed of his own destruction—or so the priest told them. (John Keane sought to remember the parable.) "The parish is burgeoning," Father McShane had said. The school was bursting at its seams. Mr. Krause was a Lutheran so he might not be fully aware, but Father McShane, in his pride and boastfulness (through my fault, he told the men) had assured him that eight Masses were offered every Sunday morning—seven, eight thirty, ten, and one—in the church and simultaneously in the auditorium, and still there were folks standing in the aisles. There were double shifts of kindergarten in the school, morning and afternoon, to accommodate all the children. Building the gym was only the first step. Once it was up and Masses could be held there on Sunday mornings, then the old church was coming down and a new, larger one would take its place. Father McShane was thinking of something "in the round" to suit the new liturgy.

But of course Mr. Krause knew the Mass schedule and the school schedule at St. Gabriel's. Also the hours of the Mothers Club meetings and the Holy Name Society meetings, the basketball games, the first communions and confirmations. Father McShane said three, sometimes four Masses on Sunday mornings, but he had never once edged his way into Mr. Krause's little store after any of them, never found himself pressed cheek to jowl with thirty other parishioners vying to order cold cuts or potato salad or those marvelous doughnuts from Mr. and Mrs. Krause, their two sons, and the daughter who worked the counter. He'd never reached an arm through the crowd outside to throw some coins into an open cigar box and grab a Sunday *Daily News* before they were all gone. Father McShane had forked boiled ham and rolled pieces of Swiss cheese onto paper plates, added a dab of good mustard and some coleslaw, snitched a green olive from the tray, in living rooms after funeral Masses or at backyard graduation parties, but he had never thought to note how these always came from Krause's store.

The parish is burgeoning, he'd said, and no doubt Mr. Krause saw housewives holding wrapped trays of cold cuts high over their heads, like Copacabana chorus girls, as they maneuvered through the Sunday-morning crush. Husbands sent back to get a good-size container of rice pudding. He saw St. Gabriel's kids in their uniforms coming in for sodas, for chips, for a quick perusal of the candy displayed beneath the counter, saw them handing their mother's scribbled shopping list to him over the deli case, or ordering a bologna hero because there had been no time this morning for making lunches. And now added to that vision, thanks to Father

McShane and his (he was the first to admit it) big mouth, bricklay-
ers and electricians and plumbers and painters filling the place every
lunchtime for however many years or months it took to build the
gym and the eighth-grade classrooms, and then to tear down one
church and put up another.

Mr. Krause understood that the old places were fading, the dairy
farms and the potato fields and the clapboard houses of the last century, and nostalgia over the loss of a past that had never been his
had made him momentarily lose sight of the present, and of the in-
disputable fact that there wasn't a storefront anywhere on Long Island that could beat this location. When Father McShane returned
with his generous offer and a copy of the architect's drawing that
graced the cover of each pledge form, Mr. Krause said simply that
he'd be a fool to sell.

How, then, would they break ground in the spring?

From the far end of the priests' dining room, Pope John XXIII,
even in profile, looked benevolent and amused. The men on the
building committee had wondered, only half joking, if they had to
wait for his canonization before they could send the good old man
their petitions or if they couldn't start praying to him even now.
With Mr. Krause's store stubbornly in place there was only a sliver
of street access available to the school—a narrow driveway, an alleyway, really, bordered by the cinder-block wall that divided the
church parking lot where the bulk of the new building was to sit
and the Dumpsters that served the small strip mall on the far corner.
The design, the one printed on every pledge form the men had delivered and returned, displayed on a gold easel in the church
vestibule and in Sister Rose's office at the school, sent to the bishop,
approved by the diocese, would have to be scrapped, utterly
changed. Father McShane swallowed another burp. "None of these
people," he said, indicating the stacks of pledges, "will feel he's
gotten what he's paid for."

Is it too early, the men asked, only half joking, to pray to Pope John? Or would they have to wait till he was a saint? Wasn't anyone in heaven more or less a saint?

If that's the case, Mr. Marrs asked, does anyone here know any recently deceased architects?

The six men and the three priests and the accountant all turned their eyes to the living architect who stood above the plans that were spread across the dining-room table with his cheeks puffed out and his brow furrowed. Thus far he had donated his work, both time and material, with the hope that he would then be selected to design the new church, but he could not very well afford (he was considering the best way to say this) to do it all over again, gratis. He could offer them, he said, two options. He could turn the entrance around—he pretended to pick up the building with thumb and forefinger—put the back of the gym and the new classrooms to Mr. Krause's backyard, but then the spanking-new entrance of steel and glass that Father McShane was so fond of would face only the cemetery.

"Unacceptable," the pastor said.

Or—he moved the building again—he could turn it to the side, facing the alleyway and the cinder-block wall. Goodbye green lawn, but the white statue of Saint Gabriel might easily be moved into the lobby. And the alleyway, at least, could accommodate a car or a truck or a school bus that needed, for whatever reason, to pull up to the front door. It was a compromise no doubt, the architect said. Not nearly as grand as the original, but they could break ground in the spring and have the gym going in a year's time. Which meant the new church could get started and it was the new church, after all, that would be the showpiece.

"It seems a shame," Father McShane said, "that one man's intransigence will leave generations of St. Gabriel's students in an alley."

Collectively, the men bowed their heads and considered this.

The six men on the building committee had jobs that only vaguely qualified them for the task—Mr. Keeley was an electrician, Bill Schultz managed a bank, Mr. Kozlosky sold insurance, both Mr. Keane and Mr. Battle were with the telephone company, Lou Pintaro owned a garden center—but each of them was happy to concede the point when the architect replied that a man had to make a living and provide for his family, first and foremost, come what may. No one could blame Mr. Krause for that.

It was late. No one could blame the men for wanting this business to be concluded. They had work tomorrow. They were missing *Bonanza*. Mrs. Arnold was waiting in the kitchen to clear away the coffee cups and get home herself. Father McShane folded his arms across his chest. He called the men by their first names, Robert? Bill? Jerry? John? Larry? Lou? And one by one they all agreed. It was not ideal, but it was a solution. With Mr. Krause dug in like this, there weren't many alternatives. Mr. Marrs said, "Those Krauts do dig in," and the men laughed, pushing back their chairs. The matter was settled. The new church, then, would be the showpiece.

In the cold black sky over the rectory parking lot, there was Orion, as he'd always been. And always would be. Jacob had drawn the constellation once and labeled it "O'Ryan." At dinner tonight, Michael had announced that a kid in school asked if Jacob was a Jew. Michael thought this was very funny. Jacob had brushed it aside. So what, he'd said. Jesus was a Jew. There was something rehearsed in the boy's reply. John Keane wondered if one of the nuns hadn't provided it to him, against another kid's teasing. Across the dinner table, his wife had bowed her head, more effective than catching his eye. Fourteen years was no time at all in the life of an I told you so.

Mr. Keane got into his cold car. Let the engine run a bit. The other men were pulling out of the drive and he saluted them as they drove past. They had done the work of their church. Solved the question of Mr. Krause. At home, there would be a light left on in the kitchen for them, or a lamp lit in the living room. A wife under a caftan, watching TV, or in bed, asleep already, or pretending to be. The scent of dinner still in the air. A child (probably Michael, but maybe even Clare) still awake. Some of them might open a beer or pour two fingers of scotch. Or walk the dog. Read the paper.

They were either immortal, or they were not. It was prayer, all of it, this talking to the dead, or it was howling at the moon. At the winter sky. At Orion. O'Ryan. It was another bit of misapprehension, another mistaken imagining—the dead pope hearing their prayers, his parents, his brother Frank, all the angels and all the saints, the other Jacob. Or it was true.

Absolutely, Mr. Gallagher.

Positively, Mr. Shean.

At home, his wife was at the dining-room table with Jacob. What distinguished this room from the priests' was the clutter of bills and magazines on the server, the simplicity of the small chandelier (the priests' was Waterford), the dust. A portrait of a pretty little girl in a wide-brimmed hat rather than the old pope. She had his history book before her and her forehead in her hands. Jacob was sitting quietly to her left, looking ready for sleep. "It's late," John Keane said, coming in, but she ignored him.

"Battle of Hastings," she said and he answered, dejectedly, in his new voice, "1066." His face was changing, too, growing thinner and longer, balanced somewhere between homely and beautiful.

"Magna Carta?" There was silence. The boy frowned. Swallowed hard, perhaps resisting tears. His Adam's apple, also new, looked swollen. His father had an impulse to turn away.

From the couch in the living room, Michael called out, "1215," and Jacob slammed his fist on the table and, standing, threw back his chair. "I'm going to bed," he said, and his father might have reprimanded him if the boy had not also said, turning slightly toward them, "Good night."

Mary Keane looked up at her husband. Her face was colorless and worn, as dimpled and lined as a potato. She ran her finger down a double page of dates and names and places. The end-of-chapter review. "He doesn't know half of this," she said.

He shrugged, walked through the living room where Michael, lounging on the couch in his pajamas, said, "It's easy."

His father said, "Don't be a smart aleck," and then, when he had hung up his coat, "Get to bed."

Upstairs, in their room, Michael said, matter-of-factly, as if it were the middle of the day. "Battle of Hastings, 1066, Magna Carta, 1215 . . ."

"I'm asleep." Jacob had his back to him. His voice was muffled.

"I thought Jews were supposed to be smart," Michael said. In the dim light from the hallway, he couldn't tell at first what his brother had thrown at him—it missed anyway and hit the floor. But then he saw it was the flashlight Jacob kept at his bedside and the potential pain it might have caused filled him with indignation. They were on each other in seconds, legs and arms and blows struck into ears, into shoulders. The overhead light came on—if they hadn't expected that it would they would not have begun the battle—and their father barked a single word. He dragged them apart, both of them splotched red in the cheeks and across their shoulders and throats, but whether from blows or their own fury, their father couldn't have said.

He grabbed them, both of them panting, by their shirts. Their mother was in the doorway with Clare in her arms and Annie was next to her. "Enough," was what he said.

He shoved them both down on the edge of their beds. "Sit."

They glared at each other, across the short space between their beds, believing, each of them, that there was no greater flaw in all the vast design of the universe than these two made brothers, condemned to this same small room. Only their father between them, saying words, kept them from colliding again.

"Flesh and blood," were the words their father was saying, standing between them. Michael's eyes fell on the black flashlight, rolled just under Jacob's bed, and he pointed to it as if it could bear witness. "He threw the flashlight," he said, before his father cut him off. "Your own brother," their father said, raising his voice again. "Who," he asked with his finger in the air, "who do you think you'll have on your side when your mother and I are gone? Who do you think you'll be able to turn to when you're as old as I am and there's something you need—a buck or two, or a piece of advice, maybe just someone you can ask, Remember when? Your friends? Your Little League team?" He waved his broad hand. "They'll be scattered to the four winds. They'll have forgotten your name." He paused, as if waiting for them to speak. And then he said, "Your family. Your flesh and blood, that's who you'll have. If you're lucky. Your two sisters. Each other. That's who you'll have."

Michael held out his arm once more. "It could have really hurt," he said, trying again; the occasions when Jacob struck the first blow were so rare. Their father put his hand in the air. "Enough," he said again. "Apologize," he said, suddenly weary. "Then say your prayers and go to sleep."

He walked past them, past their mother and the two girls, turning off the overhead light as he did. Into the darkness, with Clare in her arms, their mother whispered, "Think of poor Uncle Frank."

"He threw the flashlight at me," Michael said, all in a rush.

His mother peered into the shadowed room. His sisters, little Clare and Annie both, stared at him too, duplicating her eyes.

"Think what your father would give," she told him, whispering, "to have his own brother beside him for just another night." Then she walked away.

Jacob was slipping his pale feet under the covers, awkwardly, as if his feet were much bigger and his legs much longer than he could manage. He threw himself at his pillow like a landed fish, put his back to his brother and pulled the blanket up over his shoulder. After only a second or two of silence, he said, "Sorry, Michael."

Michael said nothing. He remained seated on the edge of his bed, the lumpy whorls of the chenille bedspread just under his palms. He looked into the lighted hallway, heard his mother putting Clare back into her bed, and asking Annie to put her head down. Then he heard them praying, "Ever this night, be at my side . . ." Next door, Mr. MacLeod was playing his piano again, each note just a slight vibration against their bedroom wall.

Michael had only a vague recollection: Uncle Frank had looked like their father, only ugly. A broader, taller, bizarro-world version of their father with more hair and bigger teeth and a white handkerchief that he would mop his maroon face with, like Louis Armstrong. He drove Cadillacs and always spoke to them in a voice like Donald Duck's. When he visited, mixed nuts and chips with onion dip were served, and they would hear him downstairs late into the night, telling long, loud stories that involved a multitude of voices—Porky Pig, Ed Sullivan, Jimmy Durante—stories that made his parents scream with laughter. Sometimes, lying in the dark, listening, missing most of it, he and Jacob would laugh, too.

Michael watched his mother cross the hallway to her own room. Heard his parents' voices. On the floor by his feet, just under the fringe of Jacob's bedspread was the flashlight he had thrown. Quickly, Michael bent down and picked it up and then slipped into bed with it. He turned it on under the blankets, put his fingers over it to see if he could count the bones. Turned it up to the ceiling. He wrote his name, drew a face. The light went off in the hallway. He moved the beam over Jacob's back, the bedspread and the blanket, his dark head, his ear.

He moved it down the length of his brother's body and over the wooden footboard of his bed, past the dresser they shared, out the door. Leaning out over his own mattress, he saw the light catch the doorknob of the linen closet, the door to his sisters' room. He willed the light to push the door open a bit more. He could then move the beam over Annie's face, play it across her eyelids.

"Michael," he heard his mother say from his parents' room. She was trying to keep her voice low, but not whispering. "Go to sleep," she said. She sounded not exactly far away but heading there, as if she had stopped in the middle of her leaving. "Do you hear me?" she said. He imagined she was speaking to him from over her shoulder, just as she was stepping out, maybe through one of her bedroom windows, maybe following his father, her hands on the window frame, her foot on the sill, their father already gone before her (when we're gone, he had said) into the night. "Put out that light," she said, over her shoulder, as he imagined it. And he did. In the darkness, he felt more certain of their absence. His parents had left the house and if he called out "Mom?" only Jacob and the girls would hear him. If there were a knock at the door tonight, it would be left to him to answer. He would take Jacob's flashlight. He imagined Pauline, scratching at the glass, wanting to get in. Lying alone in the darkness, he formed the words in his mind, willed them across the room, but did not speak them out loud. "Sorry, Jacob."

Instead, he whispered, "Mr. MacLeod is tinkling on his piano again."

And then they were both laughing in the dark.

THEY SHOULD HAVE COME EARLIER in the day, but it was a World's Fair, after all, and there had been much to distract them. Now the sun was low and orange, radiating heat like a glowing coal. The asphalt that had been wet and clean this morning—hosed down by jumpsuited workers intent, it seemed, on lending the paved-over park a hint of morning dew—was now gummy and pliant underfoot. Now heat waves rose from it, smeared the air and made a mirage of the shoes and the ankles and the pink knees of the passing crowds. The painted benches had grown too hot to sit on. The shrubs and sparse trees were limp. Now the jumpsuited men walked listlessly, clicking their long-handled brooms against the opened and closed mouths of their long-handled dustbins. The passengers in the sleek Glide-a-Rides, erect and smiling earlier in the day as they tested a bit of space-age transportation, now slumped in the molded plastic seats or gazed out from behind their sunglasses, unimpressed even with the future. It was the end of the day.

In another hour, the sun would dip into the Hudson and the humidity would begin to give way. In another hour—by the time they got through the exhibit—the lights in the trees and on the pavilions and under the fountain that surrounded the Unisphere would draw the eye up, to the spires and the arches and the silvery searchlights of the fair, to the stars themselves. But not now. Now every head was bent under the day's accumulated heat, every grimy collar and darkened arm ring exposed, every stranger's arm or bare shoulder—as they joined the line outside the exhibit—was sticky, unpleasantly cool.

"We should have come earlier," Mary Keane said, although, she supposed, earlier the line might have been longer still.

Beside her, Annie stood on her toes to glimpse the distance to the entrance and then leaned out to see how many more had joined the line behind them. There was solace in the seven or eight—and now another four—who would have to wait longer still. She stepped back into place. There was a tall, older couple ahead of them, the woman fat, the man slightly stooped. Behind them, a younger couple, but not so young that the woman didn't look a little foolish, hanging—in this heat—on the man's hairy arm.

They had already missed the exhibit twice. Once, the first time they had come to the fair, when they had Clare and the two boys, who had balked at waiting an hour and a half to see a statue. Once again when their father was also along. After only ten minutes on the long line, he had shown them his wrist and declared that if they were not all in the car in the next half hour it would be a nightmare on the Grand Central.

(Because he was a man who always knew precisely when they must all be in the car, knew precisely the minute after which the trip would be in vain, impossible, a nightmare. "Look at the time," turning furiously on his wife as if she were both the single force delaying them and the single reason in all the world that he sought to wage this battle. It made little difference if their arrival or departure was meant to be precise or merely eventual, he held his wrist in the air, his fist clenched as if he would bring it down on their heads if they failed to understand—tapping the face of his watch—that time was against them.)

But now they were just the two—mother and daughter—and

while Mary Keane, in deference to her husband's habit of mind rather than out of any impatience of her own, reprimanded herself for not getting here earlier, she also made calm accommodation for what would clearly be a long wait: a later bus home, was all, she told herself. A phone call to the boys to tell them to fix some spaghetti. Another to Pauline, who had Clare for the day. Nothing else to stop them, really, from finally seeing this through.

"Probably," she said to her daughter, "it's best to have left this for last. Probably after you see this you won't want to see anything else."

Together, months ago, they had watched on TV as the statue arrived. Or at least they had seen the crate that contained it as it was lowered from a ship. One of the world's most profound and precious works of art, taken from Rome for the first time in history. The television showed men reaching up to touch the wooden crate as it slowly descended. Carved by the artist in his youth, nearly five hundred years ago.

And the line was moving. Shuffling, really, as if the hot asphalt pulled at their feet, and with so little distance between them all that each step brought the bump or brush of another body, a bare forearm, a soft hip. The touch of a toe against your heel. Among the fair's sweet, pervasive smell of Belgian waffles, there was a stirring of human odors, perfume and aftershave and sweat and hair warmed by the sun. The odor of breath as they all turned to one another to say, "At least it's moving."

The tall old man in front of them wore a yellow plaid shirt, short-sleeved. Although his arms were tanned, his puckered elbows were chalky. He had missed a belt loop in back. Beside him, his wife was fanning herself with a map of the fair. Despite the heat, there was a white pillbox hat pinned to the back of her head. She wore a floral shirtwaist dress and the flesh beneath her arm moved like a pink hammock filled with something heavy. She turned to the mother and daughter to say that the lines had been terrible all day long. They'd waited forty-five minutes to see It's a Small World. More than an hour and a half at the Bell Pavilion. There was an orange plastic dolphin on her dress, a gift from the Florida exhibit. She said they'd brought their son along, who was on leave, but he'd already gone back to the hotel to cool off. He told them he did enough standing in line in the army.

For Annie, the lines, the crowds, the restricted view while she waited, were all part of the fair's adventure, like being led, blindfolded. At the end of every wait—it had been happening all day—wonders were revealed.

(She and her mother, who did not drive, had steered a green convertible into the dark, past dinosaurs and the invention of the wheel and into a shimmering city of tall white towers, the threshold of tomorrow. They had sat—after the hour wait—in a moving theater as a mechanical family, as real as her own, lived through the 1800s and the 1900s and into the next century, only their faces unchanging. They'd watched gray dolphins leap out of a blue pool and hang suspended above the ordinary Queens skyline. They'd walked quietly through the spiced air of Asia, where tiny chimes sounded softly and incense was burned, and through a chilly Alpine village that actually smelled of snow. They'd sat side by side in a moving chair that took them past lunar bases and underwater farms and along a glittering continental highway while a voice like God's told them, whispering softly into their ears, that the present was just an instant between an infinite past and a hurrying future.)

The line shuffled forward three more steps. Constricted by the space between them, Mary Keane reached back carefully and pulled her blouse away from her spine. She felt a bead of perspiration roll down her back. And then another. Cascading, she thought. "I'm melting," she said. Behind them, the man with the woman on his arm was reading from a guidebook. Annie felt the edge of the paper against the back of her head.

"They shouldn't have moved something so old," he said. "Something could have happened to it." And the woman on his arm made a sympathetic noise and then seemed to readjust herself, as if she were turning in bed.

"God, it's hot," she said and Mary Keane turned to nod at her, "Isn't it, though?" Farther behind them there was a family, parents and two teenagers, limp shouldered and unhappy. Then what might have been a church group of pastel men and women, all with name tags and crosses on their breasts, fanning themselves with identical paper fans printed loudly with the name of an Atlanta funeral home.

Above the rooftops of the Belgian Village, the sun had gone from orange to red—so fiery now it might have been lifted from some creation tableau itself. Might more appropriately have been shining down on tar pits or boiling mud. As Annie leaned out to look back (the line was longer still) and then forward (no shorter ahead), the red sun struck the gold dome of the pavilion and sent her ducking back into her place. Now a vertiginous edge of purple outlined everything she saw. She saw heads turned away from the sun. Shoulders moving slowly forward. The man's speckled hand that had missed a belt loop this morning reaching up to wipe perspiration from his sunburned neck. His wife was turned around again to say to her mother they had one son in the army and one in the Marines and another one married and back near home. And Mary Keane replied four, two boys and two girls.

Something prehistoric, too, in the scaly flesh of the woman's throat as she turned to speak to them, chin and neck indistinguishable. Her voice was worn.

She said she should have gone for four and had a girl, too.

Daughters will wait with you to see something like this. Not boys. "Although my boys are good to me," she said. "They're good boys."

The woman turned to Annie, taking her in with small eyes, perhaps assessing what she'd missed. Suddenly, she asked, "Did you see the Carousel of Progress, honey?"

And her mother answered, "Yes we did."

"The Magic Skyway? Futurama? The Moon Dome? Did you talk on the picturephones?"

"Oh, yeah," Annie said, knowing her mother wanted her to say yes, not yeah.

"What I want to know," the woman said, raising her voice, nearly shouting, "is what if you just got out of the shower, and your picturephone is ringing? Do you answer it?" She laughed, her open mouth full of silver and gold. She shook her head and wiped a tear from her eyes. "That's your future, honey," she said to Annie. "Not mine or your mom's." She leaned back, her wide arm touching Mary Keane's damp shoulder. "We'll be well out of it, don't you think?"

The man in the plaid shirt, as husbands will do, was staring straight ahead, ignoring the conversation, as if both women were strangers to him. Even in this heat, Mary Keane was aware of a certain pleasure in being relieved of the burden of a husband.

"We sure will," she said, agreeably.

But then the woman suddenly raised her arm, the pale skin swinging, and gestured toward the fantastic rooflines and white towers, the sky lifts and the monorails.

"The only thing I hate to think about," she said, "is how all this will be knocked down when the fair is over."

Other than the slow shuffling forward and the fanning of maps and brochures, there was the rise and fall of cigarettes to mouths, the tossing of them onto the asphalt. A couple up ahead occasionally left the line to chase a toddler. The man behind them was saying "Michael-angelo," and the woman on his arm was saying, "Meekel, Meekel-angelo."

They shuffled forward. In the boredom and the heat there were only the tender backs of necks to consider, arches of ears, puckered elbows, freckles, birthmarks. The variety of head shapes and hair colors. What wash-day mishap or expense spared or birthday gift or Simplicity pattern had led to those clothes on that body on this day. A missed belt loop. A plastic purse. A bleached beehive. A baggy pair of Bermuda shorts. A lip held over a protruding tooth. You had to pity anyone in long pants or black socks. Women in white gloves. Soldiers in uniform. You had to pity the man behind them for the hair on his arms, the woman's weight against him.

The fat woman, mopping her thick neck with a small tissue, turned again to say that the long wait would be worth it. "It'll be like a once-in-a-lifetime trip to Rome."

With her purse in the crook of her arm, Mary Keane reached out to run her fingers through her daughter's thin hair, gathering it bit by bit to the top of her head. She twisted the hair into a topknot and pulled three bobby pins from the purse to hold it. Annie reached back tentatively to feel her bare neck. "Better?" Mary Keane said and Annie said, "Yes," although one of the bobby pins bit like a tooth.

The line moved again. Mary Keane leaned down and blew a soft stream of air onto her daughter's neck, miraculously cool. Annie closed her eyes briefly. "How much longer?" she said at the same time the woman behind them said, "Not much longer." They turned, mother and daughter, to meet her eye, but it was the man she was addressing, leaning against him, holding on to his arm. There was a diamond engagement ring on her hand. You had to pity the length and thickness of her brown hair, the weight of her chin on his shoulder.

They shuffled forward again. Now they could hear faint music coming from the building, and with the next step forward they could smell, if certainly not yet feel, the air-conditioning inside.

Someone up ahead, an official, cried, "No pushing, please," in what might have been an Italian accent. They felt the line grow slack at the reprimand. And then it moved forward again.

The fat woman was now talking to the woman ahead of her. "What if you'd just stepped out of the shower?" she shouted.

"Pee-aye-tuh," the man behind them said and the woman, laughing deep in her throat said, "Pee-aye-*ta*."

Here now was the official who belonged to the voice, perspiring in a red jacket and gray pants. He waved his arms like a traffic cop although, at the moment, they were standing still in front of him. "Almost there," he was saying, smiling at them all. His accent not Italian but Long Island. "That's it"—as they moved forward— "won't be long now."

As if responding obediently to a command, the line pressed itself together, tighter still, heads, hands, shuffling feet. (Annie briefly placed the heels of her palms to the damp yellow shirt of the man in front of her and then drew them away.) Chests to backs and the woman behind them leaning, it seemed, over Mary Keane's shoulder. "No pushing, please," the man said again.

The sun had nearly dropped out of sight although the sky glowed so vividly with its afterimage that it hardly mattered. The heat still gave the thick air a slow pulse. The crowd pressed together and her mother took her hand, moving. For a moment Annie forgot just what it was they had been waiting to see. And then they were inside.

Cold air and a low Gregorian chant, eyes struggling to adjust to the change. There was the smell of incense and of new paint. Glass cases along the walls and the impression of red and gold. Golden arcs of light. Red carpet at their feet. The line held, still shuffling, past cases of jewels, now, or books, or vestments, or small ivory models of churches, paintings of saints and priests. The volume of the choir's voices seemed to rise slightly as they moved forward, wavering the way the heat outside had wavered. But the heat was already forgotten. "Keep moving, please," someone said.

And then the line broke. Wheat from chaff, Mary thought as red-jacketed guards counted them off, said, there—four rows in descending order—back there, please, here, down there. A brusque tap on her shoulder and she and her daughter were hurried forward. Down here, please, keep moving.

No choice in the matter, it soon became clear, because what they were being directed to was a moving walkway, four ascending rows in a kind of amphitheater of moving walkways. There was the uncertain first step, the tug of the rubber tread against the soles of their feet, and then, through no effort of their own, the slow movement forward into the dark. Mary Keane and her daughter were in the first row. The air grew colder and the holy chants nearer, even as the faces and the bodies and the clothes of all who had waited—though they were still beside them or above them in the darkness—disappeared. There were only whispers and stirrings, a child's voice, and then not even that.

Mary Keane put her arm across her daughter's chest, pressed her close so that the little topknot was just under her chin. Annie took her mother's arm in both hands.

In the absence of all color and all other light, the white marble held every nuance and hue a human eye could manage. Here was the lifeless flesh of the beloved child, the young man's muscle and sinew impossibly—impossible for the mother who cradled him—still. Here were her knees against the folds of her draped robes, her lap, as wide as it might have been in childbirth, accommodating his weight once more. Here were her fingers pressed into his side, her shoulder raised to bear him on her arm once more. Here was her left hand, open, empty. Here were the mother's eyes cast down upon the body of her child once more, only once more, and in another moment (they were moving back into the darkness) no more.

The white light reflected dimly off the faces still within its reach and then disappeared from them, lamps extinguished, one by one, as they were slowly drawn away. Somewhere among them a woman was weeping. Slowly, the moving sidewalk delivered them all through the darkness to the four ascending doors where they disembarked, step carefully please. Flesh, hair, clothes returned to them in the low light of the rest of the exhibit. A low, golden light that was nevertheless painful, accustomed as their eyes had become to the dark, and despite how briefly they had been in it.

Outside, the heat was a comfort, momentarily, on chilled shoulders and arms. The lights had come on in the park, in the trees, in the tall clock towers and the soaring pavilions and under the fountains that surrounded the Unisphere. It led their eyes up, for a moment. There were stars but also a stain of red on the western horizon, against the quickly descending night. There was the later bus to catch from the park to the terminal in Jamaica, and then the second bus to the intersection where they would call home and John Keane, unhappy about the late hour, would come in the car to fetch them.

A T PAULINE'S APARTMENT, Clare was already asleep on the couch. Pauline listed all they had done together that day—an excursion to the fabric store and lunch at a diner, two cute gingham aprons run up on the sewing machine, cookies baked and nails painted and a walk around the corner for Chinese—making each occasion sound, to Mary Keane, like a compensation Pauline had rendered, since attached to each one was some surprise, on Pauline's part, that Clare had done none of these things in exactly this way before. "And she said her mother only knew how to make Christmas cookies."

Mary slipped her hands under Clare's arms, lifted the sleeping child to her shoulder, felt the weight of her, and how, not quite asleep, she tightened her arms around her mother's neck, brushed her fingers against her mother's hair. Pauline was handing a shopping bag to Annie, the folded aprons, the cookies, a few odds and ends, "Little presents," Pauline said, "nothing much," proudly enough. The apartment was close, dimly lit, full of the scent of Pauline's perfume. In her weariness after the long hot day, in her anger over her husband's unreasonable impatience, in anticipation of the bedtime routine that was still waiting for her at home, Mary Keane looked at the peaceful rooms with some envy.

Which Pauline saw, of course. At the door, she asked, "Is he

waiting downstairs?"—meaning John Keane. And when Mary nodded, Pauline said, "You'd better hurry then, you know how he is,"
and laughed to show she would not be married to bald John Keane
for all the tea in China. In her laugh was every confidence Mary had
ever shared with Pauline about her husband's failings, every un-
guarded criticism, every angry, impromptu, frustrated critique of
his personality, his manners, his sometimes morbid, sometimes inscrutable, sometimes impatient ways. A repository, Pauline and her
laugh, for every moment in their marriage when Mary Keane had
not loved her husband, when love itself had seemed a misapprehension, a delusion (a stranger standing outside of Schrafft's transformed into an answered prayer), and marriage—which Pauline
had had sense enough to spurn—simply an awkward pact with a
stranger, any stranger, John or George, Tom, Dick, or Harry.

A repository, Pauline and her laugh, her knowing eye, for all
that Mary Keane should have kept to herself.

In the elevator, Clare heavy in her arms, she told Annie that
Pauline was intolerable, sometimes. Really. "I don't just bake cookies at Christmas," she said resentfully, and Annie agreed although,
at the moment, she could not recall any cookies her mother had ever
made that were not shaped like Christmas trees or snowmen.

Her mother said, "You know," and then paused. She recalled,
briefly, the sacred music and the white stone and all the soaring aspirations of her faith: gold domes and ivory towers and in the darkness, light. She considered, too, how tired she was, Clare's head
heavy on her shoulder, the child's heels digging into her hips. How
annoying Pauline could be. "You know," she said again, "Pauline
doesn't speak to Helen anymore, the girl she went to Europe with
last year." She looked down at Annie. "And she's fallen out with
Adele, too, from the office. Even though they shared a cabin on that
cruise and were best pals for a while there." She hitched Clare up on
her shoulder. Annie transferred the heavy shopping bag from her

right hand to her left. "I wouldn't mind sometimes," her mother said, "if Pauline got mad and stopped speaking to us for a while. It would be a nice break."

Watching the light move behind each number as they descended, Annie laughed and said, "I know."

"It would be nice to untangle ourselves a bit," her mother said. Clare stirred against her shoulder, moved the fingers she had placed in her mother's hair, tugged.

Mary Keane and her daughters rode the rest of the way down in weary silence. It was an unkindness, she knew, what she had just said about Pauline. Words said in conscious defiance of all the gentle aspirations of her faith. But it was also true, what she had said. Just as it was true that there would be no untangling herself from Pauline. Not with Clare already so fond of her.

THE CHURCH had gone to pot. It had gone to seed. It had been minimally repaired for the last five years and come Monday the dismantling would begin. Any parishioner wishing to purchase one of the old pews should have already called the rectory. There were shingles missing from the exterior; the bell, for safety's sake, had long ago been removed from the belfry. The green canvas awning that had once shaded the entrance and the tall brick steps that led from the street had been torn in the '60 hurricane and never repaired. In '64 it was taken down altogether and now only the metal frame remained, a crisscross of bare ironwork against the sky. The choir loft, also for safety's sake, had been off limits for as long as most of the children in the school could remember. A rumor spread among the younger ones, Clare Keane included, that the unused staircase at the back of the church, with its wide marble banister and its velvet rope (and its scent, when you got near it, of incense and attics) was an entrance to heaven. The painting across the high ceiling, of John the Baptist pouring water from his palm over the head of a beautiful Christ, was itself marred by water— there was a misshapen, ominously gray cloud in the blue sky above their heads, another stretched across the saint's feet and over the savior's knees. The stained-glass window high above the altar— Saint Gabriel with his halo and his wings—also leaked. On a bad day, the water ran down the wall and over the crucifix and behind the gold tabernacle. The filigree on the old altar had chipped away. No one remembered the last time the organ had actually played.

On the Friday before the last Sunday, all the children in the school were led into the church for a farewell prayer, and just as Father Hecht said, "The old makes way for the new," Marilyn Giovanni in the fifth grade slammed the back of her head into the back of the pew and with an echoing, inhuman cry, rolled onto the worn carpet of the center aisle. It was an epileptic seizure. Mrs. Ryan, who taught the third grade, had an afflicted child of her own and knew just what to do, and superstition in this day and age was well to be avoided. But the Bible itself was full of misdiagnoses and who could help but wonder what it was the devil would have objected to—the old or the new? Was it protest that made him seize the little girl at that moment, or celebration?

("Nonsense," Father McShane said to the younger priest. "I'm ashamed of you." And then, with a wink and a crooked smile, "They talk about the Irish.")

On the corner in front of the church, the boys waiting for the high-school bus watched the workmen carrying statues over their shoulders like huge dolls. They saw them carrying the large framed oil paintings in both hands, Our Lady of Perpetual Help, stained with the smoke of votive candles, of forty years of petitions, and Saint Pius, still clean, carried like suitcases to a waiting van. The old wooden pews, eased out through the front door and down the old steps like streamlined, oversize coffins, were either placed in the van or—as in some final reckoning—carried to the lawn in front of the rectory where they were labeled with the purchasing parishioner's name. Then a high chain-link fence went up around the old church and the wrecking ball came and in no time it was all splinters and smoke.

Jacob Keane, waiting at the corner with the other boys from his high school, in a jacket he had not grown into and his school tie, swore that the smell of incense still came from the hole where the church had been. He made the other boys pause and sniff the air. Yes, they nodded, their chins raised, they could almost agree. The road in front of the church seemed to grow more congested every morning. There was the thick diesel smell of county buses and school buses, delivery trucks and flatbeds, so that even on a spring morning at seven there was hardly a trace of new leaf or daffodil or even the cool dawn in the suburban air. But Jacob told the other boys, "You can still smell it," and with their fingers in the fence they paused, raised their noses. Those who had once shared the belief that the stairs to the old choir loft led to another world, to heaven itself, considered briefly the possibility that some sort of holiness lingered everywhere, perhaps just beneath the shell of earth and sky. Jacob wondered as well. Then Michael told a joke about a workman in a church who hammered his thumb and cursed. A nun who was praying nearby said his bad language had made Our Lady cry. She pointed to the statue. "See the tears?" the nun said. The man shook his head. "She's only crying cause I hammered a nail into her backside to hang up my coat."

The laughter outran the mystery. Michael was pleased to see his brother blush. The joke, he was pretty certain, had come from Uncle Frank.

But if there was inspiration in the lingering smell of incense, there was incentive in the church's rising frame. The new church was to be in the round—a spaceship, some of the older parishioners complained, a circus tent—and every afternoon when the boys from the Catholic high school left the bus, they could mark the progress that had been made that day, at first in the dark stakes and poured concrete of the foundation but then, more clearly, in the skeletal web of steel and wood. By summer, a number of them had begun projects of their own—backyard tree houses and storage huts and potting sheds. Tony Persichetti and his father worked on their attic, transforming the space the developer had left as bare beams into a bedroom and a bath. Jacob and Michael Keane, making a case for privacy, for a place to gather with their friends that was not the kitchen, where their mother would have to break things up to make dinner, or their bedroom, where their sisters could listen at the door, convinced their parents to let them finish the basement— which meant to cover the cinder-block walls with knotty pine panels, to drop a white ceiling, enclose the furnace with its own room, and replace the shower curtain at the entrance of the tiny bathroom with a real door.

Their father took them to the lumberyard, bought them levels and tape measures and boxes of nails, cartons of two-foot-square linoleum with which to cover the concrete floor. Every evening that summer, when he returned from work, he changed into his old clothes, put on the army boots he wore for all household chores, and went down to assess the boys' progress, to offer corrections and advice. With the help of a do-it-yourself manual, father and sons figured out the wiring for the fluorescent lights, got the door hung right, laid a checkerboard pattern across the floor. The old couch and the train table were donated to St. Vincent's and their father agreed to splurge on a six-piece set of Danish modern from Sears, which gave the new room a sleek, science-fiction look that Mary Keane found cold, although it inspired in her sons a sense that their own modern futures, part Buck Rogers, part James Bond, were finally upon them.

In only a matter of months, Michael learned that the cheap foam cushions of the Danish modern sofa will buckle on you when you press a girl too ardently into its frame.

THE PARISHIONERS on that first Sunday seemed both reluctant and awed, filing in not down a single central aisle but along any number of aisles that fanned out from the semicircle that was the altar. The faces in the new stained-glass windows were all angles (Mary Keane thought they looked vaguely Danish modern themselves), their robes all long bright shards of color. The crucifix suspended above them was a long swoop of gray steel intersected by a small crossbeam that seemed hardly the breadth of a man's arms. There were no recognizable statues of any sort and the Stations of the Cross were merely white rectangles of carved stone, the Passion barely discernible within them. Because there were no corners, there were few shadows in the new church. The confessionals were small rooms, with actual doors (John Keane tested one on the way out, assessing how well it had been hung) and doorknobs, not curtains. Between them, behind a large plate-glass window, there was what Father McShane seemed delighted to call the "Bawl Room," a soundproof room for mothers with small, noisy children. He pointed it out three times in his dedication sermon—it might have been the sole motive for the new construction—and Mary Keane, who throughout the service grew progressively dissatisfied with the too new St. Gabriel's, added to her criticism of the place the fact that a baby's cry or a toddler's shouted phrase added life, and sometimes even laughter, to a Mass, which was, after all, supposed to be a celebration, not a dirge. She imagined the Blessed Mother with baby Jesus in her arms, standing behind the plate glass, the child's mouth moving but not a sound getting through. Beside her, her husband noticed how the new pews lacked the small brass hat clips that had been secured to the back of every pew in the old church (spring-loaded, felt-tipped clips that Michael would stealthily snap at least once every Mass, a sound like a gunshot echoing through the place). He understood there was no longer a need for them—so few men wore hats anymore (he blamed JFK with his thick hair and his big Irish head for changing the fashion)—but the lack of them added to his dawning sense that the new church had turned the stuff of his own past, his own memories, into something quaint, at best. At worst, obsolete.

And yet, the smell of the incense from the censer was the smell of the incense of old, and the stately movement of the priests in their robes as they walked down the aisles swinging them, sending the pale smoke into the air, their free hands placed gently over their hearts, was as it had always been. At his shoulder, Jacob's bowed head and thin folded hands reassured him somewhat (and told him the three hundred a year for four years that he'd spent on his Catholic high school might actually have purchased the boy something). Beside Jacob, Clare had lost her initial, openmouthed fascination with the saucer-shaped ceiling and was now simply studying her sister's hand (which Annie, limply, had allowed her to take into her lap), studying especially the latest boyfriend's thick high-school ring, which Annie had made smaller with a welt of yellow yarn. Beside her, Michael sprawled in the pew (three hundred a year for three years with not much to show for it), his eyes cast down not in prayer but in a kind of wry embarrassment for how utterly mistaken everyone around him, everyone who had ever had a hand in the construction of this place, seemed to be.

As soon as the priest said, "The Mass is ended" ("Thanks be to God," was the only response Michael joined in on, saying it loudly and sarcastically and always adding, just loudly enough for his siblings to hear, "Let's cruise"), Michael was in the aisle, out the door, the first to grab a fresh Sunday *News* from the pile outside of Krause's store.

He carried it and his ritual bottle of Sunday-morning root beer back to his parents' car. They were delayed, touring the new church (his father testing the confessional's sturdy doors, his mother with the girls on either side of her clucking her tongue at each white and nearly indiscernible depiction of Christ's suffering). Sitting on the warm hood of his father's car, Michael watched the people leaving the church, getting into their own cars, pulling out. He saw Lori Ballinger walking behind her parents, her legs tan, her hair glossy in the sun, and he raised the bottle of soda in a debonair salute. She waved back, smiling.

When Jacob joined him ("They're talking to people," was his only explanation for their parents' further delay), Michael said that he had seen her. "She's cute," Jacob said.

"A nice girl, I hear," Michael added, emphasizing nice so that Jacob would know he hadn't said "good."

Jacob knew, and showed that he knew with a slight smile. He put out his hand and his brother passed him the soda, although he said as he did, "Get your own." Jacob took a drink and then passed it back. It was a taste that made him feel ten years old.

"Where the hell are they?" Michael said. He leaned back on the hood, his knees raised. "Why the hell didn't you take your car?" The sky was clear blue above them, hardly a wisp of cloud. He felt sometimes that all he did anymore was wait. He put his hand in his pants pocket and found a stubby pencil from the golf course where he caddied. He sat up. "Let's walk home," he said. "I'll leave a note." He wrote across the clean border at the top of the Sunday comics. Propped the entire paper up on the windshield and secured it with a wiper, left the empty soda bottle beside it. His father's car, a '65 Ford, was, he told Jacob, a piece of junk.

Jacob shrugged. This summer, as a graduation present, his father had given him three hundred dollars toward his own car, a little Capri. The puzzle he had studied in high-school religion classes—why the rich were so ungenerous, why the suffering of the poor, the fixable suffering, was so seldom fixed—began to solve itself for him the first time he drove off alone, in his own car. There was want, as the Brothers at St. Sebastian's had referred to it. But then there was, he suddenly understood—alone, unfettered, pressing the accelerator, palming the wheel—I want.

His brother leaped off the hood—the percussion of the metal bending in under his palm and then bending back again. "Let's cruise," he said again.

They walked together, down the alleyway that ran in front of what they still called the new gym, past the modern entryway. Saint Gabriel, with the shoulders of his folded wings rising up over his head, was mere shadow behind the plate glass. They emerged from the alleyway into the sun, passed Krause's store, where there was still a crowd of customers inside, pressed against the door. They cut through the parking lot of the strip of stores beside the school, turned toward home. It was the route they had walked together for years, when they were students at St. Gabriel's and then again when they had come to this corner to meet their high-school bus. That was over now. Jacob was starting St. John's in the fall. Michael would be hitching a ride to St. Sebastian's with some friends, his senior year.

Jacob said, when they had reached the orderly streets where the houses, each nearly identical, began, "I called her once."

"Who?" Michael said. He was thinking of how much money

he'd lost today, not caddying. Giving in to his parent's request that they all go to the first Mass at the new church.

"Lori Ballinger," Jacob said.

Michael looked at him. He was about four inches taller than Jacob, and still growing, he was sure. He straightened his shoulders. "You asked her out?"

Jacob nodded, smiled a little crookedly, making fun of himself. Given the look, he didn't have to say how it had turned out, but Michael asked him anyway.

"She turned you down?"

"Yeah," Jacob said. "She said she was busy."

Michael considered this. He considered saying, Well, that took courage. Instead he said, "When was this?"

"Last year," Jacob said. "Junior prom."

He stood still on the sidewalk. His brother kept going. "Holy shit," he said. "You asked Lori Ballinger to your prom?"

Jacob shrugged, shaking off Michael's astonishment. Michael caught up with him. "She was dating football jocks in grammar school, man."

"Really?" Jacob said.

Michael fell into stride beside his brother. "You should have asked me," he said. "I would have told you to forget about Lori Ballinger."

Jacob shrugged again.

The route was all familiar—gray sidewalks and driveways, green rectangles of lawns, cars, bicycles, houses, and trees. The familiar streets. He and Jacob could name nearly every family as they passed. The O'Haras' house, the Krafts', the DeLucas', Levines', Persichettis'. They'd been in most of their kitchens or front hallways, they'd collected paper-route payments or candy on Halloween, gotten glasses of water or Kool-Aid from them on hot summer days. As he walked beside his brother, Michael's recollection of those days made them all seem soft-focused and gentle, an easy roundness about things that had since given way to something thinner, something grown sharper in a threadbare sort of way. Maybe it was the clean-edged aluminum siding that had replaced the aging shingles on most of the homes, or the sleeker cars, or the sun catching the chrome on Tony Persichetti's motorcycle in the driveway, where he once would have left his bike. Maybe it was just the sense of it coming to an end, his time in this place, his childhood. Maybe it was that the place had worn thin only for him, that he was already worn out with waiting to leave it and get on.

He said to his brother, "I can't wait to get out of here. One more year." He said, "I don't know how you can stand it, not going away."

Jacob shrugged again. His father had told him: "I can pay for private-school tuition, or I can pay your room and board. I can't do both. There are four of you to put through college."

"I don't mind," he said.

Michael looked at him again. Someone, some girl, had told him once, "Your brother's nice." And then added, as if it pained her, "Too nice, if you know what I mean." He hadn't, not exactly. He thought again of Lori Ballinger. Jacob had made a plan and worked up the courage and called her and asked her to the prom and she had shot him down and through it all, he'd never said a word. About any of it. Through it all, he'd pulled his blankets up over his shoulder and faced the wall. Michael would hear him sometimes, the mattress, the deep sighs. No doubt Jacob heard him, too, when his turn came. Tempting as it had been to say, across the short space between their beds—"Are you jacking off?" "Are you crying?"—Michael never had. Not out of any kindness, he knew, but in exchange for future consideration, when the agitation under the covers, the tears, would be his.

"I think the new church is bullshit," Michael said. He had only the slightest hankering, like the first hint of hunger, to start a fight.

Jacob shrugged again. "The other one was falling down."

"They could have fixed it," Michael said. "Instead of spending all that money."

Jacob said nothing. They were almost home. The Rosenbergs' house, the Lavins'. "Putting the screws to guys like Dad," Michael said. "Making them cough up the dough to make McShane look good. It's bullshit."

"You gotta have a church," Jacob said.

"Why?" Michael asked. The MacLeod house, him with the musical aspirations and the Orange Crush hair. Michael was certain that if Jacob had told him what he was thinking, he would have said, There's no way you can go with Lori Ballinger, give it up. He would have saved him from whatever it was he had felt when she said, No, I can't. "Why do you have to have a church?" More belligerent than he'd intended.

Behind them, they could hear Clare calling, jokingly, "Oh, boys." She was hanging out the window of the car. The car was slowing down, passing them. "Yoo-hoo," she said, waving her headband toward them. In the front seat, their mother and father were laughing.

They both waved back. The car swung into the driveway ahead of them.

"People need a place to go," Jacob said.

"Why?" Michael asked again. "What for?" And when Jacob shrugged, but smiling this time, as if he knew they both knew the answer, Michael said, once more, "It's bullshit."

J OHN KEANE LAY IN BED and held a running argument with the
pain. It was a terse, dismissive argument, the kind he might
have with some idiot shop clerk or dishonest mechanic, the kind of
hopeless, useless, beneath-your-dignity argument that you know
you should walk away from but don't. Can't. Raising your eyebrows at any bystander or eavesdropper as if to say, Can you believe this idiot? Can you believe I'm bothering to talk to him?

The boys, before they left for their summer jobs—Jacob was
cutting lawns again this summer, Michael caddying by day and
pumping gas at night—had knocked together a number of two-by-
fours and, following his instructions, had rigged it with a pulley and
a rope. They had then wrapped the rope around one of his old,
paint-spattered army boots, across the instep and up through the
laces, and weighed the other end with a dictionary and half a dozen
volumes of their grocery-store encyclopedia. Following his instructions (they were good kids, both of them), they had slipped the
boot over his right sock, adjusting the whole contraption until his
leg was pulled taut, nearly suspended over the damp mattress, and
the pain that had woken him two nights ago, all unbidden and unaccountable, met its match with this new pain—a disciplined, intentional pain—intended to be the cure.

Michael had hesitated at the bedroom door. This was at about eight-fifteen this morning, Mary downstairs getting the rest of them out of the house. If anyone was going to say this two-bit attempt at traction was an eccentric, half-assed scheme, it would be Michael the wise guy. But Michael merely waved his arm—a long, thin arm, softened, nearly blurred by the fair hair that covered it—and said, "Take care."

He had lifted his own arm, the mold from which the other had been formed, and said, "Sure I will."

He had a bottle of aspirin by the bedside, a cold cup of tea, a tube of Ben-Gay, even, his wife's idea, a tumbler of scotch, but he resisted resorting to any of them just yet. Yesterday, the boys had moved the portable TV into his room, close enough so he could reach the dial and the antenna (another jerry-rigged affair with rabbit ears and a coat hanger and aluminum foil), but he resisted that as well. The house was empty now—the boys at their jobs and his wife and the two girls off to a matinee in the city—and silent but for the whir of the fan on the dresser, which by now had become a part of the silence as well. This was the beginning of his second day of sick leave, the first two he had taken in more than twenty years, and he didn't like the vertigo he felt at this sudden suspension of his routine any better today than he had yesterday. (He raised his chin at the army boot, at the pale blue pant leg of his pajamas: I don't like it.)

It wasn't that he was a company man, he was happy enough to use up his three weeks of vacation time every year—one week to work around the house in the spring, two in summer to take the kids to the shore. He was just mostly healthy, and found a couple of aspirin or a cold tablet taken in the morning far preferable to the silence and boredom of a sickroom. And he didn't like doctors. Mary Keane rolled her eyes every time she heard him say it. She understood that what he didn't like about doctors had less to do with what he called their arrogance and more to do with the diplomas on the wall, the golf-course tans—the disadvantage, the particular kind of humiliation a man with four children making fifteen thousand a year endured while sitting with his bare legs dangling, those missing toes, in his boxer shorts and T-shirt before a diplomaed man in a good suit who had been to Columbia University or Cornell. Once a year, he went downtown for his company physical and every year he got a clean bill of health—as had (he was quick to point out) his brother Frank two weeks before he died, which told you something about doctors.

He was convinced anyway that lingering illness and curable, or incurable, disease was not likely to get him. His end, when it came, he was certain, would be swift and unavoidable. The black coach. The sudden fall. Like Frank's.

He shifted uncomfortably on the bed, palms pressed to the mattress to ease the pressure on his tailbone. He moved his foot inside the boot. This morning, when he had shown the boys the sketch he had drawn during the sleepless night, Michael had muttered, "It looks like a guillotine. Or the rack." He had raised an eyebrow and flicked an imaginary cigarette and said in a squinting, lip-curling German accent, "Foolish man, ve have other vays to make you talk." But Jacob, who if he had been another kind of oldest child might have had the courage to dissuade his father, to point out that they were not setting a broken limb, that this was not the Wild West and it was high time a doctor be consulted, said simply, "Dad thinks it will help," and then led Michael to the basement where there was still a small, leftover pile of two-by-fours tucked away in the furnace room.

It might have been more fitting for them to have rebelled, and he suspected that were he a younger man, a younger father, they would have. But the solemnity with which the two of them had come, one after the other, into his bedroom yesterday morning revealed something. Here he was out sick for the first time in more than twenty years and here they were standing over him, dumbstruck and wary, their fear of his dying sprung into their faces as if from the very moment their mother had awakened them with the news that sometime during the night, something had gone wrong with Daddy's leg. He suspected that they followed his instructions for the weights and the pulley and the contraption that was to support it not so much to humor him in his pain but to coax themselves into believing that he was still in charge, that they were still under his care.

And then the sound of them pounding the wood reached him from the basement, and it was all he could do to cast aside as utter nonsense his own morbid thoughts regarding coffins and crucifixes. It was only a bum leg, after all. Sprung on him in the middle of the night.

He stirred again against the mattress, tilted his head back against the mahogany headboard. He tried to gauge the movement of the sunlight across the white ceiling. There were the blue shadows cast by the valances of his wife's curtains, the reflection of light in the mirror above her dresser, in the glass of the children's school photographs, in the blank face of the TV. The pain stretched its own legs for a few seconds, reached up over his thigh and across his back and into his chest and arms. In response, he moved the toe of the boot, then bent his knee to lift the weight of the books that pulled against it, matching pain for pain, the unbidden with the intentional, in some vague theory that the one would defeat the other, that the one was preferable to the other. When he reached for the aspirin on the bed stand, he saw that his hand was trembling and he whispered a quick "Son of a bitch." It was an ongoing and unwinnable argument with an idiot.

And yet it was an argument he could not resist.

He swallowed the aspirin without water, tossing them one at a time into the back of his throat, the second one catching on his tongue. What he was hoping to put off for as long as possible was the inevitable slipping out of the boot and off the bed, the awkward, gimping trip across the hallway to the bathroom.

There was an old hockey stick on the other side of the bed, another basement resource the boys had fetched for him, meant to serve as a crutch, although using it had made him feel like some Old Testament prophet leaning on his staff.

"Like Charlton Heston," Michael had said from the doorway of his own bedroom last night. It seemed to John Keane that over the past two days, one or the other of his sons was always lounging casually in the doorway whenever he got himself up and hauled himself across the hall to the bathroom. Had he been a younger father, they might have simply thrown him over a shoulder and carried him across.

He lifted his hand to wipe the perspiration from his lip, raised and lowered his good leg and then slipped both hands under the thigh of the bad one and slowly raised it until he could feel again the weight pulling against his foot.

And then the pain again, wire thin this time, through his leg and into his gut and reaching up to hook the corners of his mouth.

He turned his head, waiting for it to pass. The fan on the dresser was humming, though it offered no breeze. The Saran-wrapped sandwich and the pile of magazines his wife had left for him on her side of the bed, the damp bedsheets themselves, gave off a nauseating yellow sheen and in his impatience with it, with the pain itself, he pulled at the leg again.

The pain answered in kind.

It was a ridiculous argument. A stupid fight. And yet, he raised his chin defiantly at the speckled boot. There were white dots of paint from the living room, bits of pale green from when he had done the boys' room, pale pink from the year Clare was born. Other colors, no doubt, were he to examine it more closely, two decades' worth of housekeeping chores done in these boots, painting and gardening and leaf raking, the very peacetime pursuits the army, in giving them to him, had sought to insure. Pursuits that the pain, on this hot still morning, now easily reduced to foolishness. He had wasted his life with painting and gardening and leaf raking. He had squandered his time.

With his hand under his thigh, he lifted his leg again. The pulley squeaked a little, slowly turning. Foolish man, Michael had said. Ve have other ways. Well, no, not squandered. There were his children, after all.

In the mirror above his wife's dresser, he could see the reflection of the crucifix that hung over their bed, the tiny gold Christ curled against the thick cross. Thick in this particular case, he knew, because behind the tortured figure on the ivory cross there was a secret compartment that contained two candles and a vial of holy water, the accoutrements of Last Rites. It had been a gift from the priest who married them, a reminder, no doubt, that their marriage bed might also be the bed in which they would breathe their last. It had not been difficult for them, bred-in-the-bone Catholics, Irish Catholics, even at the beginning of their lives together, to imagine the final scene: the candles flickering on the bedside table, the holy water glistening on his forehead, the hushed air, the dim lights, the children kneeling at his bedside, and his wife, her hand over his, assuring him, assuring him, forgiving, in the last minutes left to them, assuring and forgiving. Certainly, they had said till death do us part, but it wasn't until they'd opened the priest's present (he recalled the wrappings of the other gifts spread across the living room of her father's apartment, her pretty beige going-away suit, the nervous anticipation he had felt, opening a few packages while they waited for the cab that was to take them to the city) that the scene became vivid for them both—the crucifix spread apart, the thin white tapers lit, the dim room where he would breathe his last.

It was a scenario he no longer deemed likely. His brother had clutched his heart and hit the pavement on Thirty-fourth Street, already gone.

He lowered the leg again, heard the pile of thick books, tied together like a schoolboy's satchel, hit the floor. Pain such as this had a tendency to reduce everything, every effort, every belief, to brittle plastic, easily shattered. It could shatter the notion of Paradise opened by a single, wracked body hung on a cross. It could shatter any hope you had that you were worth more than the bustling of your ordinary days. It could remind you easily enough that death was no more or less than the choke and sputter of a single muscle, the sudden exposure of gut and bone, your skin turned black in the cold.

If you didn't argue against it, the idiot pain, the very things you'd based your life on could shatter.

His eyes went from the reflected crucifix to the blank gray face of the television. He could make out his own reflection there, sitting up against the headboard. His chest and shoulders in his pale pajamas, his bald head, his face, which in the reflected shadow and distorted sunlight caught by the blank screen, was suddenly the face of his brother.

It had happened before: one of his sons would be talking in another room and he'd hear, for a moment, Frank's laughter. His niece once raised a hand, turned her head, and it was Frank's gesture. He would raise his own chin shaving and there he'd see his brother, briefly, briefly.

Even now his own reflection in the blank gray face of the TV set had become simply his own again, too bald, too gaunt for Frank. But the glimpse, nevertheless, had been well timed, and as if to acknowledge it, small gift that it was, he pulled at the leg again. He held his breath again as the pain flared. No realistic person expected a full-fledged visitation, or even hoped for one—it was, surely,

what they meant when they said "laid to rest"—but still there were
tricks of the eye or of the mind that could satisfy even someone like
himself, who, steeped in superstition as a child, had long ago
learned to resist it. Surely there were assurances, even for the most
reasonable of believers, that pain wasn't all, in the end. That something would trump the foolishness of body and bone, day after day.
Frank's face, glimpsed briefly, assuring him, his own heart, his spir-
its, rising at the mere possibility of once again seeing his brother's
face.

He recalled that all the pain of that rainy day—the endless Mass
at Incarnation, the traffic-choked ride to the cemetery—had been
for Catherine, Frank's daughter. All the dignity, resignation, joyful
hope of resurrection the rest of them had mustered, as one must, to
get through the day, undermined by the poor girl's tears. She cried
a torrent through it all. Thin as a willow in her dark sweater and
skirt, bent over in the pew or under her mother's arm at the cemetery. A scrap of tissue in her hands and the pale red hair falling over
her face. Too young to be so wracked by grief. Too pretty, too
newly formed to know that particular kind of disappointment. Afterward, back at the house, he had knelt beside her chair and said,
"Your father will be with you for the rest of your days," and she,
nineteen at the time, had looked at him with her red eyes and said,
"I'll never stop missing him."

Six months later, when he gave her his arm on the day she was
married, he felt himself a poor substitute, although she had whispered her gratitude, leaving the scent of her lipstick on his cheek
and his ear. She had married a kid from Greenwich, a wealthy boy
who had a seat on the Stock Exchange now. They lived in Garden
City and had refused so many invitations, to Clare's christening
party, to her first Holy Communion, to confirmations and gradua-
tions, even to a few odd Sunday suppers, that he and Mary had sim-

ply stopped asking. "She moves in different circles now," Ellen, Frank's wife, had said, with more pride than disappointment, although many of her invitations were also refused.

Last he saw her, just last year, he was waiting for his wife and the girls outside A&S when Catherine, in a beige Cadillac, pulled into the parking space beside him. It took him a moment to recognize her, and she was out of her car by the time he waved at her through his own passenger window. Then he opened his door to get out and greet her. But she was already walking away, her head down. There was another woman with her and she was the one who glanced over her shoulder when he called. But neither one of them paused.

He looked again at his reflection in the TV set. You'll be pleased to know that she drives a Cadillac. That she's doing quite well, her own daughter growing, Ellen tells me. A big house in Garden City. I can't say that it didn't cut me like a knife, Frank, standing in that parking lot. I can't say that I didn't see some of it in you, while you were here, with your own Cadillacs every other year, your Chivas Regal and your fancy beer, a certain fascination, when we were kids, with the society page.

He lifted the leg again. The pain, he realized, was constant, there was only the illusion of ebb and flow.

His eyes went again to the crucifix above his head, reflected in the mirror. The strained arms, the arched spine. All that effort to open the gates of heaven for us and we (he thought) probably spend our first hours among the heavenly hosts settling old scores with our relatives.

Absolutely, Mr. Gallagher.

He pulled at the leg again—it was only stubborness that made him continue to believe that what he was doing was therapeutic.

A T NOON MARY CALLED from the city. They had met Pauline at Penn Station and now they were having lunch at Schrafft's before the show. It was hotter than heck. They were looking forward to getting into the cool theater.

And then, with (he would have said) much hemming and hawing, she asked him cautiously (she was building up to something) how he was feeling, if he'd gotten any sleep, if he could eat—and, finally, if his contraption was doing him any good.

He said, Yes it was, believe it or not, and he knew immediately that the lie had taken the wind out of her sails.

Still, she said, "Pauline says it's a slipped disk."

"Pauline's the expert, then," he said.

Her silence was a remarkable concoction: hurt, impatience, recrimination, blood-red anger, fear, worry—the kind of concoction only a long marriage can brew. Rising behind it was the faint clatter of dishes, the hum of restaurant conversation.

"No," she said finally. "But a gal from the office had a brother-in-law with the same problem. Just woke up one morning with a terrible pain. Down his leg. A slipped disk."

His wife would replace the natural laws with anecdotes. No gravity until someone's sister's cousin's husband had fallen down the stairs. Night and day mere rumor until a girl she used to know in high school was stricken with insomnia, or burned to a crisp by the sun.

"Is that so?" he said placidly. "Same exact thing?"

"Yeah," she said, with some hesitation. "More or less. You know, his leg."

The line clicked to say their three minutes were up and instead of getting off, she said, "Hold on," and dropped another dime into the phone.

"Right or left?" he asked when the coin had been swallowed.

"What?" she said.

And he repeated more emphatically, "Was it the right leg or the left leg? Of this fellow just like me?"

She paused and then said, "Very funny," to show that it wasn't. "Pauline read an article about it," she said. "It happens to a lot of men. It's evolution. It's the price men pay for standing upright."

Pauline, he thought, would be happy to learn that there is a price men pay for standing upright.

"Tomorrow I'm calling the doctor," she went on, the very reason she had dropped the second dime into the machine. He could see her do her little "so there" nod. There, I said it.

"What are you going to call him?" he asked her.

When she hung up the phone he could hear her say "Stubborn" before the receiver hit the cradle. He could not be sure if she was speaking to herself or to Pauline, or perhaps to the two girls, who would also nod. Maybe only to a waiter, clattering dishes.

An hour later, Jacob returned, banging into the house as he tended to do, always sounding like a drunk on a stage set. He moved around the kitchen a bit, clink of glass and clatter of silverware and slam and then slam again of the refrigerator door. When he poked his head around the doorway of the bedroom, he had half a sandwich in his cheek, the other half, dripping mustard and pickle relish, cupped like a small creature in his hands.

"How are you doing, Dad?" he asked, stretching his throat to get the food swallowed as he spoke. John Keane could not help but wonder how many years would have to go by before it would occur to his son that maybe he should have come up and asked after his father before he made the sandwich.

"Better," he said.

And then Jacob began nodding, that long, low, exaggerated nod that he and his friends so often substituted for speech. "The thing's working, then," he said.

His father shrugged. "Seems to be."

"Good enough," Jacob said, still nodding. He was not quite meeting his father's eye. "You want me to put the TV on for you?"

Although it was within easy reach and the last thing he wanted, he said, "Sure. That'd be great."

Jacob's sneakers were grass stained and there were grass stains like brushstrokes on his skinny calves and his khaki shorts. Not just slower and shyer than his brother, but shorter, too: you could see in his legs, in the way he walked, that at nineteen there was no more growth in him, that the sudden, surprising adolescent transformation his father had imagined for him all through his childhood was not going to occur. It surprised him. The men in his family were all of a good size. He thought, not for the first time, how strange it was that his son should take after no one so much as his long-ago namesake, the other Jacob.

John Keane watched the boy as he carefully edged himself between the bed and the TV on its rickety stand, turned it on, fiddled with the antenna, leaning a little, his back to his father. He smelled like mown grass, sun, and air. There was some sinewy strength in his tanned arms and in his hands. A young man's strength, a young man's compact body under the loose, sweat-limp T-shirt. It was another kind of pain—a sweet, heart-dropping pain—what he felt for his son, what he felt for the boy's young body, his awkwardness, his earnestness, his life ahead. And he suddenly found himself pulling against it, deliberately, with an opposite and equal weight, meant, like the contraption that bound his foot, to provide equilibrium. There were his failings as well. There was the question, after a less than successful first year, of whether he'd go back to St. John's in the fall. ("Good money after bad," he had told the boy, after Jacob's last set of grades. He'd said, "I've got four of you to put through college, you know.") There was the draft. There was the chance that the military would be the making of him. There was the chance of Vietnam.

Jacob stepped back for a moment, watching the TV—two soap-opera characters, a man and a woman, arguing intently, another woman shown wide-eyed, elaborately eavesdropping from behind a closed door. Jacob watched them all with utter absorption as he finished his sandwich. His father could see the small crop of sparse beard along his son's jawline, under the fair, sun-touched skin. He needed a haircut, but these days they all did.

When a commercial began, Jacob turned to his father as if he'd just come to. (It was the heart of the boy's trouble, John Keane would have said; he was too easily absorbed.) "You want to see this?" he asked and his father waved a hand. "Christ, no," he said. "Turn it off. Get your shower."

And then he reached out to touch his son, to playfully slap him on the back, but he missed and paid the price for the awkwardness of the movement with another neon-bright rush of pain. He pulled some air through his teeth, he couldn't help it, and Jacob paused, looking down on him from beside the bed, and then, gently, put a hand to his father's shoulder. His face was white under his tan and his dark hair fell into his eyes. "Dad," he said with some alarm, and then paused. And then, in another tone altogether, he said evenly, "What can I do for you?"

There was some comfort to be discovered, no doubt, in the odd connections, and repetitions, in the misapprehensions themselves, some pattern across the years that would convey assurance. He had said to that other Jacob, in a prayer, What can I do for you?—and now here was his own boy, that other's impulsive namesake, saying the same. Some pattern in the coincidence, the connectedness, some thread of assurance that was woven through the passing years—but he was in too much pain now to discern it, if it was there at all. He put his fingertips to his son's arm. "Get your shower," he said. "I'm fine."

When Michael returned, he leaned into the bedroom and said, "How you doing, Dad?" and "The Met game's on" in the same breath. He turned on the television, sat on the edge of the bed. He, too, had the smell of the outdoors on him. The smell of the golf course. The smell of the wider world. At the first commercial break, Michael looked over his shoulder at the boot and the rope and the pulley and the wood, at his father's suspended leg. He tested the rope a bit. "Maybe we should patent this thing," he said. "We can write to the army and buy up their old boots." He laughed. His father glimpsed the face Michael would wear as a grown man, the blue eyes and good teeth. It was handsome now, in its youth, but it would be no more than pleasant, perhaps, in middle age. "If they don't all have jungle rot by now," he added.

Jacob had joined them to watch the extra innings. He was in the chair beside his father's bed. He was showered and dressed, a short-sleeved shirt and cutoff blue jeans. There was a girl who took up his evenings this summer, although it was Michael who, his father noticed, had a pink bruise on his neck, the shape of a small bite.

"Tony Persichetti," Michael was saying, "said in his letter that the skin comes off with his socks."

Downstairs, their mother and the girls were just coming in. Clare was the first to climb the stairs. She hesitated for a moment at the door of the bedroom before her father called her in, and then she leaped easily up onto the bed, rattling the mattress and the magazines, the plate with the untouched sandwich and every plate, it seemed, in her father's fragile spine. He put a hand out, "Go easy," he said. Michael turned from the game to say, "Watch it, nimrod." Only slightly subdued, she perched herself on the pillow beside her father, patted his bald head. "We had fun," she said.

Then Mary was in the doorway, in her skirt and blouse and stocking feet. Her hands on her hips. "Are you ready to get out of that thing?" she asked.

John Keane saw both boys bow their heads.

"No," he said simply. "It's helping."

She looked to the boys, as if they would corroborate her skepticism. But they were having none of it. She looked especially at Michael, who might have been her surest ally, given all the times in the past he'd stood against his father, over politics, over hairstyles, over mandatory Sunday Mass. "Honestly," she said, moving into the room, gathering the clutter from her side of the bed. "I hardly think this is the solution."

"It's helping," he said again.

She only glanced at him. "You don't look like you've been helped," she said.

It was Clare who was absorbing the discussion unabashedly, through her wide eyes.

Now Annie appeared. She was talking—these days she was always talking—and both boys raised their hands to hush her. She walked around the bed to join them in front of the small screen. The runners scored. Michael leaned forward to slap Jacob's hand, jostling the mattress. Clare threw her hands up in the air, and then around her father's shoulder. Impatient, Mary Keane was leaning over the bed, gathering the magazines.

In fact, he would die alone, accompanied only by the high-pitched pulse of the hospital machine, his last breath missed even by the nurses who were distracted by the changing shifts. None of them gathered at his bed, no candles lit. The offending leg already amputated in the doctors' routine efforts to save him.

With the plate and the magazines in her hand she said, "Do you want the boys to help you get to the toilet before dinner?"

He knew he would have to manage it sometime within the next twenty minutes (ten minutes, now that she had brought the subject up), but he said, "No. I'm fine."

He recognized the tactic: she'd humiliate him into a doctor's office. Using words like toilet when she never said toilet, thought it unrefined, just to get him annoyed enough to make an appointment.

"Maybe I could get you a little bell or something," she said, as coy as she might ever have been at twenty-one. "You could ring it when you need to go."

No doubt this was Pauline's plan.

He glanced at the TV. He felt the pain roil a little, threatening a larger blow.

"Why don't you all go downstairs and have your dinner?" he said, calmly. Because she would see every bit of it in his face, she saw everything in his face.

"Send me up a piece of steak," he said.

Clare brought the tray, walking with it through the slatted rosy sunlight that now stretched slowly, leisurely, the stroll of time, across the ceiling and the far wall. He'd just returned from the bathroom and the old army boot, its tongue lolling, lay in its coil of rope at the foot of the bed. He had an impulse, in his daughter's presence, to throw a blanket over it. It occurred to him that he had reached an age (he remembered Mary's befuddled old father) when his surest convictions could be transformed into mere foolishness in the blink of an eye.

"Put it here," he said, dragging the straight-backed chair to the side of the bed. She put the tray down, kissed his cheek. There was something of the metallic odor of the hot subway about her still, the odor of his own missed commute home. All of his children scented with the wider world.

She was talking about the day in the city and what the man at the token booth had said, and what Pauline had said, and who she swore she saw in the lobby when the intermission lights flashed though she couldn't really be sure. He surveyed the tray. A piece of chuck steak and mashed potatoes and green beans. A roll and butter and a dish of canned pears. Sitting on the edge of the bed, with both feet on the floor, he was aware of a certain numbness taking over his leg. He couldn't eat a bite.

"The Spanish Inquisition," she said, and he looked up at her, thinking, perhaps, she was repeating Michael's joke about the rack. Again he had the impulse to cover up the empty boot. But she was, he quickly gathered, talking about the play. The tickets had been a gift from Pauline. Someone in his office told him they could well have cost sixty dollars apiece.

"They're all prisoners," Clare was saying. "In a dungeon. And there's this long staircase." She raised her arms, illustrating it. Her skirt was short, too short (he resisted interrupting her to mention this), her knees still chubby although the rest of her body had grown lean. "And Cervantes comes down. The prisoners attack him and then they put him on trial. In order to defend himself, he tells them a story. And then he becomes Don Quixote and all the prisoners are the other characters. So the whole play is like the story he tells, while they're waiting in jail."

She pulled off the headband that held back her hair. Scratched her head. The sunlight from the window was on her back. "He's this old man and he's read so many books about chivalry that he goes crazy and thinks it's all real. He thinks he's a knight, Don Quixote de la Mancha. And only one of his servants goes along with him, Sancho Panza. And they go out on a quest. He sees a windmill and thinks it's a monster."

"Titling at windmills," he said. "It's an expression."

"Yeah," she said. She slipped the headband on again, it was a habit of hers. "But it was really good the way they did it. The windmill was just this huge shadow at the back of the stage."

He picked up his fork. Tried, and failed, to lift the bum leg. The pain, he realized, was far preferable to the numbness. She was on about the sleazy inn that Don Quixote thought was a castle, the servant girl ("A slut really," she said, catching his eye for a second to see if he disapproved of the word—he did) he thought was a beautiful damsel.

He wondered briefly if she would end up wanting to go on the stage herself. She was pretty enough, he thought. But then all the little girls her age struck him as pretty.

The cure they came up with, she said—he had missed just who "they" were—was mirrors. (She said it mear-ras, the way her mother did. A touch of Brooklynese carried out to Long Island.) They surrounded the old man with mirrors, she said. And made him look at himself. Made him see.

She paused and said, "You're not hungry?" But he shook his head, lifted the warm roll. "I'm listening," he told her. He would give himself another minute or two before he tried moving his leg back onto the bed. It was possible that he'd have to call the boys for help. It was possible that he'd lost all use of it. "Did it work? The dose of reality?"

She stepped back a little. Now the sun was on her shoulder and her hair. Downstairs, he heard Michael saying, "A nine iron, a fucking nine iron," and Jacob laughing, Annie, too. Their mother shushing the bad language. His brother Frank somewhere, in the boy's laughter. And what a vocabulary his youngest child would take into the wider world. But Clare was attending only to her own tale.

"Yeah," she said, dramatically, "but then you see him in bed and he's dying." Her eyes didn't fall on his own bed, the empty old boot, or on him in his pajamas. But there was, perhaps, a catch in her voice, a sweet change of pitch as she went on. "Sancho Panza's there, and his niece. But he doesn't remember anything about being Don Quixote. Not even when Dulcinea comes in. She's kind of cleaned up. She wants him to remember, but he tells her he was just confused. He says he was confused by shadows. Like the windmill thing."

She paused. Looked at her father and shrugged. He suddenly realized that she was about to cry.

"That's too bad," he said. He knew enough not to laugh at her. He had already offended her, more than once, when he'd teased her about her easy tears. Downstairs, the water was running, the kitchen chairs were being pushed back from the table. He broke the roll in two and handed her a piece. "Did you have your dinner?" he asked.

She took the bread. Held it in her hand. "But that's not the end," she said, caught up in it now. Not just her mother's accent but her delight in the sound of her own voice, once she got started. He smiled, watching her. The only way to temper the outlandishness of a father's love was to weigh it against the facts of your children's imperfections. She was a plain child, truth be told, not as pretty as her sister. "Dulcinea sings the impossible dream song and, really slowly, he begins to remember. He starts to get out of the bed. Sancho helps him. All of a sudden he knows he really is Don Quixote. Really."

And then, to his great surprise, she began to sing. Her voice was sweet, lower than he would have expected, although surely he had heard her singing around the house a thousand times before. But now she was singing for him, much as she used to do when she was very small, her hands at her sides, her eyes half closed. The cotton skirt not too short, perhaps, but wrinkled from the hours she'd been sitting. The little-girl knees, although her body was growing lean. She sang and he was both enchanted and embarrassed by her earnestness. Both hopeful that neither of the boys would come upstairs (Jacob would only roll his eyes but Michael would sing along with her, mocking, howling the words, *to run, where the brave dare not go ow ow*), and yet wishing that they would because there was something painful in it, watching her, another kind of pain altogether than what he'd been fighting these past two days. The boys had their lives off in the wider world, he thought, but girls, his daughters, they had lives far wider and far more inaccessible, right before his eyes.

The room was lit with the thick yellow light of a summer evening. The leg was numb and as certain as he was that he would find a way to heal it—or that the doctors would—he knew, too, that some part of his future had been retracted, foreshortened by the pain. That it had added, if only by a month or a year or two, to the time she would have to miss him.

She sang, she seemed to know all the words.

THE LOTTERY was held three weeks before Christmas, which made something biblical about the whole ordeal, or at least, Mary Keane said, medieval.

When all the days of the year had been called, she said to her husband, her mouth held crookedly—a grim joke in the face of what they could not change—"Maybe if the piano player had skipped practice that morning, Jacob would have had a different birthday." He nodded; it was a joke, given its intimate circumstances, no one else could share, and even he, all these years later, felt himself blush. "Maybe if you'd married George," he said.

And then he took Clare's hand. She was bundled up against the cold. They were just going out for a breath of fresh air. At the foot of his driveway, pulling his garbage cans to the curb, Mr. Persichetti paused. Tony's birth date, as it turned out, would have been a lucky one, if he hadn't already enlisted and gone over and come back home again, hollow-eyed and furious, after all he'd seen. "Hooked on drugs," Mr. Persichetti said. He might have just learned the phrase.

Mr. Persichetti told Mr. Keane, "Shoot him in the foot. Break his legs before you let him go."

Clare looked up at the two men. Her father gripped her hand

and Mr. Persichetti stepped back and then forward, his face shadowy in the night.

"No, honey," he said, touching her wool cap. "Don't pay attention to me." And then he glanced at her father, his eyes catching the dull streetlight. "I was there when you came into the world, you know," he said, cheerfully, as if cheerfulness now could erase the terrible thing he had already said. She told him she knew. She had come too soon. She had come inconveniently. Pauline had only just put on her hat when the call came, on her way out to the movies.

"I was the very first person," Mr. Persichetti said, "to welcome you into this crazy world of ours."

And for the second time in that hour, John Keane felt a flush rise to his cheeks.

A ND YOUR BROTHER?" Mrs. Antonelli said because it was Michael Keane she remembered, all the hours he had cooled his heels on the leather couch before her desk, waiting to see Sister Rose, the principal. Jacob, sitting before her now, had left no mark on her memory—which was understandable enough, given the number of children who passed through St. Gabriel's, a hundred graduates each year, six or seven hundred more since Jacob Keane had been an eighth grader. As secretary and (she liked to say) palace guard for Sister Rose, Mrs. Antonelli had far more contact with the troublemakers anyway. Michael Keane had been one of them. Jacob, clearly, had not.

"He's upstate," Jacob said. "College."

He was a nice-looking boy—dark hair and dark brows, green eyes. But he was also slight, narrow-shouldered, not much bigger, perhaps, than he'd been when he left here. It was Mrs. Antonelli's belief that God should have made all men tall and broad—out of fairness. Her own husband was six foot three. She thought of this as an accomplishment.

"Good for him," she said, and then wondered at the contrast her words implied, for Jacob had just told her that he himself had left St. John's and was now headed for the army. "And good for you, too," she added. "For answering the call."

Jacob smiled shyly. He wore blue jeans, which she did not approve of, and a tattersall dress shirt rolled at the sleeves, which was all right. "Thanks," he said, politely, although they both understood he'd had no choice in the matter.

"And you'll have the GI Bill when you get back," Mrs. Antonelli said. "That's how my husband put himself through Fordham."

Jacob nodded slowly. "It's a great thing," he said, and then looked at her, his large green eyes and a girl's dark lashes, nothing else to say.

Mrs. Antonelli glanced down at the work before her, but she had taken off her reading glasses when the boy came in (here to pick up his sister for a dentist appointment, although the mother had sent no note), so everything was a blur. From the room beyond came the sound of Sister Rose on the phone, speaking in the clipped rhythms of her professional voice. From down the hall came the drone of a class repeating its times tables. "I suppose it seems like just yesterday that you were here," she said, making conversation.

The boy merely moved his head, as if uncertain himself whether he wanted to say yes or no.

The office was paneled in dark wood, and the light from the small window was yellow. There was a statue of the Holy Family in one corner, a flagpole bearing the white-and-gold diocesan flag in another. There was a crucifix and an oil painting of the pope on the wall behind Mrs. Antonelli's desk, and the portrait of Our Lady of Perpetual Help from the old church on the wall behind Jacob's head. There was the gently overpowering odor of Mrs. Antonelli's perfume—a powdery scent that was neither fruit nor flower nor spice, like nothing in nature Jacob could think of—and despite the terrible familiarity of the office, the long halls of the school, the sound of the children reciting their lessons, it was this scent alone that brought him back to his years here, years of terror (he'd been a shy child and the nuns with their sweeping skirts and clicking beads had all but made him mute), years of grace (because he was also a good child, chosen above all others to carry messages from his teachers to Mrs. Antonelli's desk). He briefly studied his hands. Mrs. Antonelli's perfume brought him there again and put off all that was ahead of him not simply by a few hours but by years.

And then Clare was standing in the doorway, beside the eighth-grade boy who had been sent to fetch her. She wore her beanie, and her pigtails had already begun to fray. There were Band-Aids on both of her knees, above the navy blue kneesocks. She wore the school's plaid jumper, a new one that still hung on her stiffly, and under the wide white sleeves of her uniform blouse her bare arms seemed as thin as sticks.

Jacob stood. The car keys were in his hand.

"Please tell your mother," Mrs. Antonelli said, standing as well, "to remember to send a note in next time."

Jacob nodded. "I will," he said. And then, "Thank you." And then, head down, "Sorry to disturb you." He put his hand out to allow his sister to go before him through the door. "Nice to see you again," he said.

Mrs. Antonelli doubted very much that Jacob Keane would find the army to his liking. She looked up to see the eighth grader, a brazen thing, nearly six feet tall, who still lingered at the door with his shirttail out, hoping for another assignment from her to keep him from going back to class. She dismissed him and then sank into her chair. She put her glasses on and Sister Rose's lovely handwriting—a perfection of the art, she always said—came clear to her again. She said a prayer: Let them find something easy for the poor kid to do. A desk job in Germany. Lifeguard duty at a base on Okinawa, as a neighbor's boy had done. Amused to find how the world had turned since she was young—Germany and Okinawa now safe places for an American soldier.

But there was something unlucky about the boy. She would not have said tragic, just unlucky: his small stature, the awkward attempts at good manners, the apparently unsuccessful years at St. John's, the draft. Getting sent to Vietnam would be of a piece with all that. And what opportunities for bad luck would he find over there? Mrs. Antonelli had no children of her own, and so felt herself more clear-eyed about such things. There were kids who were born with luck on their side and others who simply weren't. It wasn't about intelligence or good grades, not even necessarily about good looks (although there was luck in that, too). It was chance, plain and simple. Kids born lucky and kids who never got a break. It was fate, perhaps, although she supposed God came into it somewhere (she couldn't say how, except, perhaps, that God had his favorites, too). She saw herself, some months from now, telling Sister Rose, who would not remember him, how Jacob Keane had come to her office not long ago, just before he went in, to pick up little Clare and take her to the dentist.

Two boys from St. Gabriel's had already died in the war. Neither was memorable to her as a student, although she had attended both funerals, sitting behind the three eighth-grade classes who had filled up the back of the big round church, warming it a bit, for both boys had been buried on cold winter days. From where she sat, the flag-draped coffins and the stooped families in their dark clothes had seemed rather a long way away. Although she had heard one of the mothers say, simply enough, "My baby."

Mrs. Antonelli touched her glasses to make sure they were still there, for Sister's blue ink and fine letters had once more lost their clarity, and the steady yellow light briefly wavered. She looked up. The tall eighth grader was in her doorway again, his shirttail still out and his tie still crooked, a white attendance sheet from Sister Savior in his hand. His face and his hair, all his edges, a blur, through her tears. An angel himself, through her tears.

In the narrow alleyway beside the school, Jacob paused and

then leaned down to whisper into his sister's ear. "It was a fib," he said.

He leaned down, out of the autumn blue sky, out of the cinder-block wall, out of nothingness (she would say later) and into awareness, into memory. His eyes were green and his lashes long and thick. There were marks on his face, freckles, lingering acne, nicks from his razor. There was the trace of a beard. He leaned down and put his lips to her ear and said, "It was a fib," a buzz against the soft bones that made her raise her shoulder and giggle. Surely not her first memory of him—he had read to her when she was still in a crib, he had sat beside her on the stairs waiting to be called down on Christmas morning, at the dinner table he had spoken to her through his raised milk glass, the milk bubbling with his words until their father said, "Enough"—but surely this was her first clear memory of his face, leaning down to her out of the autumn sky.

There was no dentist appointment, he said. He had the car keys in his hand. He started walking again. He just wanted to take her for a ride, he said. She hurried to keep up. They were in the alleyway. On one side was the long cinder-block wall that separated the school property from the strip of stores and the parking lot next door. On the other, the low steps and wide glass doors of the gym. The alleyway itself was a magnet for lost mimeographed worksheets and loose-leaf paper, for candy wrappers and brown lunch bags and the yellowed wax bottles, many of them marred by teeth marks, that had once been filled with sweetened, brightly colored liquids, purchased from Krause's store. There seemed to be a constant wind blowing along the ground here, full of sand and grit, and she felt she was racing through it, following him. He had the car keys in his hand and they jingled like a cowboy's spurs as he led her around the cinder-block wall and into the parking lot next door, where he had left his car. He unlocked the door, opened it for her. "Hop in," he said. There was a thin terry-cloth cover over the old leather seats. It seemed to be attached with rubber bands. It slid underneath her as she climbed in, but it was soft to the touch. He slammed the door, walked around the back of the car. He had parked under the single tree in the lot and a few leaves, yellow and gold and rust colored, had drifted onto the red hood and across the windshield. He got in the car, put the key in the ignition. "Let's just drive around," he said.

She said okay, although still she expected the drive to end at the dentist's office—the eighth grader who had fetched her had said so, and so had Mrs. Walters when she called her to the front of the class. She could already smell the cinnamon and alcohol of the place. Hear the hateful sound of the drill. The office was in the basement of the dentist's house. There was a long concrete stairwell, damp and steep, that went down to the door. The floor of the waiting room was black and white. There would be a shoe box full of charms and toy jewelry from which she could pick two when it was over.

Her brother put his arm across the seat and slowly backed out of his space. He drove first through the length of the narrow lot, past the candy store, the hardware store, the five-and-dime. "That's where the 'hoochie-koochie-koo' man used to stand," he said. He pointed to a row of shopping carts in a corner near the grocery store. "When I was your age," he said. "He was just a crazy old man, always kind of drooling. If he got close enough to you, he'd pinch your cheek and say, 'Hoochie-koochie-koo.' " He looked over his shoulder as he turned out of the lot. He was smaller than their father, but he had the same seriousness when he drove. "People said he was shell-shocked. From the war." He made another turn, driving slowly, slower than she could walk. "I don't know when he stopped being there." He drove past the bowling alley and told her he'd been on a bowling team in eighth grade. He was so bad, he said, that he never broke a hundred. He said he used to sit there and pray, waiting for his turn. Just one spare, he used to say. Not even a strike. You don't have to make me good, he used to tell God. "Just average." He looked at her and laughed. She laughed, too, mostly because it was the middle of the morning and she was supposed to be in school and she wasn't. She was sitting beside her brother in his car. He raised his arm and pointed and then quickly returned his hand to the steering wheel. "That's where we used to go for our polio shots, when we were little. And then they changed it to those little sugar cubes."

"Oh," she said.

"I guess they worked," he said. He looked at her. "I've never had polio, have you?"

She laughed, not exactly certain it was a joke. "No," she said.

He put the turn signal on again and once more pulled out into the road. It was a familiar route, the one that led from the church or the school to home, but it was made strange and new by the fact that it was mid-morning and she should have been in school, by the fact that she was alone with her brother, in his car, and they were driving even more slowly than she could walk. They passed the playing field at the back of the school, beside the cemetery. Without a word, the two of them turned their heads to watch it go by. The grass was balding and the fence behind home plate was bent and torn. There was still something of summer's dust over the whole thing although the leaves on the trees at the far end were yellow and red. They turned again, down another street, this one lined with houses like their own. Lawns and driveways and sidewalks. Jacob named the friends who lived in some of them—Louie, Kevin Malloy, Ted Fish. He told her a story about one Halloween. He turned again. Lori Ballinger's house. Michael took her to the prom. Bobby Kent's house. Bobby cried in sixth grade when people wouldn't stop calling him Clark. He turned again. Now they were off the familiar route to church and school and she began to suspect once again that he was taking her to the dentist.

"Did you ever see this house?" he asked her and once more raised his hand from the steering wheel. She looked. A house like all the others but as they passed she saw that the bushes beneath the front windows were scattered with garden gnomes, maybe a dozen of them. And then that the front steps were full of ceramic animals—dogs, geese, rabbits. And then, as they passed, that the garage door was painted with a huge, colorful portrait of the Blessed Mother, surrounded by stars and rainbows. "Not sure what's going on there," he said.

She said, "It's pretty."

They passed a woman pushing a baby carriage. Lawns with sprinklers going. He reached to turn on the radio. He said, "Don't let me hear you listening to anybody but the Good Guys while I'm gone."

She said, "I won't," and remembered for the first time that last night before she went to bed her mother had said that when she got home from school today Jacob would be gone off to the army. Like their father had done.

He turned again, the signal making a ticking sound, and she recognized the street once more. They were nearly home. "Do me a favor," he said. "Scoot down." She looked at him, unsure. "Scoot down," he said, more urgently. He put his hand on the top of her head, over her beanie, and pushed her a little. The terry-cloth cover slid with her. He did not increase his speed. "Just in case Mom's looking out the window," he said.

All she could see were the tops of the trees and the blue sky, but she knew they were passing their house, the driveway and the lawn, the white shingles and the dark red trim, the sheer white curtains in the front window and the drapes upstairs, in their parents' room.

She knew her brother had turned and was looking at their house over the top of her head. It was like a dream of passing her own house and not turning in. There was a slow song on the radio and the *tick tick tick* of the turn signal seemed to mar it somehow. Jacob looked down at her over the rolled-up sleeve of his arm. Her beanie had come down over her forehead and she had buried her chin in her chest. He glanced back at the street and then reached out to touch her thin elbow. "Okay," he said, softly. "Sit up again." But the terry-cloth cover was slipping under her and it was more of a struggle than she would have imagined. She wiggled and pressed her palms against the seat and raised her legs and pulled at her skirt. Her saddle shoes flashed black and white beneath the dashboard. He watched her, his eyes going back and forth from the windshield. "Jeepers," he said, finally, when she had settled herself, pushed the beanie to the back of her head. "A little spastic there," he said, and although he was smiling, not teasing, she pouted at him anyway, for saying spastic. He reached out again and put his palm on her head.

They drove on, through an intersection and up a hill and then around the front of the high school with its long row of gray doors. Past the football field and the tennis courts, then, turning again, back among houses that over here were all single-story with long front lawns. He gave names to only a few of them. He was mostly listening to the music, only occasionally, softly, singing along. His sleeves were rolled up and his arms looked strong to her, although his hands, fingers and nails, were pale and thin, like her own. He said, "This can be Michael's car when he gets home from school, Thanksgiving and Christmas. But Dad's got to go out and turn the engine over every other day or so. Remind him."

She said okay. They were driving back down the hill. She could see the wiry spire stuck on top of St. Gabriel's round roof. There was the stubble of a beard on her brother's cheek and his hair brushed the collar of his shirt. She was beginning to feel the first pinpricks of doubt, or guilt. The morning was growing long. The sun was now hot through the windshield. She was supposed to be in school. Surely it was not her first memory of her older brother—he had once helped her make a bus for dolls out of a cardboard box and pushed it across the living-room carpet, from bus stop to bus stop—but it was, perhaps, the first memory in which she saw him distinctly, on his own, apart from their house and their family, separate. He took his hands from the steering wheel one at a time and rubbed the palms against his jeans. He glanced at her again. "Got me a ticket for an aeroplane," he said, and grinned, but stopped at a light at the next intersection, he leaned his head back and blew air at the cloth ceiling. He closed his eyes and for a moment she was afraid that he had forgotten about her completely. But then the car behind them beeped to get them going again. "Hold your horses," he said, his eyes on the rearview mirror. There was a brown scapular, a small picture of the Sacred Heart, dangling from it. They were now passing the far side of the church and her school, the cemetery and the gray incinerators.

"I don't want to get yelled at," she told him.

He nodded slowly, as if she had said much more and he was slowly, bit by bit, agreeing with it all. He pulled into the parking lot beside the church and walked her only to the door of her school. He pushed the door open for her and she walked under his arm, from the heavy autumn sun to the cool shadows of the hallway. The entire school was reciting the prayers before lunch—Sister Rose's voice on the PA sounding from every classroom, the children's collective voice following along—Our Father and Hail Mary and Bless us, O Lord, and these Thy gifts, which we are about to receive from Thy bounty . . . She walked along the shining linoleum, down the stairs, and pulled back with a start as she began to turn into the wrong classroom. By the time she found her own, the prayers were over and the children were reaching under their desks for their lunch boxes. When she saw Mrs. Walters's powdered face, smiling at her, she began to cry, all unaccountably until she felt the woman's hand stroking her head and realized that somewhere along the way she had lost her beanie. In the parking lot where they played during recess, she recruited a pair of friends to help her search for it, but with no luck, although one of them spotted Jacob, coming through one of the doors of the church and called to Clare. She looked up just in time to see him leave.

LATER THAT AFTERNOON, on the plane, his first flight, he leaned his head against the window and tried to distinguish the streets and highways and parks below, looking for the thrill of spotting something familiar. He looked for the church and the school, certain they would be his surest landmarks: the roof of St. Gabriel's, from up here, would indeed look like a flying saucer. The school and the gym made identifiable, from up here, by the way they jogged around Mr. Krause's store. But the plane was banking already and wisps of cloud touched the rising wing. He could not get his bearings. Down below, there were green yards and long gray roads and more baseball diamonds than he would have imagined. There were the blue ovals of backyard pools. There was the Unisphere and then the stadium and then the spires of the city, a glimpse of limitless ocean before the plane banked again and the clouds took over. He sat back. He was aware of an obligation to say something to the woman beside him—she was a smallish woman, older than the girls he knew, younger than his mother, she was already reading a paperback—but he was uncertain of the protocol. Where you headed, maybe. Or, Good book? Fly much? He was leaving home for the first time and already he saw how ill equipped he was, how unready. He could not make conversation with strangers, and yet conversations with strangers were perhaps the first thing required of him in his new life. He touched his seat belt. Put his hands in his lap. He closed his eyes and thought to pray but all petition was undermined by Jesus' superior prayer, on the night before his death: Your will, not mine. Jacob wanted only to say, Take care of me. Give me a break. The change of light in the cabin made him open his eyes again. The plane had cleared the clouds—they now ran like a great white field just below the wing, they were touched with gold—and the sky was a solid blue. "Incredible," Jacob said, and the woman beside him put down her book and leaned forward, their shoulders brushing, her hair smelling fresh, like green leaves. He had a memory of the scent of green willow leaves on yellow, pliant stems, small starbursts of blood on his palms. "Isn't it pretty?" she said.

IN JUNE, Susan Persichetti found a job at the Woolworth's in the mall—the cosmetics counter, which was fun and gave her a chance every once in a while to slip a lipstick or a bottle of nail polish into her purse. She had to wear a smock, a pale blue polyester thing, all the employees did, and by early August she was bringing it home and putting it on over her clothes in her bedroom before she went downstairs and out past her parents to work.

Her room was in the attic, the long, dormered space that had been left unfinished by the builder (although he did provide the center-hall staircase that led to it), and paneled and plumbed rather inexpertly by her father and Tony while he was still in high school. She'd borrowed the room while Tony was in the army and now that he had left home—for good, it seemed—the space was hers alone, but it still retained the dark scent and insurmountable dreariness of a boy's room: oak paneling and brown shag carpet and a wooden toilet seat in the bathroom. She didn't mind. She had even kept a couple of her brother's old posters on the far wall.

Putting her smock on over her clothes, she skipped down the stairs, her car keys in her hand, and cried, "Going," to her parents, who would always look up from the couch or the table or the television and then—if they were in the same room—look at each other to confirm how they both understood that this summer's quick glimpses of their teenage daughter breezing in and out the door were mere prelude to her leaving them for college in another year. And then for the rest of her life. But the look they exchanged acknowledged, too, how pleasant it was to know that for her, stepping off into her life, there would not be the quicksand that had met Tony: the army, the war, the year away in which the child they had known was lost, utterly drawn down, sucked under by the troubled, angry, silent young man he had become.

"Drive safely!" they cried back. Or, "Be careful!"—cheerfully, because girl children went off but they also returned, bringing grandchildren and their own solicitousness to their parents' old age.

Sometimes her father would begin to sing, teasing her, "I found a million dollar baby in a five and ten cent store."

It was amazing, she learned, what you could find out. There was no sense looking under A in the phone book, for instance, you should look under W instead: Women's Health. Women's Medicine. (Woman itself sounding in their mouths like a newly coined word—not ladies, not girls anymore, but women.) Information filtered down from a college-age friend of a co-worker at Woolworth's that one of the clinics in the city was in the same building that held a famous hair salon everyone at school was talking about going to. She called the clinic from a pay phone. She needed proof of age and three hundred dollars and if she hadn't had a pregnancy test yet, they would do one there. Also someone to accompany her home.

She wasn't eighteen but she could use Annie Keane's phony birth certificate and driver's license, the one she used to get into bars. Although Annie had hazel eyes and hers were brown, they were both five foot five or so and slim. Annie said she'd come with her, too, so no need to call the boy—"The Jackass" was how Susan now referred to him—who had stopped calling her himself early in July. There was only the matter of the money.

She had saved seventy dollars so far this summer. Annie loaned her fifty from her own savings and then two more ten-dollar bills, filched (on two separate occasions) from her mother's lingerie drawer. Susan added thirty-five of the fifty dollars her father had given her to shop for fall clothes—indulgently, because her mother wanted her to use her own money—saved by buying a single sweater and then going into the dressing room to put a blouse and a kilt skirt into the same bag. The trick—amazing what you could find out—was to go to the better departments of the nicer stores where there was usually only one saleslady working the floor (a plump grandmotherly type in this case, whose daughter had gone to Mary Immaculate Academy as well), and no one counting hangers as you moved in and out of the dressing room, looking for another size.

She added the next thirty of the thirty-seven dollars from her second-to-last paycheck.

In her blue polyester smock, her arms pressed against her stomach, she drank a Coke and smoked a cigarette with Jill O'Meara who had come into Woolworth's just as Susan was going on her break. They sat together on the concrete rim of a planter in the middle of the mall. It was humid, but there was that orange color at the edge of the blue sky—the beginning of a late-summer sunset. Because they had not seen each other since June—they were not particular friends—conversation demanded an accounting. Jill had had a perfectly boring summer, working at a card shop in a strip mall near her home, the backyard pool, Jones Beach, two weeks camping with her family—where, she added, a spontaneous lie, she met this guy. They went pretty far, she said, improvising, swimming together late at night, in the lake, out of their suits. He was dark-haired and blue-eyed and funny—but from Syracuse, she said, the first place she could think of that sounded like the dark side of the moon.

Susan looked at her, smiling. "How far?" she said. They were not friends, but might be becoming. Jill admired Susan. She liked her wit, her self-possession, her feline languor in the classroom, the way she slumped and curled into chairs. The way she let her eyes close slowly, never bothering to put her head down, when a teacher grew boring.

Like most compulsive liars, Jill O'Meara was skeptical of the reports others gave of themselves—the incredible dates, the wild parties, the insane mothers and alcoholic fathers—but she had always trusted what Susan had to say. Susan's brother had gone to Vietnam and had come back a basket case. (This offered in a history class discussion about the war.) She had spent a year convinced her parents were really brother and sister, they were so identically boring. (This during a retreat day at school when the girls had been broken into small groups to discuss ways to bring Christ into their daily lives.) She had written her initials in love bites around the navel of the boy she was taking to the junior prom. (This declared amid much laughter at a table in the lunchroom.)

Jill sipped her drink, nodding slowly. "God," she said, as if at the recollection of some astonishing memory. "We went far. Really far."

A laugh, sophisticated, wordly-wise, broke from Susan and she said, "Start saving your pennies now," and opened her smock and put her hand on her stomach, although what she thought of as her paunch was mostly invisible to Jill, and to everyone else.

"This ain't pizza," she said.

At the end of a boring summer (no boy at the lake or anywhere else, only a hopeless crush on the UPS guy who stopped by the card shop every day and called her Kid), the revelation, the sudden tears in Susan's voice, were high drama.

Jill O'Meara had nearly two hundred and fifty dollars in her senior prom fund. (It had been her junior prom fund last year but she hadn't found a date.) She told Susan—the summer suddenly become interesting—"I can lend you the rest. You want me to go with you?"

Susan spent the night before at Annie's house so in the morning they could walk to the bus stop. They both told their mothers they were accompanying the other to the famous hair salon in the city to give her moral support while she got a new cut. (The story would be that in the end Susan/Annie had chickened out on getting something totally new and just got a few inches cut off, you could hardly notice the difference.) They took the Long Island Rail Road to Penn Station and then rode the hot subway uptown. Of course, they didn't run into any neighbors or relatives who worked in the city, or anyone else who knew them, but that was no matter—the haircut story was already in place; they were, until they got off at the eleventh floor and not the third, precisely where they were supposed to be.

Susan filled out the forms with Annie's name and placed Annie's fake license and birth certificate under the clip on the clipboard before handing it back to the woman at the reception desk. The woman, handsome and serene, with a small face and an old-fashioned French twist, merely slipped them out from under the clipboard and handed them back to her—no question of hazel or brown. "That's fine," she said, sweetly. "And how will you be paying?"

The day before, Susan had gone to a bank near the mall and exchanged her collection of money for six crisp fifty-dollar bills, sensing somehow that the neatness of her payment would confirm the authenticity of her age. She handed these to the woman, still in their yellow bank-provided envelope. The woman merely attached the money to the same clipboard and then said again, "That's fine."

"We'll call you in a minute," she said.

It was ten thirty on a Tuesday in late August and there was no one else in the waiting room, which was very small and comfortable—a pale lavender sofa and two plaid chairs, shaded lamps that might have been in someone's living room. Annie had brought the last of her summer reading books—*A Farewell to Arms*—which she was only halfway through and Susan herself had not yet finished. "Boring," Susan said, glancing at it. "A lot of war stuff."

Although they would have said they were prepared for it, they both were startled when a woman—a nurse in a white uniform—came through the door beside the receptionist and said, "Anne Keane." After only a moment's hesitation, Susan stood.

"Good luck, Annie," Annie whispered and Susan laughed a little. "Thanks, Susie." Like the spunky, place-trading twins from a sitcom.

The nurse—square-jawed and deeply tanned but with warm brown eyes—advised Susan to leave her purse with her friend, and in that moment of turning back to hand over the strap of her bag, Annie saw that Susan was trembling, trembling slightly, almost imperceptibly, but also thoroughly, from her fingertips to her shoulders to the smooth flesh of her pretty face, lips, scalp, even the ends of her pale hair.

In that moment she saw, too, how Susan had fixed her eyes—brown not hazel—on some distant point, some point out of the room, out of this particular ten thirty on a Tuesday morning in late August, out of this strange office building in Manhattan, and onto a place after which this would be done, gotten through, gotten over.

Annie took her friend's bag but did not aim, again, to smile at her or to offer any encouragement. Later, wading through the war stuff, she wondered if what Susan had shown her in that moment—trembling, looking ahead—could be called courage. And wondered why it was assumed that courage was always put to some noble end.

Inside, Susan gave a urine sample and then undressed and was examined, and when the pregnancy was confirmed, the procedure was explained to her. The strange words: cervix and uterus, dilation and curettage, felt like a steel blade against the edge of her teeth. In religion class, Sister Lucy had said, more simply, that they break the baby's arms and legs and drown it in salt water.

Pain like a pretty bad period, the doctor said, some heavy bleeding afterward.

There was another paper to sign and she was halfway through her own first name when she remembered and went over the S and the U.

"My hand is shaking," she said, apologetically, and the tanned nurse whispered, "No worry," and gently took the botched form away.

The woman who did the exam and all the explaining was small and wiry with wiry red hair and a humorless face. She had been introduced as the doctor but still Susan expected a man to come in for the abortion itself. Someone stooped and gray in a white coat and a tie who would call her "young lady" and look at her over the top of his glasses both to reprimand and to forgive. Who might say something old-fashioned and complimentary, something like, "Well, I can see why your young man might have been carried away. You're a lovely girl."

But only another nurse came in, a pretty Asian woman who might have been alone with the doctor in the small and crowded room for all the notice she paid. The doctor said, "Are we ready then?"

The tanned nurse stood right beside her. She complimented the sun streaks in Susan's hair and then held her hand when she drew a sharp, unsteady breath at the cold touch of the instruments. She told her, "Go ahead and say 'Ouch' if it hurts," but Susan only turned her head, her eyes now fixed on the woman's white uniform, which was the same woven polyester of her Woolworth's smock. She could smell the sweet clean odor of the detergent it had been washed in. "Not much longer now," the nurse said. And, "You're doing great." She was supposed to be in what they'd called, so prettily, a twilight sleep, but the pain was on a steady rise and in the midst of it, Susan gripped the woman's hand and raised it to her own mouth to stifle a sob. There was the smell of hospital soap on the nurse's skin, sharp, medicinal, and, because of the pain, somehow cruel. It was a scent that would return her to this moment for the rest of her life.

They brought her to another room to recuperate. She had not worn a sanitary napkin and a belt since she was thirteen and the thing felt like a diaper between her legs. There was a kind of chaise longue for her to sit on, a small table beside it with grape juice and a few cookies: a kindergarten snack, a clean sheet, and a light blanket. The tanned nurse lowered the light a little further and said she would go tell her friend she was okay. She could go home in an hour or so, depending on how she felt.

"Rest a bit, honey," she said, like a mother, before she left the room.

Susan could hear the traffic rising up from the street, the bang and rattle of trucks, taxi horns, a warning shout and a whistle and then a man's laugh. She could picture the men in the street below, men pushing carts and backing vans into narrow parking spaces, men in suits, men with briefcases, going to lunch, ducking into cabs, running their hands down their ties as they walked across a subway grate. She closed her eyes but knew she wouldn't sleep. She had never gone to sleep in New York City.

An Act of Contrition started up in her head. "Oh my God, I am heartily sorry for having offended Thee," more a habit of mind than a plea for absolution. Because she could not balance any remorse against the dawning sense of relief. However terrible it might be, what she had done, it was over: gotten through, finished. However terrible it was, its immediate effect was that she could go back to school next week, her senior year. She could take the SATs, go to the prom, go to graduation. She could apply to colleges and choose one and move into a dorm in September. She could go out with her friends this weekend, maybe meet another guy. She could sleep late tomorrow (she had already asked for a late shift at the store, three to nine) and go downstairs in her work clothes and her smock—"Going"—her car keys in her hand, her father singing from another room, "It was a lucky April shower, it was the most convenient door," sweet and affectionate and naïve as he always was because he had no fear of trouble for this beautiful child, no quicksand, no terrible diversions, no nightmares to drive her from the room he and his son had plumbed and paneled with their own hands. "I found a million dollar baby in a five and ten cent store."

The tanned nurse came in again to take her temperature and check her pad. She came back a little while later to say the doctor would be in to talk to her once more and then she could get dressed and go. "Although," she said, blithely, "I'm not sure where your friend has gone off to."

Susan almost said, "Annie?"—but instead pursed her lips to show she had no answer.

The nurse glanced at her watch. "I thought maybe she'd gone out for a bit of lunch, but she's been gone a while now." She gave Susan the full, professional warmth of her brown eyes. "Pam at the desk said she just kind of flew out."

Susan nodded. She and Annie had agreed to have lunch together, if she was up for it, at a diner on Third Avenue. Vanilla egg creams and greasy cheeseburgers, they'd said.

"We can't let you go home alone, you know," the nurse told her kindly, deliberately. "Is there someone else you can call? If she doesn't come back?"

Jill O'Meara came to mind, but Susan suspected she was probably at work now. Susan didn't even know the name of the card store. Jill would be two hours coming in from Long Island anyway. The Jackass had a car—a GTO, the whole problem—and lived in Queens, and it would serve him right to get the full weight of the whole summer delivered to him in one phone call (You screwed me, you dumped me, I just had an abortion, and you need to drive me home), but she wasn't that crazy. She knew he caddied on Tuesday and Thursday anyway; she'd made enough plans this summer to casually drop by the golf course.

Slowly, she shook her head. "She'll be back," she told the nurse. "She said she might run over to Bloomingdale's." And then, when the nurse had gone out again, wondered how messed up she was to find herself praying, praying earnestly this time, that her half-assed lie was true.

The doctor, without a smile, gave her a lecture about venereal disease and a prescription for birth control and told her about the new risks a second abortion would raise. Then she handed her a small white business card, the name and number of a social worker.

Frowning at her from behind the wire-rimmed glasses, the doctor suddenly asked, in quick succession, "You live with your family? Mother and father? Are you afraid of your father? Is he violent? Does he hit you?"

After everything, Susan was surprised to feel herself blush. There was a time when she might have been afraid that her father would hit her. When she and her brother were kids, he had often shown them the back of his hand, and though they'd never once been struck, they had always flinched. But that was long before Tony went to Vietnam, and came back, and disappeared. Long before the night she saw him weeping in their father's thick arms, not like a baby or even a kid, but like a lunatic, one of her father's own patients, God's mistakes, as he called them, saliva veiling his open mouth. Or the day he put his fist through the living-room wall. Or

the day their mother told Susan that it would have been easier for
their father if Tony had been killed in the war.

"My father's never hit me," she told the doctor. "Not at all." After everything, it was the first time she saw them suspect a lie.

The nurse had just handed her the first month's supply of pills
in a little case that looked like a pink compact when she said, cheerfully, "Your girlfriend's outside."

Annie was on the same couch where Susan had left her, but it
was clear, even in the warm light of the waiting room, that she'd
been crying.

There were two other, middle-aged, women also in the room so
Annie whispered when she said, "You okay?" and Susan whispered
back, "Yeah, are you?"

"Fine," Annie said shortly, and then handed Susan her purse.

They walked down the hall to the elevator in silence. Although
they lived on the same street, although Susan's father had helped to
deliver Clare, they had been best friends only since the first week of
freshman year. At mixers with the all-male Catholic schools, they
had discovered they were the perfect boy-meeting pair: You ask the
blonde, I'll ask the brunette. They had gone on their first dates together. They had lost their virginity within a week of each other—
Annie on the night of the junior prom, Susan a week later in
gratitude for the prom and in regret for not having done it, perhaps
more memorably, then. They had gone through this ordeal all summer knowing that their places were interchangeable—that Annie
could be Susan and Susan could be Annie. Knowing, too, all they
knew about breaking the baby's arms and legs and drowning it in
salt water.

"Did you have lunch?" Susan asked her in the elevator and
Annie said, "No. Aren't we going to the diner?"

At the third floor, they got the full whiff of the famous hair salon and then watched a tall, beautiful woman get on, her frosted hair blow-dried to elaborate perfection. Stepping back to make way for her, the two girls exchanged a look behind her back, a grimace and a grin.

If Annie hated her for what she had just done, Susan thought, then she would be alone in the world, as lost as her crazy brother screaming in his dreams.

In the diner, they found a booth near the window. The cheeseburgers were perfect, flat and juicy and turning the soft rolls beneath them a reddish pink. The sweet egg creams, in frosted fountain glasses, might have been a balm for any number of things. They both put their straws in and then drew them out again and licked the white, vanilla-scented foam.

"So, where'd you go?" Susan asked, hoping to deflect Annie from saying, How was it? This morning she would have trusted her not to ask "How was it?" but now, suddenly, everything seemed tentative between them. It was possible Annie hated her for what she had just done.

Annie slipped the straw back into her drink, churned it a bit. Reluctant to speak until finally, she simply said, "I lost it." For Susan, the thick pad and the cramps and the terrible word—curettage—that set her teeth on edge, all gave way to the sudden descent her heart took. If their places were exchanged, Annie would not have done what she'd done. And there was no undoing it.

Tears came into Annie's eyes—green eyes now against their red rims. Susan saw her swallow hard before she leaned across the Formica tabletop and asked, whispering, "Do you know she dies?"

Susan felt herself draw away from the question, even as Annie seemed to lean into it. "Catherine," Annie said. "In the book. Did you know she dies at the end, and the baby's dead and he walks out into the rain by himself?"

Annie's voice seemed to twist away from her and she tried to laugh through it, suspecting she would lose it again were it not for the good cry she had had an hour ago, in a deserted ladies' room some floors below the clinic—a place she had sought blindly, flying (as the receptionist had said) from the waiting room (another pair of women had entered by then, a greenish-looking girl in her twenties and an older woman who might have been her mother) and into a nearby stairwell where the first sob had broken from her throat and echoed so loudly that she'd run heavily down the stairs just to cover the sound with her own footsteps. Out onto another floor where there was, luckily, an empty ladies' room. She had locked herself in a stall and sobbed for the unbearable sadness of the story: Catherine dead and the baby dead and nothing at all left for him—like saying goodbye to a statue, he had said—but to walk out into the desolate rain all alone.

She had cried for what must have been twenty minutes and then went out to the sink and splashed cold water on her face—knowing she should get back upstairs for Susan—and then began to cry again.

Because it was intolerable: Catherine dead and their baby dead. Intolerable and terrible and made even more so by the fact that within the same hour of her reading, the book had convinced her (there in the softly lit waiting room of the abortion clinic) that despite war and death and pain (despite the way the girl with a woman who might have been her mother seemed to gulp air every once in a while, a handkerchief to her mouth), life was lovely, rich with small gifts: a nice hotel, a warm fire, a fine meal, love.

She had studied her own young face, blotched with weeping, in the bathroom mirror. Terrible things were ahead of her: Jacob would go to Vietnam. Her father's surgery had made him an old man. And how would she bear the empty world without her mother in it? There was college to look forward to, boyfriends, marriage, maybe children of her own, but terrible things, too, were attached to any future. What you needed, she thought, was Susan's ability, her courage, to fix your eyes on the point at which the worst things would be over, gotten through. But what an effort it took.

Susan's baby, she thought, might be better off, after all, never to have been born.

And then she had cried twenty minutes more.

"I'm over it now, sort of," she told Susan, laughing at herself. "But I really lost it."

Susan said faintly, "I guess I'll have to read it." In all her calculations about what to do, about running away, telling her parents, leaving school, driving to the golf course and throwing herself into his arms, she had not considered dying in childbirth. The baby dead, too. She wasn't even sure if such things happened anymore. Although she knew the words "even death" had appeared somewhere this morning, on something she'd signed.

Annie pulled some paper napkins from the steel dispenser and held them under her eyes. "Don't," she said, laughing. "Spare yourself. You can copy my summary when it's due." Then she straightened her spine, threw back her head. She balled the napkins in her hand. "What is wrong with these people? These nuns?" It was an old refrain, but it comforted, somehow, returned them to the time before today. "What is wrong with our school?" It was their friendship's eternal question. "Why do they pick these depressing books?"

Susan smiled, knowing the tune. "That bridge thing," she offered.

"God, yes," Annie cried. "*San Luis Rey*. What was the point of that?" She held out her hands. *"Ethan Frome."*

"Oh, God." Susan had a napkin to her eye as well. "When they crashed their sled into the tree."

"Nice," Annie said.

"Uplifting," Susan added. It was their old routine. Oh, Mr. Gallagher.

"And the end of *Great Gatsby*," Annie said. "The blood in the pool from where he's shot in the head."

"And then that other guy," Susan said, warming to it, "in the poem, who goes home and shoots himself."

"Miniver Cheevy," Annie said. "And *Anna Karenina*."

Susan shook her head. "Couldn't read it."

Annie leaned across her plate, emphasizing the words. "She throws herself under a train."

Susan laughed once, like a cough.

"*Madame Bovary*!" Annie said.

"Dead, too?"

She nodded. "After about a million affairs."

Susan shook her head. "Well, of course," she said. "Sex and death. That's the message."

Annie threw the balled-up napkins onto the table. "Christ," she said, "what is wrong with them? Why do these crazy women want us to read such depressing things?"

"They want us to suffer," Susan said, sarcastic so that Annie wouldn't see how much she wanted to cry. "They want us to be afraid."

"They want us to be nuns," Annie added, so she wouldn't have to say, Oh, Susan, oh, my poor friend.

IN COLLEGE, Michael Keane was given to saying that if they were not exactly the middle children born at mid-century to middle-class parents and sent from middling, mid-island high schools to mediocre colleges all across the state, they were close enough. They were out to be teachers, most of them—industrial or liberal arts the predominant goals since any interest in science or math portended better things: accounting, engineering, med school in Mexico.

Damien's, where they drank, was not, as Michael Keane liked to say, in the most felicitous part of town: it was an ugly, desolate old house tucked among ugly, snowplow-ravaged streets that were themselves lined with more narrow, sagging houses, bent fences, scrawny trees. There was a sorry-looking baseball field across the street and the edge of a cemetery off the abandoned lot behind. The black skeleton of an old power plant rose up in the far distance, over the field, and you couldn't get to the place without feeling three, four, maybe five times the rutted thump and bump of abandoned railroad tracks under your wheels. But by their junior years most of them had had enough of the storefront bars on Main Street, the bars along the river and at the lake, the roadhouses and beer barns out past the fraternities. In the paucity of streetlight and house light that surrounded Damien's, the place could easily be

missed—there was only a bit of red neon in the window—and the
joke was that you couldn't find it unless you knew where it was.
Knowing where it was brought all of them that much closer to what
they thought of as the real life of the city. As did knowing Ralph.

He was in his early forties. Lean, a little stooped, a little
paunchy. He lived on the second floor of the old house, above the
bar. The house itself had once been a funeral parlor. Then a
speakeasy. Then, and currently, a dive. Stories that were told about
Ralph Damien said that he had dropped out of three colleges before
joining the army. And turned down an offer to attend Oxford after
beating the "head guy" at chess in a London pub. And accepted another to service a society matron in Saratoga Springs when he was
nineteen. He wore his dark hair long at a time when most middle-
aged men still didn't, and had a drooping mustache at a time when
every college student who could did too. He was languid and sarcastic and worldly-wise, a source for pot and hash as well as for beer
and schnapps and tequila—for cheap stereo equipment, sometimes;
sometimes for a stash of watches, commemorative gold coins,
leather jackets; once for sealed boxes of Chanel No. 5 to take home
to your mother.

Like Michael, most of them who hung out at Damien's were
juniors and seniors. Most of them had done at least one semester of
student teaching in some smelly local school—in their dress pants
and button-downs and ratty, poorly knotted ties. Most of them had
a pretty clear idea of what the next few years were going to be like.

But stop into Damien's at four o'clock in the afternoon with a
cold rain falling, and there would be Ralph, a joint burning in an
ashtray on the bar, the newspaper spread before him. He'd open the
refrigerator in the back room to show off a dozen choice sirloins
wrapped in white butcher paper—payback for a favor he'd done
someone. He'd berate, leisurely and with a cool amusement, some
perspiring liquor salesman in a cheap suit and a hunting jacket who

was trying to sell him piss for beer. He'd hunker down at a side table with a pair of locals, his thumb to his jaw, his fingers splayed across his cheek and then rise, laughing, slapping backs. He'd be in Aruba over Christmas, he'd tell the college kids, great little hotel, great little woman waiting for him there, the color of caramel. At ten or eleven on a weekend night, he'd ask, "Anyone want to pump beer for a while?" And then step out from behind the bar to slip his arm around the waist of the woman or the girl who had been waiting on a corner bar stool. He'd bend down first for an openmouthed kiss and then, with his thumb slipped behind her belt, walk her to the stairs.

It never occurred to Michael Keane, to any of them, it seemed, to wonder what women saw in Ralph Damien, this middle-aged townie with his low-slung jeans and paunch and long hair (and— after the Christmas in Aruba—a diamond earring at a time when no middle-aged men, no men they knew of, wore one). The hours Michael had already spent in those green-walled classrooms had given him his own pretty clear idea of what the next few years would be like, but he wasn't quite ready to believe that he'd be there, polyester dress slacks, frayed button-down, knotted tie, at thirty-five or forty. Better to imagine vaguely a life like Ralph's, to imitate his weary smile, his cool squint, his way of palming the cash register or the beer pull. His nonchalance when he returned from upstairs with the girl in tow and either threw on the lights for last call or bought shots all around, or just took up one of his own bar stools for the rest of the night, the girl's hips in his hands, her rump pressed firmly between his skinny legs.

On a night of cold rain turning to sleet late in October, Ralph put an elbow on the bar and slipped his hand under the long blond hair of a girl Michael knew—Caroline. He leaned toward her and she, stepping up on the bar rail, all graceful and delicate in muddy construction boots and blue jeans and an army surplus parka, leaned toward him. They kissed, just briefly, before she stepped back and raised her plastic cup of beer. Ralph lifted his cigarette from the edge of the bar and said, through the smoke, "You guys want to pour for a while tonight?"

He never paid anyone for working but he was generous with free drinks for those who did. Michael turned to the guy beside him to see if he was game. The kid looked blanched. Michael didn't know him very well. A transfer from Nassau Community, he was observing at the same middle school where Michael was teaching social studies that semester. Michael had introduced him to Damien's at the beginning of the year and now the kid followed him to the place after school as a matter of course. He was a surfer and didn't much like the upstate weather, but, Michael thought, a nice enough guy, a little doe-eyed and baby-faced—you'd put him closer to fifteen than twenty—and a heavy but inept drinker, which was the first thing he thought of when he saw the kid's bleached lips. But then he saw the way he looked down the bar at Caroline.

Michael had passed around a bag of miniature Hershey bars in his class that afternoon, in honor of Halloween, but a lot of the kids had refused to take one—because of their acne or their efforts to be cooler than the student teacher, he couldn't tell—so he'd brought the extras into Damien's. He took one now and slid it down the bar to Caroline, who turned as it bumped her elbow. She had one of those wide, clean faces that seem ordinary only on first glance, and beautiful hair. The girls he lived with filled their off-campus firetrap with the smell of hot rollers and singed scalp, but Caroline still wore her hair perfectly straight and nearly waist long. She picked up the candy bar and once again stepped up on the bar rail, leaning to see who had sent it.

"Trick or treat," Michael told her. There were probably half a dozen backs and elbows and reaching arms in the short space between them, so he leaned forward and said, "Come here for a minute."

He saw her glance at Ralph before she stepped down again and made her way through the crowd. He could see her smiling as she squeezed through, knowing everyone, having a fine night at Damien's. She pushed through the crowd, flushed and grinning. She put her hand on his shoulder and he put his to the back of her head, just to feel the heavy silk. It was, he understood, why he'd called her over in the first place.

"You know my buddy here?" Michael asked her because he had momentarily forgotten the kid's name.

But she shifted her hips a little and dropped her eyes for just a second before she said, "Hi, Terry."

And Terry looked casually away from her, sipping his beer all nonchalant to say, "How's it going?"

The crowd pushed her closer and Michael took the opportunity to slip his arm beneath her parka and around her slim waist. "How do you know this lowlife?" he said.

Terry was still looking straight ahead, his right leg jiggling.

"High school," Caroline said. "We went to Valley Stream Central together." She smiled at his averted face. There was something regal about her although she was not tall. She shook her hair, brushed some stray electrostatic strands of it off her cheek. The gray fake fur that edged her hood could have been ermine. "We ran into each other his first week here," she said primly. "When he was thinking about going back home, he was so lonely." She pouted a little, imitating his loneliness. "I tried to make him feel better," intimating with her smile a certain benevolence bestowed, back when he was so lonely.

Terry glanced at her from over his shoulder, his color restored. "Fuck you," he said.

"Nice mouth," Michael told him even as Caroline sighed and slowly shook her head. "He does it even quicker than he says it," she said. A few people around them laughed. Charlie Hegi, who was reaching for the bag of Hershey bars, said, "Zing."

Now Ralph was in front of them, a bottle of tequila in one hand and four shot glasses in the other. "Play nice, children," he said. Terry swung off the bar stool and immediately someone else took his place. A big guy, made bigger by his long doughboy coat. Bad skin and short arms and a ponytail that smelled unwashed. Bean was what they called him. He seemed to expand to fit whatever space was left for him, bellying up. "Hey, Ralph," he said, with that false belligerence guys like Bean substituted for wit. "Where the fuck are your decorations? It's Halloween, man."

Ralph shook his head. "Don't need them," he said. He lifted Bean's cup out of his hand, refilled it. Handing it back, he added, "They don't make decorations as ugly as some of you assholes." And then, leaning forward, "You know what this place used to be, man?" He bared his teeth, a kind of smile. "This place used to be a fucking funeral parlor, man."

Bean took this in for a second, narrowing his small eyes, and then said, "Bullshit."

"The trapdoor in the garage is casket-size," Ralph went on. "Go look." He gestured toward the center of the room, toward the juke-box and the bulk of the crowd. "From the turn of the century to the forties," he said. "One dead body after the other laid out right here. This place has so many ghosts I can't sleep at night. You want me to put up decorations?"

"Yeah, man," Bean said, none of it sinking in. "It's Halloween." But the chubby girl who had edged in beside him, Debbie, held out her empty plastic cup and said, "You told me this used to be a speakeasy."

Ralph took her cup and filled it, shaking his head like he was the weary professor and she some dumb-ass student who hadn't done the reading. "My grandfather was the undertaker," he said patiently, "but my father was the bootlegger." He handed her the cup, took her dollar. His earring caught some light. "During Prohibition," he said, and then looked at Bean. "You know what Prohibition is?" and Bean said, "Shit, yeah. I'm a fucking history major."

"Yeah, well," Ralph said. He slapped the dollar into the register. "During Prohibition," he said, "my father had something going with some Mafia guys to ship booze from Canada—in coffins. Most of it went downstate but my dad kept enough of it to get a little side business going with a speakeasy—you know what that is, Bean?" And Bean, who had a mouthful of beer, swallowed it before he nodded. "They served the stuff right next to the stiffs," Ralph said. "I kid you not. My grandfather would stuff 'em and truss 'em and then as soon as the last mourner left, my father would bring in his customers and get them stiff, too. His biggest challenge, he said, was keeping the cigarette butts out of the coffins. One time he came down here in the morning, just as the dead guy's family was coming in to close him up for good, and, holy shit, he sees the corpse has a shot glass on his forehead."

Ralph plucked a few empty cups out of hands and refilled them, collected his money. "This is a fucking funeral parlor," he said, his arms outspread. "What do I need Halloween decorations for?"

"It's not anymore," Bean said, but uncertainly.

Ralph shrugged. He'd grown tired of the subject.

And then he looked at Caroline, who turned on her smile the way you flick on a lamp. Michael had driven home with her once, Thanksgiving vacation, a whole carload of them. She lived in a split-level, the shingled part painted pink. There was a saint in a stone grotto between some bushes, a boat on cinder blocks in the driveway, and her mother already waiting for her behind the aluminum-and-glass storm door. Someone had made a joke about Mom radar.

Ralph touched his crotch, shook his head, and then turned to reach into the cooler for two long-neck bottles of beer. He made his way around the bar just as Caroline moved to meet him. He took her under his arm, the two beer bottles resting just over her shoulder, and had his face in her hair before they'd reached the stairs.

Bean murmured, "Oh man," as if he were in some mortal pain. Charlie Hegi had bowed his head and was twisting the Hershey wrappers into little bows.

Michael stepped behind the bar, but for a moment no one was ordering.

Then Terry returned. "I'm leaving," he told Michael, as if he were obliged to. Michael shrugged. He felt sorry for him, in his student-teacher clothes. By the look of his eyes, he'd either been crying somewhere or throwing up.

He put a shot glass on the bar. "Have a drink," he said. "And take off that fucking tie."

"The guy's a creep," Terry said after he swallowed. "He's old enough to be my father."

"He's old enough to be dead," Bean said. And then added, "He probably is," pleased with himself. "Probably sleeps in a coffin."

Terry said again, "He's a creep."

But Charlie Hegi looked up to the ceiling. His teeth were full of chocolate. "He's a lucky son of a bitch at the moment," he said.

The place got busy then and Charlie stepped behind the bar to help out. Michael was pouring drinks and shots and slapping the cash register with the flat of his hand and the more time Ralph took with Caroline upstairs, the more the place became his own. What he was thinking of, he found himself telling a girl with a small face and short hair and dark eyebrows that were alternately appealing and weird, was teaching for a year or two and then heading south, maybe Ft. Lauderdale or Daytona, maybe even Key West, to open a bar on the beach—work his tail off over Christmas and spring break and then kick back the rest of the year, go fishing, travel, maybe write. Not for him, he said, polyester pants and short-sleeve dress shirts and the scorn of thirty inbred seventh graders for the next forty years. Not his old man's Robert Hall suits five days a week, either, and the Long Island Rail Road to the city, the subway to the cubicle. Someone else's shot glass on your forehead when you're dead.

The girl was pretty enough, petite. She said something about wanting to be an artist as well as a kindergarten teacher. When Ralph returned, he slapped Michael on the back and said, I owe you, man. The scent of the pot they'd smoked was on him and Caroline took a bar stool in the corner and drank another beer, her hair still mussed in the back and her lips kind of blurred. Her friends seemed to stay away from her, but Ralph walked to that end of the bar every chance he got and leaned there next to her, watching the crowd, playing with her hair, not saying much.

Michael left with the short-haired girl. She was from Commack. In his room they smoked a joint and listened to Pink Floyd and then he showed her some glow-in-the-dark chalk he'd bought for his class. He wasn't sure what he was going to do with it yet, he told her, he just thought it would get their attention. Later, with all the lights out, she stood naked on his bed and drew all over the wall—pretty good drawings, he thought, some of them fairly obscene. He told her she was going to make one hell of a kindergarten teacher and then pulled her down again and wrapped his legs around her—she couldn't have weighed a hundred pounds.

When he finally took her home late Saturday afternoon, the sky was slung so low over the rusty city and everything looked so beat up and damp it seemed more like the end of winter, the beginning of mud season, than the height of fall. He went out for subs with some of his housemates and ended up at a Halloween party in one of the Main Street bars. Bean was there and at one point stumbled over to ask if Michael had a shovel in his car. He was wearing a girl's hoop earring and a bandanna. A pirate, Michael supposed, digging for treasure. "This is upstate New York," he said. "Everybody has a shovel in his car." Bean asked if he could borrow it and Michael asked if he was snowed in. They both glanced through the crowd to the orange light of the plate-glass window, to the brown and desolate street. "No," Bean said. "I'm not snowed in." "Then you can't have it," Michael told him.

After last call, he went by Damien's. He went in the back way—a set of wooden steps beside the garbage cans. This door was always open. It led to a small screened porch and what had been the original kitchen, which now stank of wood grown moldy with spilled beer. There were still plenty of people inside. Ralph had an arrangement with the police that usually allowed him to serve all night as long as he flashed the lights at one and cleared the place of most of the younger kids, and then locked the front door and turned off his sign. Michael didn't see the short-haired girl, Beverly was her name, but Caroline was there, behind the bar with a couple of girlfriends. Ralph was at a table playing chess. Michael had a beer and watched him for a while. Then he had another and played some pool. At one point, about ten of them did shots of schnapps, simultaneously, up and down the bar, laughing like this was the wackiest college stunt ever. When Michael finally left, Ralph was still at his game and Caroline was curled up in a corner under her own parka. The sky just beyond the ball field was beginning to lighten—nothing spectacular about it, just the darkness turning into a queasy kind of pink. He could see a couple of neighborhood dogs running together across the outfield, noses to the ground. He could hear some poor working stiff trying to get his car started in the cold.

There was no food in the house on Sunday and there was no use bemoaning, yet again, this part of the state's lack of decent delis and diners. Hungover, all any of the downstaters wanted was a chocolate egg cream and a buttered roll. But they drove over to campus anyway and paid three bucks for brunch in one of the dining halls. They watched the residents, mostly freshmen and sophomores, move around the table with their trays—some of them still joined to last night's date, most of them stuck in same-sex groups of friends or roommates who also hadn't scored. A girl walked by wearing torn fairy wings. Another had a tall striped hat. There was a subdued murmur throughout the room, the smell of steam-table scrambled eggs and burning toast and bins of bacon and beef bourguignonne. The staff had hung cardboard skeletons from the window of the dish room; one of them wore an apron and a hairnet. Michael noticed that most of the kids eating had wet hair and damp clothes, just out of the shower, and it made him think how young they looked, half formed. Outside, the campus, too, seemed sodden, the leaves gone from every tree but still lying in black heaps and scattered rags across the grass and along the walkways.

Then a roll of laughter came from the far end of the room. And then, following one another at a run, three guys dressed as the Marx Brothers—Harpo, Groucho, Chico. They climbed over tables, sat in girls' laps, chased one another, the whole routine. Groucho put his arms around one of the fat dish-room ladies and did the eyebrow thing. Harpo had his bicycle horn. Their costumes were excellent—theater majors, no doubt—and all their gestures dead-on. People began standing on their chairs to watch, some of them shouting jokes or bits of encouragement or merely caught up in the growing, crazed enthusiasm that made Michael think of his own students when some glorious distraction disrupted the day and sent them all to the windows—a sudden hailstorm, a screaming fire en-

gine, the milk delivery truck backing itself into a basketball hoop
on the playground.

And then, out of the blue, a boy stood up from one of the tables
and smacked a full plate of steaming eggs right into Groucho's face.
The impact floored the poor kid, sent his cigar flying. There was a
moment's pause in the general noise and Michael found himself listening for a moan of anger or resentment, but what he heard instead
was only the silence of a change in the tide. Suddenly, someone else
dove for Harpo and pulled off his wig. He saw it fly into the air,
bouncing from hand to hand until somebody else slam-dunked it
into the milk dispenser. Chico's hat, too, was being passed around
and when he appeared again among the crowd, he was hog-tied in
his own plaid jacket and someone had squirted ketchup and mustard
down his shirt. On the other side of the room, some girls were
dancing around a dog pile of guys—one of them had Harpo's horn
and was squeezing it in short bursts, like a rising orgasm. Then
Harpo scrambled free. He was naked from the waist down, cursing
wildly. He ran for the door they'd come in through, hunched over,
bare-assed and limping. Chico and Groucho followed, Groucho
turning as he ran, the nose and mustache gone, the eggs still stuck
to his shirt front and hair. He gave the room the finger and was
gone.

It took a few minutes for things to settle down. Someone else
had the bicycle horn and blew it intermittently, another guy held up
Harpo's pants and underwear and danced them around a bit. But
people were returning to their seats, finishing their coffee, picking
up their trays. Michael turned to one of his housemates and said,
"What the hell just happened?"

He shrugged. Chris was a good guy. Stocky, already balding,
laid-back, and funny. His father taught industrial arts in a Bronx
high school and that's what Chris wanted to do, too. Michael knew

he'd be good at it. Everybody's favorite teacher. Chris had made all the furniture in his room—bed, dresser, desk, bookcase, even the box he kept his dope in, intricately carved with vines and flowers, satyrs and nymphs.

He was going to get married right after graduation and they had a running joke around the house about what his girlfriend had decided was going to be their wedding song: "Time in a Bottle."

Chris shrugged, his elbows on the table. "The world is full of assholes," he said, nonplussed. "What are you going to do?" Michael could see him asking his students this very question for the next thirty years.

At Damien's that night, Michael scanned the room for the short-haired girl, not sure whether he was hoping to see her or not. There were a few people in costumes, mostly masks or crazy hats, nothing too ambitious. Some of the girls wore leotards under their parkas and little ears on their heads—black cats or bunny rabbits. The less shapely ones were kids in flannel pajamas or housewives in bathrobes, curlers in their hair. One kid—every year—in a thrift-store trench coat that he would part to reveal a piece of pink rubber hose glued to a square of brown carpet whenever he caught a girl's eye.

Ralph still didn't have any decorations up, but there was a plastic pumpkin filled with candy by the register and every once in a while he lifted it and tossed some candy into the crowd. When Caroline squeezed in beside Michael, she put her elbow on the bar and held out her hand. "Where's mine?" she asked, coyly, but a little defiantly, too.

Ralph looked her up and down, baring his teeth in that strange grin. "Where's your costume?" he said. He held the candy away from her, eyeing the turtleneck and jeans beneath her parka. "You've got to have a costume to get a treat," Ralph said slowly, as if explaining something he thought she already understood. She stared at him a second longer and then abruptly turned away. The ends of her long hair briefly clung to Michael's arm and shoulder as she turned. Then Bean moved in. He was still wearing the earring and the bandanna. He'd be wearing them for the rest of the year.

"Is he going upstairs?" he asked. He had put bits of black and gold paper over his teeth. "To get his nut?"

Michael shrugged. But Bean was watching Ralph behind the bar and didn't seem to notice. Then he leaned closer, elbowing Michael's side as if he were the one with the attention problem. "Is he going upstairs tonight?" he asked from behind his hand. "With her?"

Michael turned away from him—the bandanna was tight, digging into his eyebrows. He had a sudden recollection of Pauline's big face, bearing down on him. "Doesn't look like it," he said, and Bean, still watching Ralph, said a breathless, "Fuck."

And then he took a drag from his bottle of beer and shouted, "Hey, Ralph." The hoop earring swaying with the effort. "What's this about ghosts? I hear you got ghosts. You can't sleep at night cause of the ghosts." He looked around, noted the attention his voice had drawn. "Or is it because you're some kind of frigging vampire?"

Ralph was handing beers over the bar to outstretched hands. When he finished, he walked down to where Bean stood. He touched the corner of his mouth, the drooping ends of his dark mustache. "You know, I never came down here when I was a kid," he said softly. "There was an outside staircase we used. Straight to the second floor. I had it torn off when my folks moved south—it was a fucking death trap, it was so rotten. But when I was a kid, that's how we went in and out. I never came in here. So I never really knew when the funeral parlor changed over to a bar. I mean, to a kid, it's all the same. People are talking, somebody's crying, somebody's laughing. A fight breaks out. Every once in a while there's this creepy silence and then everybody starts talking again. All the same. Still is."

He looked at them all. He seemed to be making an effort to stay interested in his own words. "I had no problem with it. Dead guys, drunks." He shrugged to show his indifference. "All the same."

"No ghosts?" Bean said. "No ghosts keeping you up at night, like you said?"

Ralph let his black eyes rest on Bean for a minute. And then he said, "Only you guys." Michael laughed with the others. Then, as was his way, Ralph leaned forward, squinting through his own smoke. "I listen to you guys, when I'm upstairs," he said. He had his hands on the bar, a cigarette burning in one of them. "You don't sound any different from last year or the year before. Or ten years before. Or even when I was a kid trying to go to sleep upstairs and there was a stiff down here in the middle of it all. And next year it won't sound any different either."

Bean straightened up at that, pulled himself back. "Fuck, I'm out of here next year," he said. He looked around as if for corroboration, then pushed at the bandanna that had begun to slip over his eyelid. "I won't even be here."

But Ralph only grinned, patiently. The long-suffering professor. "That's what I'm telling you," he said, straightening up. "It won't matter."

He turned to toss his cigarette into the sink behind the bar, and Bean, his tongue still poking at his cheek, cried out sarcastically, "That's one hell of a scary story, Ralph," just as Caroline was squeezing herself between them. She had some of her girlfriends behind her and Michael heard them giggling and whispering, "Oh my God," before he took in everything else. She squeezed up to the bar, smiling, her parka with its dirty fake fur closed up around her neck, and her hair, except for a few strands that rose and fell with

static, tucked down inside it. She said one sharp, "Ralph," as if she
needed to get his attention. Michael looked down at her and then
looked back over her shoulder. Her legs were bare from the hem of
her parka to the tops of her construction boots. Michael looked
back just in time to see her open her coat and say, "Lady Godiva."

Beside him, Bean said, "Mother of Mercy." The bright orange
lining of her parka set off her pale body like neon. Through the veil
of her hair there were her small, conical breasts and the shadows of
her nipples, the teardrop-shaped navel carved into her stomach, the
tender fuzz of pubic hair. In the mirror above the bar he could see
all around her a dozen pale, openmouthed faces, like seraphim and
cherubim in parkas and half-assed Halloween costumes, surrounding a Madonna.

Ralph bowed his head and moved his mustache from side to
side, laughing. And then he reached into the plastic pumpkin and
pulled out a Milky Way. He handed it to her. As she slipped the
candy bar into her pocket, Ralph put his hand beneath her ear, lifting her hair as she stepped up on the bar rail to move toward him.
Bean was now doing a backbend to see her lovely bare legs rising
out of the muddy construction boots, her white, dimpled behind
under the hem of the khaki parka, and if the low-grade moan that
filled the air wasn't from him, it was from half a dozen guys in the
immediate vicinity, like a muffled howl.

When they broke apart, Ralph casually pulled two beers from
the cooler. "You mind?" he asked Michael, as if he were just running out to use the john. Michael said, "I don't mind." Caroline,
meantime, had bowed her head and let her hair fall over her face.
Ralph went around the bar, bottles in hand, and Caroline, now
holding her coat tightly closed, turned to meet him.

Because Bean was there Michael asked him if he wanted to help
out, but he downed his beer and said he was already helping, he was
on the decorating committee and did his own Groucho thing with

his eyebrows under the bandanna, and then moved back into the crowd.

Chris volunteered instead. He was wearing a sombrero and serape he'd brought home from last year's spring break and he was repeating halfhearted lines from Cheech and Chong that cracked up a group of girls reaching for their beers. Michael had known Chris since freshman year and it had seemed to him since then that the bulk of his emotional effort had always gone into staying faithful to his girlfriend back in Yonkers. He wasn't always good at it—there were too many opportunities in the dorms—and his every misstep was followed by hours of banging his head against the cinder-block walls. He hated himself, he loved his girlfriend. He wanted to be faithful. He wanted to get laid. He was breaking up with her. He was marrying her. Now that he was, finally, officially, engaged, he had adopted this jokey, old-fart way of dealing with the women at school. A class-clown kind of thing that struck Michael as terribly sad, the way he shook his shoulders and wiggled his broad backside under the serape, the way they laughed at him and then let their eyes skip over to somebody else.

When Michael looked toward the door, he saw Beverly come in with her own crowd. She was wearing one of those plastic headbands with bobbing alien eyes. Then he heard the door in the back room slam open and a few seconds later Bean was backing a coffin into the bar. He was shouting "Move!" in his dumb-jock way and people were laughing. A couple of other guys were pallbearers and Terry held the far end, bumping it into the doorjamb, the jukebox, the edge of the pool table. Some people ran ahead to grab some chairs and place them in the middle of the room. It was a gray metallic coffin and at first Michael thought it was something they had made in shop. He even turned to Chris to say, "What's this, an IA project?" But Chris shook his head. "None of those guys is industrial arts," he said.

Michael turned back as they were struggling to get the chairs under the thing. It wasn't a gray coffin but black. It was the dirt that made it seem paler.

"They dug that fucking thing up," Chris said into his ear.

It was wild. Bean, the impresario in his earring and bandanna and long coat, made a big deal of opening the lid, then shutting it, then spinning around to ask, "You want to see? Who wants to see?"

Terry was leaning against one of the tables, hugging himself and laughing. He might have been shivering.

Finally, Bean snapped back the upper half of the lid—flashing white satin—girls screamed as the thing rocked on the chairs, threatening to topple, empty. Now a kind of relieved hysteria took over the room and people began coming to the bar, shaking their heads. Crazy ass, they were saying. Bean was saying he'd found the thing in the basement. He was telling everybody it was where Ralph "really sleeps."

Terry was white-faced, swaying a little, definitely trembling. With a sudden lurch, he headed toward the bathroom. Michael saw him touch the corner of the coffin as he passed by.

Other people were touching it too, rubbing the dirt, playing with the lid. It had lent its own odor even to the smoky room, something earthy and sharply unnatural at the same time. Beverly came to the bar for a beer and as he handed it to her she said, "Do you think this is funny?" She was smiling a little, as if ready to agree whether Michael said yes or no. He said no, he didn't think it was funny.

She sipped her beer, looked at the thing over her shoulder. He still wasn't sure he liked her eyebrows, or the super-short hair, but he liked her eyes and her throat and the shape of her head. He liked the lightness of her, on top of him. The stretch of her spine in the dark.

"You want to go?" he said. And she said, "Yeah."

He told Chris he was leaving and Chris looked at Beverly, the sombrero pushed back on his head, and said, "Vaya con Dios."

After the rowdy wedding in Yonkers that June, there would be his annual backyard barbecues—famous for the Gennie Cream Ale he served long after any of them still wanted to drink it. There would be his three kids, one with problems, his tacky affair with another teacher which almost cost him everything, and then didn't. There'd be the quick cancer at forty-two and the heft of his own coffin as they got him down the steps of his church. The party later, in his backyard once again, where they decided that if they weren't the middle children born at mid-century to middle-class parents and sent from middling, mid-island high schools to mediocre colleges all across the state, they were close enough.

Michael walked around the bar and took the girl's hand. It was soft and cold and she pulled back for just a minute as she turned to put down her beer. He recalled that he also liked the way he could feel her bones, rib bones, hip bones, the small bones of her fingers through the smooth skin.

There was a heavy smell of upstate winter in the air—the smell of frozen mud, low clouds, heating oil. There was the faint spill of red neon light on Damien's narrow steps. They walked through it. He put his arm around her. The alien eyes bobbed in his face. "Dogs," she said, looking past him. He turned. There were four or five neighborhood dogs along the side of Damien's back door, where he kept his garbage cans. Michael heard their low growling before he could distinguish what it was they were pulling at. At first he thought it was a dummy, a Halloween dummy from someone's front porch. They were dragging it a bit, tearing at it. But then he saw that it was too solid and too stiff, no newspaper stuffing, and a pale hand showed beneath a dark sleeve. He wore a suit jacket and pants and a white shirt, no shoes, just like they say. The hair was thin and gray and long enough to catch on the hard mud beneath its head. As they moved closer, they saw there was still flesh on the face, the nose, the chin, the sockets for the eyes, but in the dark it looked more like carved bone. A mutt with wiry haunches was tugging at something that turned out to be the man's tie, slowly, in jerky stops and starts, the way dogs do, pulling the body into the dim yard.

She said, "Oh, God," but she was so skinny it didn't take any effort at all to turn her away with his elbow and hip, back toward the sidewalk and his car. Under his arm, he could feel the tremor in her shoulders. He could see it in the movement of the bobbing eyes. "Assholes," was all he said.

He didn't turn on a single light in his room. They made love and then slept and then began to hear his housemates staggering in, talk and laughter, a waft of dope and then popcorn. It would be the same next year. At one point, Chris opened Michael's door for a second and then quickly turned away, shutting it. A few minutes later, they heard Jim Croce through the walls.

On the wall beside them were the glowing marks of the pictures she had drawn on Friday. In long sweeping strokes of chalk she had sketched a kind of Eden, tall stalks of grass and leafy flowers and, scattered among them, the figures of men and women—long thighs and bellies, penises, breasts, arms—all entangled, or pressed together, faces indicated only by a nose or an eye or a lock of hair. Some of it had rubbed off already, or had already faded, but there was enough to see what she had aimed for: something, he thought, between pretty and crude, between a cartoon and a vision. Something you could dismiss as a joke as readily as you could claim it as the precise illustration of everything you wanted.

They were lying side by side, naked in the dark, and the old house, as it did every night, was steadily growing colder. The drawings made him think of the satyrs and nymphs on Chris's dope box, and then of Caroline opening her parka for Ralph, that motley crew of cherubim and seraphim all around her. Hail, Holy Queen. Mother of Mercy. Our life, our sweetness and our hope.

He thought how even after you'd disentangled yourself from everything else, the words stayed with you:

To thee do we cry, poor banished children of Eve, to thee do we send up our sighs, mourning and weeping in this valley of tears. Turn then, most gracious advocate, thine eyes of mercy toward us, and after this our exile show unto us the blessed fruit of thy womb . . .

Words you could dismiss as a joke as readily as you could claim them as the precise definition of everything you wanted.

Sleepless, he raised his head to look at the clock. There was a flashlight on his bed table. Shades of his brother. He picked it up and turned it on.

He told her, the light on the ceiling, his hand on her thigh, that he'd have to get up at 5:45 to get to school. Get up and shower and put on the old student-teacher costume, cords and dress shirt and tie. He told her he could take her home now or in the morning. "On my way out," he said, "to face the inbreeds."

She only stirred and then slowly climbed over him, spread herself over him, no weight at all.

MARY KEANE looked for signs of grace, good fortune, or simple evenhandedness but found none. Tony Persichetti in church this morning, home again anyway, from wherever it was he had disappeared to, but looking like an overly made-up prodigal son, what with the wild hair and the beard and the thin hunched frame beneath his camouflage coat and gray T-shirt. His father beside him—the bulk of those arms still there but the hair gray and thinned, the shoulders stooped. Another boy from the parish who'd returned unscathed, but then died in a car wreck last month at 3 a.m. on the Montauk Highway—going well over a hundred miles an hour was what the rumors said, drugs, alcohol, even suicide the rumors said. (There had been a broken engagement.) An article in the *Long Island Press* about a father lost in the South Pacific in '44 and a son, a navy pilot, three years lost in the prison camps of North Vietnam. There were the Krafts down the street—Larry no more than thirteen when the knot appeared on his knee, not yet sixteen when the cancer killed him. His brother, home in his uniform for the funeral, head shorn, stoical, refusing all entreaties to claim hardship leave (or was it, she wondered, heartsick?), to request transfer, to desert, to flee. He was back in the States now, somewhere down south, safe again. But what had it cost his mother while he was away? And what comfort could there be in supposing that the one loss saved her from the second?

Jake from Philadelphia, nineteen or twenty at his short war, and her husband—having already gained the luxury of thirty-five years—making his unspoken promise to the boy. But what did it portend: Was it a blessing or a bad omen? Had they gained their son a guardian angel or the bitter irony of a repeated fate?

Pauline at dinner that Sunday said, "I light a candle at St. Patrick's every day. For Jacob. Just like we did during the war."

On the table beside Pauline's plate was the glass with the dregs of her third Manhattan. (Too many by two, Mary Keane had told her husband in the kitchen when he came out to carve the roast, but, he said, he had asked and she had accepted, what more could he do?) Only one of the three round slices of meat he had put on her plate had been disturbed. She had merely run her fork through the turnips, although Mary had prepared them precisely for her. Daintily, she'd taken only small tastes of mashed potatoes throughout the meal, although she'd also kept an eye on Clare's plate, as was her habit, urging her to finish her corn and take some more gravy and put more butter on that roll. "Okay," the girl responded, simply, pleasantly. How old had she been when she'd discovered the knack of dealing with Pauline, her mother wondered. Or had she been born with the knowledge? Annie, on the other hand, got through every meal with Pauline in a slow burn.

"Annie's not one for finishing her milk these days," Pauline declared, her fingers touching the stem of her cocktail glass. "Is she worried about her figure?"

"No she's not," Annie said. "She's just knows when she's had enough." And suffered for her rudeness her parents' grim looks across the Sunday lace tablecloth. Now that both her brothers were gone from the house, Pauline's presence at dinner made Annie think of them all, her father included, as old maids.

"All the girls her age are constantly dieting," Mary said pleasantly, to show her elder daughter how it should be done. "They can't be too skinny."

At the door that evening as Pauline got into her fur-collared coat there was the usual back and forth about how she could easily get herself home and how it was no trouble at all for John to take her—ending, as it usually did, with the compromise of a lift to the bus stop, at least, but only if Clare could come along.

In the vestibule after she left, there was the lingering scent of her perfume, a whiff of mothballs from her fur, and something else—the good wool of her skirt warmed by her hour on the upholstered dining-room chair? Annie, on her way upstairs to read Faulkner, said to herself, "the odor of aging female flesh," and found some recompense in the phrase for the long, annoying dinner.

Her mother, in the kitchen with the dishes, understood that the question that made her stand stock-still, the water running over her hands, rose out of her sudden solitude, out of the momentarily silenced house, the midwinter darkness at the window over the sink. She understood—since she had had these moments a dozen times at least since Jacob went over—that there was no premonition in it, only a sudden surfacing of what was, of course, a constant fear: What was he doing right now, as she rinsed out the good crystal in the sink, wearing the blouse she'd worn to Mass this morning, although she'd put on slacks before dinner, the house silent around her, the boys' room empty above her, Annie reading, Clare in the car with her husband and Pauline, what was Jacob doing right now, on the other side of the world (world without grace, without fair measure, without evenhandedness, as far as she could tell)? What was he doing, her firstborn, her mildest child, and did he need her?

Had they wrested from that stranger, the other Jacob, a blessing for their son, or was it all sentimentality and superstition on her husband's part—that blood-borne fascination with the dead—that had made him tell her on that first day of her life as a mother, It's just something I'd like to do? Did the fates howl with laughter at the irony of it all or had some good fortune been secured?

She took Pauline's empty glass from the counter beside her and dipped it in the soapy water and resolved to think instead (it was how she would get through Jacob's time in Vietnam) of what could possibly have been better, given all the occasions of her life, than that morning in the hospital with little Jacob in her arms. Our baby grand. The thrill and disbelief of finding herself a mother. Even recalling it now, she could vaguely smell the ether in the air, the particular sweet odor of a newborn's scalp. And then Michael and Annie and little Clare's breathless entrance into the world. Mr. Persichetti's strong arms.

But one moment nudges the other out of the way. It was something to regret. It was something to be grateful for. She rinsed the glass and placed it with the others in the dish drainer. On the windowsill above the sink was the small replica of the *Pietà* in its clear plastic dome—Annie's Christmas gift to her the year they had seen it. She dried her hands, turned to gather the plates from the kitchen table. There was enough of the roast for the girls' sandwiches tomorrow. Pauline had been garrulous tonight—the three drinks had done it. She was no thinner than she used to be, but age was making her gaunt, hollowing her cheeks, darkening the circles under her eyes. Mary Keane carried the dishes to the sink. Upstairs, Annie turned a page. Across the hall, her brothers' room was empty. On the boulevard, the bus behind them lit the rearview mirror above Clare's head. Pauline presented her cheek to the girl for a kiss and then held up her gloved hand and told John Keane to stay where he was, she could open her own door, thank you.

There were seven people on the bus, all sitting separately, most of them leaning against windows, a few clasping, straight-armed,

the back of the seat in front, none of them white. The light inside
was a stale and ugly light, too bright, given how dark it was outside.
Pauline knew it wasn't kind to her face, this light, that it lit the fine
hairs on her cheek and chin and the powder that clung to them.
Turning to the black window, she saw her own reflection more
clearly than the neon signs and streetlights they were passing by.
She looked older than she believed herself to be.

But how Clare's skin glowed, and how pleased she had been
with the gifts Pauline had brought her today. Even Annie had
seemed pleased with the loopy earrings that were certainly not to
Pauline's taste, but that the girl at Lord & Taylor had said were just
right for teenagers. ("Something for my niece," Pauline had said, a
little white lie that she had been telling salesclerks and strangers for
so long now, she no longer noticed it herself, or questioned its
meaning. Something for my little niece, for my nephew in college,
for my sister's boy in Vietnam.) She was a black girl, the one behind
the counter at Lord & Taylor—which wasn't as nice as it used to
be—and Pauline had asked for her advice in defiance of her own
expectation that the girl wouldn't know anything, would most likely
respond with a dumb or indignant look, as if puzzled by Pauline's
strange notion that the people behind the counter were supposed to
help the people on the other side. (Or so she had put it at dinner
tonight, telling the story.) But it turned out the girl was actually
quite gracious, looked something like Leslie Uggams, and so added
to the pleasure of the nice conversation they'd had ("Something for
my niece. A teenager"), and to the satisfaction that Annie had indeed approved of the gift, was the nice story she was able to make
out of it all at the dinner table tonight, one that led to all kinds of
reminiscence about how gracious salesclerks used to be and remember when you could just say, I think I'll have it sent?

Beyond the black glass of the window beside her, Pauline saw
the blurred strips of neon signs, the dulled nightlights of shuttered

storefronts, many of them with black grates across their windows and doors. Nighttime had a different color now, on this familiar route from Nassau to Queens, different from what it had had years ago when streetlights burned a soft yellow, and you could—hadn't they said it at dinner tonight—feel safe riding the subway at any hour. That was over now. There was a drunk at the back of the bus, muttering angrily to himself. There was a fat Spanish woman nodding to sleep across the aisle. The familiar world was slowly being overrun by strangers. The smell of odd spices drifted into her apartment at all hours now, even clung to her clothes. Courtesy—a man holding a door for you, tipping a hat—was long gone. You could not take it for granted that anyone spoke English.

When she changed at Jamaica, the second bus was empty, its door left open, its engine idling. She sat on it alone for ten minutes, chilled, headachy from the diesel fuel, before she got off to ask the dispatcher if the driver was going to come. "He's coming," the man said, waving her away. When she returned to the bus, there were two people sitting in the front and she said to them, with great dignity, "I've already waited here twenty minutes and there's no sign of a driver." They looked at her impassively—a black woman and a young black man—and then looked over her shoulder to the driver, also black, who was swinging up the stairs. He ducked into his seat and as she turned to hand him her transfer he took his time stowing his things, adjusting his mirrors, taking off his gloves, and then he sat for a second more with both hands on his thighs, staring straight ahead. She had to say, "Here," and thrust the paper at him. He took it disdainfully, not turning to meet her eye. The other two passengers got up to hand him theirs and he said thank you to both of them. They passed her, going back to their seats, the boy smirking, like good students turning up their noses at the one who had just gotten the reprimand. She was alone here. Middle-aged, aging, a woman alone, making her way between her few safe havens—the

Keanes' house, her office, her own apartment—through the ugly, amber-colored night.

She sat down at the far end of the first long seat, her back to the window, her gloved hand on the silver pole. The air of the bus was still chilled from the door being left open so long. Because the door had been left open for so long, the air inside smelled strongly of diesel fuel. She sat forward, on the edge of the molded plastic and leaned down as he made a wide turn out of the terminal. And then another. Although she knew this route as well as any, she suddenly found herself disoriented and she looked out the far window and then over her shoulder and then heard herself say, shouting at him over the wheeze of the bus, "Don't you go down Jamaica Avenue?"

He may have said, "Yeah," his arms moving in wide arcs over the big wheel. He might have said nothing at all. She waited, leaning down to see where they were. Once she recognized something, anything, she would sit back and say, pleasantly enough, "Oh, I'm all turned around," and the black lady on the other side might say, "Happens to me all the time." Or the driver might say, "I just made a wrong turn," apologizing. "We're back on track now." But this was no longer the route she knew (they should have passed a Bohack's by now) and when she asked him, somewhat alarmed, "Is this the Q54?" his answer was once again garbled. She looked to the woman across the aisle, who said, "Huhn huhn," which she hoped meant yes but could have meant she didn't know. "I don't know what 'huhn huhn' means," she said, out loud, but not, she was certain, loud enough for the woman to hear. She looked out again, over her shoulder, and then reached up for the buzzer over her head, fumbling for it with her glove. She stood. "He doesn't know where he's going," she said. She was sick to her stomach from the time she had waited in the cold, and the diesel odor had made her dizzy. She reached for the pole by the door. "You're not going the right way," she told him, shouting to be heard over the engine, "I'm getting off." There was another wide turn, she held on, leaning down now to look through the glass in the door. Where were they? "You'd better let me off," she said. And in the same moment that she saw the familiar storefront of Green Point Savings go by (and perhaps, recognizing it, relaxed her grip a bit) the bus swung into the curb and the driver pulled the doors open and she felt herself thrown forward and her feet, moving to regain her balance, stepped instead into the well of the stairs. She cried out, lunged forward, missed the handrail and then felt herself collapse, giving in to the fall, the harsh bang of the rubber tread against her hip, against her thighs, her good coat and good skirt, surprised herself at all the noise she made, against the fiberglass and the steel and the *oof* of her heavy flesh, her arm and her shoulder and her face against the curb. Blind pain, and then there was the feel of the cold air against her stockings, against the bare flesh at the top of her thighs. She struggled to pull down her hem, to cover herself but her arm was pinned, her body immobile. She was aware of voices, none of them urgent, it seemed. Spanish, perhaps laughter, strangers conferring above her in what she hoped was a dream. She would have cried out, if she could. There was dirt in her mouth and the taste of blood. And then a hand, soft and large, calloused, or perhaps it was a glove, touching the good wool of her skirt, pulling its warmth down over her bare legs.

The Keanes were asleep when the phone rang, although Annie was awake, her bedside light still on, Clare breathing softly across the room. She was writing in her diary and when she heard the phone, it was well past midnight, she raised her pen, skipped a line, and then wrote down, "Here it is." And then waited. Through the wall she could hear the tension in her father's voice, the effort to be alert and comprehending when he had just woken from a deep sleep. He seemed to be saying, Yes, yes.

She'd had a vision, once, of what would happen to her if her brother was killed in the war. She would not become one of those folk-singing peace-sign hippies, she knew, she would become instead something outrageous, something screaming, full of rage, burning things, tossing flaming bombs. How else would anyone get it, get what it would mean to lose Jacob? Now she saw that she would merely close the book in her hand, get out of bed, go into her parents' bedroom. It would mean their small family made smaller still. Her father's limp more pronounced from now on, her mother steely somehow (she thought of Susan's eyes, in the abortion clinic, getting through this). Michael more disdainful, Clare too babyish for a little longer. Crying jags for her, when she got drunk. No more effort or inclination to record it all in her little diaries, to remember how it had all played out.

Her father said, "No, not her sister. Just a friend."

Pauline was going to be kept in the hospital for a few days at least, and of course they could have visited her in the morning, but there had been some questions about psychiatric history and her mother felt it would be best if they went right down there. Pauline all alone, she said. She must be so scared. Her father had already dressed and gone down to warm up the car. Annie stood in the doorway, watching her mother run a quick comb through her hair.

"The woman is such an ass," she said, loud enough to wake Clare. "I thought it was about Jacob." It seemed the crying jag was going to happen anyway.

Her mother took her briefly in her arms, she smelled of her familiar lotion, warmed by sleep. "I know," she said. "It startled us all. But the army doesn't call. They send a telegram. Or they come to the door. And not in the middle of the night, I should hope." Then she backed away, brushed her daughter's hair. "It'll be over soon," she said. "Things are winding down over there. He'll be home before we know it."

Annie followed her downstairs. She watched her get into her

coat in the small vestibule. "You'll be all right?" her mother said. "We won't be long."

Annie could hear the idling engine of her father's car. "Poor Dad has to go to work tomorrow," she said, but her mother missed the accusation.

"And you have to go to school," she said. "Go back to bed." Then she asked again, "You'll be all right?" and Annie said, impatiently, "Yes."

The front door stuck a little before her mother got it open. Annie could see the headlights of her father's car, the wet glimmer of frost on the black windshield. "Lock up," her mother said, over her shoulder, and with a small smile, "and don't let anybody in," because there were other things to fear, out there in the darkness, even if the army didn't come in the middle of the night.

It was full daylight by the time her parents returned. Annie had gotten Clare up and dressed and they were eating cereal with Susan Persichetti, who was giving Annie a ride to school, when they came in to say that Pauline was all right—a lie by the looks on their faces. Annie saw them glance at Clare. A broken wrist and a broken nose and some bad bruises. Upset, though, their mother added. "The fall," their mother said, "kind of threw her for a loop." And then, again to Clare, "She'll be fine, really. Although," she added—and now she glanced at Annie—"she might have to come stay with us, for a while. When she gets out. We thought she could have the boys' room, for a while."

Annie glanced at Susan and then said, complaining, "What about when Michael comes home for the weekend?" After only the briefest pause, "What about when Jacob gets back?"

Her mother held up her hand. Her lips were pale. Her hair was littered with gray. "I'm not saying all year. I'm saying till her wrist is healed. Till she's herself again."

Annie said, "Who wants her to be herself again? I'd rather she be someone else." And Clare cried, "That's mean."

But her father, who was watching the coffee percolate on the stove with something of Jacob's own distracted absorption, looked at her over his shoulder and smiled. He'd liked the joke.

"I think it's mean to make the boys sleep in the basement," Annie said.

Susan laughed. "Hey, I sleep in the attic," she said.

"Well, the attic would make sense," Annie said. She turned to her mother. "Let's put Pauline in the attic. Like Grace Poole."

But her mother, buttering toast, was thinking of something else. "I don't know who you're talking about," she said shortly. She was about to lose her temper. "It will just be for a few weeks."

"Your mother has enough on her mind," their father said.

There was only the smell of coffee, the sound of the pot over the blue flame. The heater in the basement ticking on. "It'll be fine," Clare said into the quiet, as if she were the one to settle things. "The boys won't mind. It will be fine."

There was more silence and into it Annie whispered, "Bet she never leaves."

As the girls were going out the door, Mr. Keane asked Susan, his voice low, if her father would be around this afternoon. He'd like to call him. Susan said he was usually up by noon.

Standing in the small vestibule, Annie asked him, impatiently, in a way that conveyed her disinterest in both the question and the answer, "Why?" The lack of sleep had turned her father's skin to gray parchment. It had hollowed out the skin around his eyes. Just last evening he and Pauline had sat in the living room together with their cocktails, discussing retirement and pensions, the high cost of living on Long Island, the bargain that was Florida.

"They're talking about sending her over to Creedmoor," he

said, quietly, shielding Clare. "For some treatment." And to Susan: "I'd like to ask your father about that."

The girls left the house, walking down the front steps into the icy morning cold. It occurred to them both that a year ago, they would have put their heads together and laughed wickedly at the news. They would have said, the loony bin. Perfect. Annie would have said, I knew it all along. She had already said, Grace Poole. But it was a cold morning, the dry air seemed scoured by the cold, and in their shortened uniform skirts and thin jackets they were both shivering by the time they reached Susan's car at the curb. It would not be worth the effort it took to make a joke out of it all. The cold was bitter enough. Between the sidewalk and the curb the grass was frozen, each small blade frosted white. Annie heard it crunch beneath her feet as she reached for the passenger door. Tramp, tramp, tramp.

There was a car approaching from the opposite end of the street, the white of its exhaust no doubt exaggerated by the cold. Susan leaned over and opened the lock for Annie. Annie got in. Susan already had the heat blasting and the radio turned up and an unlit cigarette between her lips. They were late, but they were seniors, they were obliged to be late. The car passed them, moving slowly in what might have been an illusionist's elaborate billowing of exhaust. Last night, when she'd gone back to her bed, she'd picked up the diary and written, underneath, "Here it is," "Well, maybe not. Silly me. Only Pauline." She and Susan stopped at White Castle for doughnuts and coffee and then spent five minutes in the school parking lot brushing powdered sugar and cinnamon from their plaid skirts. The old nun at the front desk, Sister Maureen Crosby, although the girls called her Chuckles, waved them away as they began to fill out their late slips, saying, with exaggerated patience, "Just get to class, ladies." And they had only just turned away, heading toward their lockers, when the nun said, "Hold on, Miss

Keane." Annie looked back; the nun was squinting at a small strip of paper, as if it were a bit of late-breaking news, just in. She was soft and shapeless, slump shouldered in the black suit she now wore instead of a habit, a mouth breather, as solid as gray granite, as dependable, as immobile. The challenge was to get her to laugh just once during your four years at Mary Immaculate. "Call home," she said.

There had been the car, of course, in its cloud of smoke, dreamlike, slow-moving, reading house numbers, perhaps. Chuckles lifted the phone from her desk and placed it on the counter just above her. "Don't dawdle," she said. The lights in the office were bright. They were bright against the linoleum in the hallway behind them. "Miss Persichetti, you can get to class," Chuckles said, but Susan, standing close to her, murmured, "I'll wait."

"I am quite sure," Chuckles said, as nuns did, "that Miss Keane is capable of calling home without your assistance."

But Susan shook her head, lied easily. "I've got my stuff in Annie's locker. I have to wait for her." She touched Annie's arm and said, "Go ahead, I'll wait." And then walked with her anyway, the few steps back to the desk. She knew, of course, what it was like to dread every message, every phone call, every change in the day's routine. She knew what it was like. She watched Annie dial home ("Don't each of you girls have your own locker?" Chuckles was saying) their eyes meeting briefly as she waited. Her mother said only, "Daddy's coming to get you." And then she was in Susan's arms.

IV

MR. PERSICHETTI was good enough to come along. Mary Keane was in the backseat and she touched his shoulder with her gloved hand to say, "This is good of you." He shook his head, "No trouble," he said. It was a wet, gray morning, cold yet somewhat humid: the terrible winter being edged out, once again, by spring. There were green spears of crocus, mere buds against the dirt, under front windows and along the edges of lawns. There would be daffodils soon, too, she knew. Then forsythia, azalea, rose, and rhododendron.

She leaned back against the seat, folding her hands in her lap. Up front, her husband said, "Do you take the Cross Island or go side streets?" and Mr. Persichetti said, "At this hour, the Cross Island's fine." At this hour, the neighborhood was quiet, and somewhat sodden from last night's rain. John Keane drove cautiously, as was his habit. He wore his topcoat and his fedora—he would head for work as soon as they brought Pauline home—and beside him, hatless, wearing only a thin Windbreaker, Mr. Persichetti looked like a youngster. "I cut over to Northern Boulevard," Mr. Persichetti said, "when it doesn't look good."

Mr. Keane nodded. They passed the church and the school, the row of shops. From the backseat, Mary said, "I think Susan and

Annie actually left for school early this morning. They said they wanted to see the juniors get their rings."

Mr. Persichetti turned a little in his seat. "That's a first, hey?" he said.

"They're the big shots this year," John Keane said. "They think they run the place." He touched his turn signal, pulled cautiously into the mid-morning traffic. "Next year they'll be lowly freshmen again."

"Coeds," Mr. Persichetti said. He was both poking fun at the word and revealing his pleasure in the thought. "Can you believe it? Those two? College girls."

"Lord help the professors," Mary Keane said.

"Lord help the boys," Mr. Persichetti said with a laugh because girl children went off, but they also came back. They were a comfort in your old age, in your sorrow over lost sons.

The three of them rode silently for a while, looking out at the passing homes.

As they neared the hospital, Mr. Persichetti sat forward, a hand on the dashboard, showing John Keane where to park. "It's short-term," he said. "But then when she's ready you can pull right up to the door."

Inside, he took them just where they needed to go. In his element, Mary Keane would have said, walking them assuredly through the halls to the desk where the paperwork was waiting and an orderly talking to another nurse looked up and waved and said, "What's a matter? You're back already? They didn't let you in at home?"

"Can't get enough of this place," Mr. Persichetti said, laughing. When the nurse said she'd call to have Pauline brought down, Mr. Persichetti waved her away from the phone and took Mary Keane's arm. "We'll get her," he said gently. And to her husband, "We'll go up and get her. It'll be easier."

The floor of the elevator was wet, with streaks of mud, as if
people had been coming and going all night. Mr. Persichetti pushed
some of the dirt with his shoe and said, "Sheesh," disapproving. He
pushed the button for Pauline's floor and then looked up at the row
of numbers, his hands in the pockets of his Windbreaker. He turned
to Mary Keane as the elevator began to rise and said, "I'm the regular mayor of this place, you know," and then, as if to prove his
point, the elevator stopped and the doors slid open and another orderly appeared, a middle-aged black man, pushing a wheelchair in
which a pale, dark-haired boy was slumped, his long thin arms
raised before his bent head, waving. The black man said, in military
parody, "Mr. Persichetti, sir," and Mr. Persichetti held out a hand.
"Darrin, my man," he said. Then he grabbed the pale, yellowed
hand of the boy in the wheelchair, gripped it firmly. "How you doing, Larry?" he said. The boy, head down, neck twisted, his mouth
veiled with saliva, said a tortured, "Good. Real good."

"Behaving yourself?" Mr. Persichetti asked. And the boy drew
out a long, "Yes, yes."

"Yeah, I bet you are," Mr. Persichetti said sarcastically. He
looked up at the orderly and winked, and then at Mary Keane, as if
they were all in on some joke the young man would never understand. For a moment, she thought this cruel, or just childish, on Mr.
Persichetti's part, but as the elevator rose again, she saw how he
kept the boy's hand in his, clasping it between both of his own, and
then, briefly, tightening his grip before letting go when the doors
opened again. Alone with him once more, she said, "I don't know
how you do what you do." But Mr. Persichetti only shrugged. "Oh,
Larry's a piece of work," he said, refusing her the larger meaning.

The hallway on Pauline's floor was no worse and no better than
Mary Keane had imagined it would be. There were all the usual
hospital smells, food and urine and disinfectant, along with the
smell of the old building itself, a subway smell of dust and metal.

Some of the patients were in the hall, tied into wheelchairs. Old women, mostly, or so it seemed, hair streaming and yellowing eyes, glimpses, here and there, of bruised flesh under the limp white and speckled blue of the hospital gowns. "Hello," one or two of them said as they passed by, Mr. Persichetti with his hand on her elbow. One or two of them called out a name. Mary Keane tried to smile at them all. "Hello," she said, passing by. "How are you?" A lifetime of friendliness. A shout went up briefly, from one of the rooms, and then a low moaning. At the end of the hall there was a dull window of either smoked glass or grime, black wire inside its frame, and she had a moment of utter disorientation because although she knew they were on an upper floor, that the elevator they had just ridden had risen, she believed, for just a moment (perhaps it was the subway smell of the old tile walls), that they were underground.

Mr. Persichetti stopped briefly at the nurse's station—she was glad for his hand on her arm—and then he led her down another corridor. She had some guilt that she had not visited Pauline before, not since the night she fell, that Pauline had been alone all these weeks in this place. But she knew too that she could not have done it, in the midst of all that these weeks had held. In this corridor, another woman, her dark skin stretched thinly over her bones, sat in a wheelchair with her head bent into one hand and her long fingers held up over her face, touching her eyes and her mouth. Her other hand, in her lap, was white-palmed, empty. She was the weary image of every sorrow women knew. Seeing her, Mary Keane felt herself absolved, at least briefly, of all she had neglected in these past weeks. Were she to bend down and speak to this woman she would say, "I have buried my child." She would ask, "And you?"

"Here we are," Mr. Persichetti said, and with his hand on her arm guided her into Pauline's room. She was in a chair by another opaque window, crossed with wire. Her hair was longer than she usually kept it, swept back from her face and showing a good line of gray roots, but she looked well, even younger, perhaps—Mary was surprised to see it—than she had that last night at dinner. It might have been that she was more rested, or better fed. It might have been that she was no longer drinking (psychosis brought on by depression and alcoholism, was what they had said), although never in a million years would she have guessed that the drinking was a problem. It might simply have been, Mary Keane was suddenly sure it was true, that Pauline looked better without her makeup. Her complexion, she had always been glad to point out (usually just after Mary had complained about her own), had always been good.

She crossed the room and kissed Pauline on the cheek. There was only the hospital bracelet on her wrist. Not a hint of the broken nose. Or the shock treatment. "You look good," she told her and Pauline said, as she might of old, "What's new?"

Mary found herself speaking more loudly than she wanted to, the way you spoke, mostly inadvertently, to an invalid or a child. "We're going to bring you back to our house, Pauline," she said, leaning down to her in the chair. "You're going to stay with us for a while." Pauline nodded. Mary was surprised to see her fur-collared coat was laid out on the bed. Pauline was dressed in the clothes they had picked up for her when they emptied out her apartment, gray pants and a pale blue sweater, although someone had given her an old white cardigan as well, oversize and somewhat pilly. The only indication, perhaps, that Pauline had been changed.

"I know," Pauline said. She looked to Mr. Persichetti, standing at the door. "Sam told me all about it."

Mary turned to look at him over her shoulder. He shrugged, his hands in the pockets of his Windbreaker. "Oh, I've been stopping by," he said. "Checking up on her. Seeing how she's been doing." He looked at Mary Keane. "Being the mayor and all," he said. And then he added softly, "I knew you had your mind on other things."

"That was good of you," she said, and wanted to say more,

but the floor nurse was bustling in with the wheelchair, shouting instructions, pulling prescriptions from her smock, referring to Pauline in the third person. Mr. Persichetti pushed the wheelchair back to the elevator, Pauline staring straight ahead as they passed through each corridor. "Goodbye," Mary Keane said to the women who spoke to them. "Take care." Pausing for a moment when a shuffling old woman suddenly clasped her hand, holding it between her own as Mr. Persichetti had done for the boy on the elevator. This woman was no older than she. Her blue eyes seemed to race back and forth across Mary Keane's face as she told a nonsense tale—my sista, was all she could get, my motha, my sista—that grew more urgent as it grew more incomprehensible. The floor nurse stepped between them. "That's enough, now, Marion," she shouted. Mary Keane said, walking on, "I'll pray for you." The name of Saint Dymphna came to mind.

In the elevator, she resisted the memories the whiff of hospital food and of ether wanted to bring. She had been a patient herself only when her children were born, a visitor most recently when Michael had his tonsils out and Jacob had appendicitis and her husband had the surgery for the slipped disk. When her children were born, she recalled, they had marked each homecoming with a bakery cake, thick with sweet icing, and she felt some guilt again that she hadn't thought to have anything special at home for Pauline.

When they were settled into John Keane's car, she and Pauline in the backseat, the two men once again up front, Pauline said, "This is very nice of you," and crossed her hands in her lap. In the pale light of day, she now seemed older without her makeup, with that sad line of gray along her temples and her forehead. Mary planned a trip to the beautician for both of them, lunch afterward, somewhere nice, a stroll through A&S. As the car pulled away and into the street, Pauline suddenly sat up, something brief and childlike in her eyes, a spark of fear or confusion. And then, haltingly, she sat back again. She turned to Mary. "That raincoat doesn't suit you," she said. "You're not good in black."

Mary only smiled.

"You've lost weight, too," Pauline said. It wasn't a compliment.

At the house, John Keane gave Pauline his arm to help her up the steps. They paused in the hallway and he took her coat and hung it in the closet, as if this were just another one of her visits and the world hadn't altered utterly since last she was here.

They had lunch in the kitchen, the three of them, and then John went to work and Mary walked Pauline upstairs. The last time she had slept in this house, when Clare was born, she had been given Annie's room, but now they made a right at the landing. She was to stay in the boys' room instead. It was nice enough, a little chilly after the overheated rooms of the hospital. Mary pulled open the drawers of the oak dresser the boys had once shared. She had lined them with floral paper and arranged all of Pauline's underclothes and nightgowns and sweaters inside. She had brought her jewelry box, her gloves, her drawerful of saved *Playbills* and greeting cards.

John Keane had arranged with Pauline's landlord that the apartment be sublet, for a year. Just, Mary told her, until Pauline was back on her feet. He had spoken to her company, too, and an early retirement for medical reasons would assure her of most of her pension. Pauline nodded. Her coats and her dresses, her dressing gowns and her good skirts were hanging in the boys' closet. "You've been busy," Pauline said, not—Mary glanced at her— exactly approvingly.

"You've been sick," Mary said, gently. "That fall . . ." and would have said more, but Pauline held up her hand and said, "I know all about it." And then added, with a tremor to her jaw. "I know where I've been."

Mary Keane touched her throat. "And do you know," she asked, "what we've been through?"

Slowly, Pauline nodded. Her pale, plain features might have been carved of stone. "Sam told me," she said. "I'm sorry for you."

Mary would have put her arms around her then, might have broken down herself and wept with Pauline for what they both had been through. But that had never been their way. They were not sisters, after all, they were friends, office friends. And what had bound them all these years had more to do with how their acquaintance had begun (for how could you pray with any sincerity if you were also hoping to ditch the annoying girl at your side?), with habit and circumstance, obligation and guilt, than it had ever had to do with affection, commiseration. There had been a trick in it too, their friendship, something far more complicated than "feed my lambs." There had been the trick of living well, living happily in her ordinary life under Pauline's watchful eye. Of living well, living happily, even under the eye of a woman who always saw the dashed tear, the torn seam, who remembered the cruel word, the failed gesture, who knew that none of them would get by on good intentions alone, or on the aspirations of their pretty faith.

"I'll never get over it," Mary said. It was a phrase she had kept to herself, until now.

The boys' room was small and narrow. She and her husband had taken the pinups and posters from the walls in preparation for Pauline's coming, they had moved the desk and the old hi-fi and the record albums and the portable TV to the basement where Michael would sleep when he came home to visit, but they had left both beds here.

Pauline turned an impassive face to her, standing between the two beds.

"I don't expect you will," she said.

And then there was the sound of Clare coming in. Clare coming through the front door, dropping her books in the vestibule. "Maaa?" They heard the girl's footsteps on the stairs. "Here," her mother called. And then she was in the room. Her coat and her hair were wet with rain. She smelled of pencil shavings. Of the halls of St. Gabriel's.

"You're here," she said to Pauline, and easily went to her, put her arms around her, as her mother had not, her cheek against her breast. "How do you feel?" she said, gingerly. "Are you better?"

Pauline, with something of her old dignity, said, "Oh, yes. Much better."

At dinner, there was the new configuration at the table: Annie had taken Michael's place and Pauline sat beside Clare. Afterward, Clare sat in front of the television as Michael used to do, watching while she did her homework. Sitting in the chair behind her, Pauline said, "Doesn't the TV distract you? Wouldn't you rather sit at the table?"

And Clare shook her head. "No, I'm fine." Her hair had gone wavy from where it had been wet and it caught the TV light at its ends. "Can you really concentrate?" Pauline said and the girl nodded, "I really can."

The boys' room was chilly after the overheated rooms of the hospital, but it had a pleasant smell: there was a box in the bedside drawer that contained sticks of incense—Pauline put it to her nose—a smell like an old church, just after Benediction, a smell that ran just under the other, ordinary smells of clean sheets and the lingering scent of dinner. She turned back the plaid spread. Both beds were made up, but she chose the one nearest the wall to avoid the light from the hall that came under the door. She was well asleep when she felt Clare's hands on her shoulders, patting her softly, and had a momentary belief that she was in the hospital again, that another patient had wandered in.

But Clare laughed a little in the darkness, whispering, "Is that you? I can't see."

Pauline said, "Yes, it's me."

She heard the girl moving away. "Okay," she said. Heard her pulling at the sheets on the other bed, getting under the covers. "I sleep in here sometimes," she said. "When Annie stays up reading." She was only a voice in the darkness, but even in the darkness, Pauline would have known the voice.

"That's all right," Pauline said.

They were both silent. There was, perhaps, some faint music, piano notes from next door. Pauline was beginning to see a little more, some thin light behind the curtains, perhaps the outline of the girl's small body under the spread. In a moment, she could hear her breathing softly, sweetly, into the dark.

THE GIRLS had heard it through the night: rain drumming on the roof and rattling down the drainpipes, rain amplifying, giving voice or music (depending on their dreams) to the sound of passing cars. They had ridden to school this morning with the metronome shush of windshield wipers thrumming at their temples, erasing one thought, then another, then another as it formed again. Riding the school bus or in their fathers' cars with their sleeves and shoulders damp, their loafers and the crowns of their heads darkened with rain.

They felt the dampness of it still at 10 a.m., second period, as they moved into the classroom, their books in their arms.

The overhead lights had not yet been turned on, nor had the teacher arrived, so here was an opportunity to sprawl, for a minute. Put your head on the desk.

Outside the mullioned window was a slate-gray sky, a dark lawn, a black hedge that hid the road, although they could see the headlights of cars behind the tangled shrubs, low beams moving as if through water. There had been general consensus this morning, on the radio at least, that were it not for the unseasonable warmth of the day, there would have been two feet of snow.

The raindrops ran in fits and starts across each pane. The morning light, filtered through the rain-spattered glass, turned the colors in the unlit classroom into various shades of gray.

Clare Keane folded her arms across her books and rested her forehead in the crook of her elbow. She closed her eyes and the sound of the rain and of her shuffling, murmuring classmates grew hollow and distant, veered from noise to echo to dream.

Beside her, Barb Luce slumped at her desk, then stretched her legs to straddle the chair legs of the seat in front of her. Idly, she took inventory: penny loafers, navy kneesocks, dimpled knees, bare thighs—winter pale against the pleated plaid wool of her skirt—a nick of dried blood between knee and skirt hem from this morning's razor. She licked a finger and put it to the scab, assessed the smoothness of the shave with her fingertips. Knees were always tricky.

There was a general yawning, a leaning forward and a leaning back. A lethargic unclipping of hair clips and a clipping back up again. A roll of Life Savers was passed around, its plume of unraveled wrapper like a lengthening stream of smoke as it went from hand to hand. A clicking of candy against teeth. A general whisper, Did we have homework in here? Did she give us homework?

Monica Grasso shuffled her books and said out loud, "I don't want to be here," but opened her notebook anyway and reviewed (the Diet of Worms, the Council of Trent), just in case.

The rain was steady, no particular wind to drive it or to vary its rhythm. Cynthia Pechulis pulled her hair up into a ponytail at the top of her head and Dawn Sorrento, sitting behind her, saw in the lovely declivity between her neck and spine the fine blond hair Cynthia had been born with.

They were all fourteen or fifteen in identical plaid skirts and navy blue blazers, white blouses with soft collars.

Kathleen Cornelius, her large face drawn, her lips parted, noticed that the blackboard glimpsed through her lashes bled a little at the edges but snapped to again when she opened her eyes wide. She tried this a number of times until her attention was diverted by the floating dust motes that appeared in the gloom of her lowered lashes. They were perfectly round, transparent, either dust motes or sloughed skin cells, bits of dandruff, perhaps, or perhaps merely an optical illusion, her own blood moving behind her cornea, illuminating the defects, snags, infinitesimal genetic mutations in the sticky fabric of her eye.

The interval of idleness grew longer. Was it possible there would be no class today?

Clare Keane dreamed she was still at the breakfast table. Her father was watching the coffee percolate on the stove. Annie (who in the dream was not really Annie) was stirring her cereal. Pauline was spreading soft butter on a pinch of sweet roll, covering her fingertips with it. Much to Clare's surprise, Annie picked up her cigarette lighter which she had unaccountably left beside her plate and struck the flint three times.

"Good morning, all," Sister Lucy said. She stood at the door, her index finger held under the three light switches as if (Clare thought) she was hoping to keep three little noses from sneezing. "In the name of the Father," Sister began, as she walked in, not blessing herself because she held her crutch in one hand and her large leather briefcase in the other, "and of the Son."

Overhead, the trio of fluorescent lights merely buzzed, then clicked, then flashed angrily, before coming to full, obedient light as Sister Lucy limped into the room. One by one, the girls raised their heads, touched a pencil, stored some books beneath their desks, praying with her all the while. Clare Keane had a red spot on her forehead, marking the place where her face had heavily met her forearm. Kathleen Cornelius closed her mouth.

Now the long windows pressed back the dreary day, reflected

rather than filtered—showing them now, as they glanced toward it, their own white faces, dimly described—foreheads and cheeks, some chins, only blond hair, nobody's eyes.

Sister Lucy's desk at the front of the room now seemed as yellow as an egg yolk. She leaned against it and pulled the cuff of her metal crutch off her wrist. She rested the crutch beside her and then turned back with one uneven step to lift herself, her small and slightly twisted torso in its black dress, up onto the desk. She rearranged her body, palms pressed to the desktop, lifting her thighs once, twice, getting comfortable. Her legs in their black shoes and black opaque stockings swung girlishly.

This was not remarkable to them. They had seen her do this many times before.

She placed her folded hands in her black lap. Sister Lucy had a round face, dark though graying hair drawn back into the white band of her headpiece, large, deep-set eyes, and a small nose. Her full cheeks were pocked delicately with scars, as if marred by rain.

"Today," she said, softly, beginning. And then paused. She had a slight overbite, a delicate fuzz above her lip, small and perfect teeth. She was known never to raise her voice, although what she did instead, for discipline's sake, was described by the girls as "the hairy eyeball." But there was none of that in her look now as she waited for their attention.

"Today," she said again, her feet no longer swinging but hooked together and drawn back a bit, beneath her desk. "Today, girls, marks a terrible anniversary. The anniversary of the decision that allows women in this country to kill their own children."

In the stillness that followed, the girls moved their eyes toward each other. Barb lowered her head and murmured, "Don't tell my mother," into the soft collar of her shirt, which caused one or two of the girls around her to lower their heads as well.

The sound of the rain only made the silence in the classroom seem more deliberate and profound as Sister Lucy waited, once again, for their full attention.

"I was three years old when I came down with polio," she said. It might have been another topic altogether. "My father left us as soon as I got sick, even though my mother was expecting. Her fifth. He moved in with a woman he'd been visiting since before my older brother was born. My father was a welder," she said, as if that explained something. "Subways and bridges. Dangerous work, but he was very good at it." She shrugged, looked briefly at her hands, which she half opened, as if offering herself something from her own palms. "He had needs my mother couldn't meet," she said before she looked up again. "That's all we were told about it. And the fact that if he had gotten polio, too, we would have been destitute. But he took care of us. He sent money, he visited. He still took my brothers to ball games. He just never lived with us again."

She closed her hands. They were pale white against the black lap. The girls had their eyes on her now. Barb Luce wrote something in her notebook and moved the book to the edge of her desk so Clare Keane could see. It said, "As the World Turns."

"My mother was given a series of exercises to do with me. They involved lifting and bending my legs. They were painful. I don't re-member that they were painful to me but I'm sure they were painful for her. She would sometimes strap me down on the dining-room table. Or have my brothers hold on to me. My brothers have told me how I would scream. And how my mother would cry, just tears running down her face as she was lifting my legs and bending them, and pressing them down again, the way the doctors had told her. All the while she was expecting."

Sister Lucy's little chin moved up and down, the way it did when she wanted to be reasonable, consider all sides. "Of course, we weren't alone in the world," she said. "I had an aunt and an un-cle and a wonderful grandfather. We had some very nice neighbors.

And people from church helped out. It was really only later, as an adult, that I realized how hard it must have been. For my mother."

She straightened her spine, pulling her hands closer to her waist, as if she felt a chill. "In the first place, I think she must have been humiliated," she went on. "Four, five children in a row and she hadn't met his needs." She smiled a little, only one corner of her small mouth. It was clear she did not expect them to get her full meaning. "And I know she worried. Every mother worries, but what worries my mother must have had, in those days. I don't know when she slept. I remember seeing her, long into the night, sitting up at our bedroom window with her rosary." Sister Lucy stopped again, peering down at them all from under her thick eyelids. The sound of the rain had mixed itself with her tale so that the girls were imagining polio, pregnancy, bridges and subways and long nights at bedroom windows as all a part of the same dark weather.

She smiled once more. Her lips were pink and smooth. "But my mother took me to the clinic and she took me home and she did the exercises the doctors told her to do. And she fixed our meals and washed our clothes and kept the apartment clean. All the while she was getting bigger and bigger with the new baby. All the while she slept alone and woke alone and sat alone through the night after she'd put out our lights."

One of the girls made a sympathetic sound and Sister Lucy's eyes briefly fell on her. "Girls," she said, as if to correct something. "In an abortion, a child is pulled from a mother's womb. If the child is very new, an embryo, it is a simple enough thing to do. There is more blood than flesh. If the child has grown any, arms and legs must sometimes be broken, or a skull must be cracked. There are some procedures, I am told, in which the mother's womb is filled with saline, salt water, the baby essentially drowned like a kitten and then flushed from the mother's body." She paused only briefly.

"In college," she went on in her soft way, although she saw how

Kathleen Cornelius's open mouth had reshaped itself in horror and how Monica Grasso was glaring at her from under her bangs, the class wit, the class iconoclast, on guard, as Monica was always on guard, against Catholic double-talk and propaganda, "you will probably read the story of Medea," glancing at Monica to indicate that she might learn something here. "It is a play by Euripides. If you know the story of Jason and the Golden Fleece, you already know something about Medea. She was the sorceress who helped Jason defeat the dragon and gain the Golden Fleece. Jason and Medea marry. They have two sons. But then Jason leaves her to marry the young daughter of the king. To form a more advantageous alliance, he tells her. More power. Especially for their sons, who will have as their half brothers the royal sons he plans to have with his new wife." She smiled again, mildly. "An advantage for them all.

"But Medea doesn't think so." She raised her pale eyebrows. "She is outraged. Humiliated. And in her rage against her husband, she murders their children. She chases them down. Stabs them to death, her own children. It's a terrible scene. The chorus— remember how in every Greek play there's a chorus?—the chorus calls her a woman of stone, or iron, to have done such a thing. She is hateful beyond all other women. She has put a sword through her own children."

Now Sister Lucy looked outside, to the dark lawn and the black hedge and the rain striking the windows. She watched a pair of headlights as they moved dimly behind the hedge. It seemed to her to be something like her own idea, the point she had hoped to make, moving through the black tangle of memory and emotion and outrage and words.

She turned her eyes back to the girls. "Of course, I thought of my parents when I first read *Medea*. I couldn't help but see the parallels. That's the thing about the Greek tragedies, isn't it? Centuries later, there are parallels." She paused and then added, sounding more like herself. "Although, as we'll see tomorrow, Saint Augustine had no use for the Greeks."

She paused again. She seemed to have lost her train of thought. Some of the girls wondered if they should open their notebooks. "I don't know," Sister Lucy went on, "if my mother ever felt any of Medea's anger. Or if she considered what it would be like to deprive him of this last child, the one still in her womb, the one he had abandoned even before she was born."

Sister Lucy leaned forward a bit, her hands on the edge of the desk, and as she did, her right hand brushed her crutch and it began to slide. Quickly, adeptly, she reached for it, steadied it. And then she lifted it and placed it across her lap.

"Girls," she said again, more forcefully, as if she were now girded for battle. "The men who make our laws see women as being as capable of murdering their unborn children as men have always been of abandoning them. They see all women as equals to Medea, should the circumstances arise. They are blind to women like my mother who put their children above all else, who labor and worry and die . . ."—she paused, her large round eyes seeming to search for the word, her two hands clutching the crutch she had placed across her lap. Her voice had not risen an octave. "Die tired," she said finally, and then raised her eyebrows as if she was surprised to discover that the word she had searched for was such a simple one. She looked again to the long wall of windows.

For a moment, they all listened to the rain. It hit the windows without rhythm or pattern, as listless as tears. A few of them thought of tears.

The light outside gave no indication of how much class time was left, but Sister Lucy knew instinctively that the time was short and she was losing the thread of what she'd meant to say.

She turned back to the girls' faces. Some of them were looking away, playing with their fingers or studying their pens. Two or three were staring cross-eyed at the ends of their long hair. But more still were watching her, their faces serious, lovely, still emerging from the faces of their childhood, and raised toward her now as if to catch the solemn rain.

"Iron or stone," she said again, trying to remember the thread. "That's what they'll say about you. A woman made of iron or stone."

Sister Lucy looked down at her crutch. A few of the girls, only partially attentive, tried to remember if that was good or bad, to be iron or stone. Clare Keane thought that her mother had been like iron, in the cold pew at St. Gabriel's on the morning her brother was buried. Clare knew she had been grateful for it, the cool stone of her mother's face and hands. The iron of her arm.

Barb Luce wrote in her notebook again. Clare glanced at the page. It said, "Things are tough all over."

Then Sister Lucy looked up again, dry-eyed.

"I realize we've gone off syllabus today," she said softly. "Sometimes circumstances make their demands. We'll return to Saint Augustine tomorrow. And Saint Monica, of course." Nodding at Monica Grasso, who suddenly raised her hand.

"Yes," Sister Lucy said, expecting a question about this week's quiz, the paper due next Friday, expecting the obliteration of all she had just said by the girls' preference for practical priorities. "Yes, Monica," she said.

Her thick black hair, straight and silky and falling well below her shoulders, caught the white fluorescent light, broad sparks around her face. "When abortion is illegal," Monica, the captain of the debate team, said clearly, "women die."

Kathleen Cornelius turned in her seat as if she'd been stuck with a fork. "But babies die when it is," she said. Two or three other girls cried out in wordless agreement.

"You can't legislate morality," Monica snapped back. "Look at Prohibition."

Now the class was alert, and Sister Lucy saw that even the indifferent students were interested: not so much in the substance of the debate as in the joy of the rebellion.

Kathleen, having spent her rhetorical trove, looked rather desperately back to Sister Lucy. The other girls looked to her as well, some of them smirking, some anxious, others only curious. At their age, Sister Lucy recalled, she had craved piety, undaunted innocence, even naïveté. Now, worldliness was all they wanted. Sophistication.

She held up a hand, put a finger to her lips. "Girls," she said. "We're not here to debate."

"No kidding," she heard one of them say.

"Thousands of babies are killed," another girl said.

Under the sudden ringing of the bell, Monica cried, "Thousands of grown-up babies died in Vietnam. Why didn't they pass a law against that?" There was laughter. Barb Luce looked quickly at Clare.

When the bell stopped, echoing, there was only the familiar sound of the whole school population, four hundred girls, stirring, standing, pushing back chairs, picking up books. They shook out their skirts and pulled up their kneesocks and flipped their hair. Sister Lucy watched them as they passed her desk, the crutch across her lap.

Monica Grasso, ever mindful of her grade, said, "Good discussion, Sister." And Sister Lucy nodded, smiling, disdainfully perhaps.

Clare Keane, passing by, glanced briefly at the nun. Unlike so many of the teachers at Mary Immaculate, Sister Lucy had never before spoken about her life—her parents, her childhood, her time outside of school. Never a word about her crutch and her limp. It had lent her a certain dignity, her reticence. Clare thought it gave her a kind of professionalism. Now she wondered, glancing briefly at the nun, if Sister Lucy would take it all back if she could. If, given the way the girls were shaking off her story—her mother's poor life, her father's, all that sadness—laughing, moving on, following the bell, Sister Lucy now wished she had kept it to herself. Instead of turning it into a single day's lesson for a bunch of heedless teenage girls.

Joining the crowds in the long hallway, Clare checked the books in her arms. She was headed for geometry. This year, much to her own surprise, it was the one class where she felt sure of everything.

HER HUSBAND was exquisite. Ginger-haired, as the British would have put it, but the two American girls would have said ginger as well—although not for the color but the taste: gingersnaps, gingerbread, ginger ale. Some mild and easygoing spice that nevertheless prickled the tongue.

He was sitting cross-legged on the floor, surrounded by wineglasses. He wore brown corduroy pants and a shirt that was a soft, autumn-evoking shade of gold, an ascot—a pattern of greens and browns—tied loosely at his throat. His ginger hair curled over a broad forehead that might have been deeply tanned earlier in the year but was now faded and freckled, a burnished ginger itself, as were his cheekbones, his handsome man's dimpled chin. His eyes were brown or dark green, the whites bright against his skin.

"Loo paper," he said by way of greeting. And held up a single sheet. "The cheapest kind. Nothing like it for getting lint off the crystal."

Professor Wallace had a hand to the small of their backs, ushering them in. "David," she whispered, reverentially, bending to place her cheeks beside theirs, as if David were some distance away, on a pedestal perhaps, and, like his namesake, carved out of white marble. "My husband." And then, straightening, raising her voice. "Two more of our American students."

Gracefully, he stretched out his legs and stood, sweeping up two of the glasses in one hand, the faint sound of a bell ringing. He studied their faces carefully as they introduced themselves. He was not as tall as he'd seemed sitting, not as tall as his wife, but it made no difference to the girls, who were just now noticing the long apricot lashes. "Some wine?" he asked. "We have a lovely Chianti." And then turned to a sideboard, marble-topped and piled with books. And then turned back. Asked over his shoulder, "Or do you American women prefer whiskey?"

"Wine, thank you," Annie said, but Grace pushed her glasses up her nose with her index finger and said, "Whiskey."

Annie bowed her head as she accepted the glass of wine, afraid that if she met his eye, her hand would tremble. "My dear," he said, handing it to her. And then to Grace, "I've got just the thing." He reached for a square decanter. "Straight up or on the rocks?" he asked and Grace said, shuffling a bit, "On the rocks." There was a silver ice bucket and silver tongs.

Professor Wallace's face wore the expression Annie would have liked to wear, or would work at wearing in the future. Under Professor Wallace's long nose, her mouth was a thin, wry grin. Her small black-brown eyes were warm and understanding and forgiving. They said she understood that Grace had probably never had whiskey before in her life and would probably not like it when she had it, but that an attempt was being made here, at worldliness, at sophistication. An attempt on Grace's part to undercut the stumpy body and the dowdy clothes and the reputation she had already secured, six weeks into the term, as the smartest but dullest of the fifteen American students studying this year at the university. An attempt to promote the impression that beneath the cliché of smart and plain and studious was something like uncharted depths, even danger. Whiskey, indeed, Professor Wallace's smile said. Well, yes, of course, go ahead, her smile said. You will not be the first unhappy girl to seek to transform herself here, go ahead.

As if the injunction had actually been spoken, Grace stuck her nose into the stubby glass as soon as it was in her hand and took a large gulping swallow, sliding the ice cubes into her lip and knocking the rim of the glass against the bridge of her glasses. Coughing a little as she swallowed, of course.

Mr. Wallace, David, was either the most gracious man on earth or simply oblivious to the pretense and the struggle. He took Grace's elbow as if this were only one of many evenings in which they had met for a drink and a chat—as if, Annie thought, Grace were an old, dear friend in elbow-length satin gloves, a tapered cigarette holder in her left hand rather than the trademark (already) crumpled bit of Kleenex. He led her to the couch. "Do sit," he said and then held his hand out to Annie, indicating a red velvet chair with brown fringe. "My dear," he said again, warmly, as if she were indeed.

There were piles of books beside the chair as well—old books with dark covers, the room was scented with them—and as soon as she sat, a dark Siamese cat curved around the pile to her left and brushed itself against her legs. "That's Runty," Professor Wallace said. She herself was wrapped in a large velvet shawl, as black as her lecturing robes but spotted with gold beads, trimmed with a bit of lace. She had lifted her glass from somewhere—another crystal goblet, only half full of the nice Chianti—and now held it beside her ear as she stood, looking down on the cat, one arm across her middle, the other resting its elbow in her hand. "So named for the obvious reasons," she said. "Bozo's around here somewhere. And Tommy, the tiger-striped."

Both girls added to their growing list of things to love about

Professor Wallace the fact that her cats had nonliterary names. "But Runty," she said, "is the sycophant."

And that she did not ask them, as an American professor might do, if they knew the meaning of the word.

Six weeks ago, the American students had stumbled out of Professor Wallace's first lecture with their breaths held, tripping over one another to be the first to say, out of earshot of their humorless British counterparts, "My God, the Wicked Witch of the West," to imitate her accent as she said, trilling it, "Edmund Spencer's *The Faerie Queen.*" But six weeks into the term, they were all enchanted. She had only to turn up a corner of her thin mouth in the middle of a lecture, or to raise a single eyebrow as she recited, or to touch her hand to her breast as she made some aside ("*As You Like It,*" she had said, "not, necessarily, my dear ones, as I like it") to get them all grinning, clutching the edges of their small desks, leaning to see that the other Americans in the lecture hall had gotten it too, the wry pun, the witty reference, the experience they were all having, basking in her brilliance, growing literary and worldly-wise, nearly British.

When they discovered, on a bulletin board crowded with Carnival flyers and club schedules, tutorial appointments and reading lists, a small index card that said Professor Wallace is home every Thursday evening, followed by brief directions—the bus number, the shop on the corner, "fourth house in, red shutters"—it had taken some time for any of them to get the courage to take her up on what the English students told them was simply an opportunity to have a nice meal. But one of the American boys—Caleb, a bit of a sycophant himself—had gone along with a pair of African students in the third week of the term and returned to tell the other Americans of curry and Sauternes and incredible conversation. One by one, the others made plans to go, Annie knowing that she and Grace would have to go together since it was Grace who had sat beside her on the flight from Kennedy. Grace with whom she'd eaten dinner and watched the movie and exchanged biographies with blankets up to their chins and their faces turned to each other like lovers. Poor Grace who, it sometimes felt, had slipped her hand into the crook of Annie's arm during those five hours and kept it there ever since. Her own private Pauline.

David bent down to scoop Runty from her feet. "I don't mind," she said, but then he was crouched before her, brushing the cat hair from her trousers, touching her instep and her knee, the cat pressed to his golden shirt. "Come what may," he said softly. "He'll be in your pocket by the end of the evening." He smiled up at her, his face rising over her lap as he straightened. The strong cheekbones and the dimpled chin, the adorable lock over the forehead. He paused, speaking to her from just the other side of her knees. He lowered his voice, as if to share a secret. "We don't want to encourage him too early in the proceedings."

Professor Wallace stepped forward to take the cat from his arms. Annie noticed that there were cat hairs, too, along the hem of her sweeping black skirt. And that she wore soft leather booties and bright purple tights beneath it. Like a character from D. H. Lawrence. Or Virginia Woolf herself.

"Thank you, darling," he said. Side by side, the extremes of their physical beauty were startling. Professor Wallace all hooked nose and bun, white skin and black hair, David soft and warm-hued. One to be photographed, the other painted. Professor Wallace turned, spinning her skirts a bit, and disappeared through the door beside the server. Mr. Wallace sank to the floor once more, behind his ring of crystal goblets. "Now," he said, looking up at them both, "which one of you is from Binghamton?"

The girls exchanged a look. Grace, with her whiskey, had not allowed herself more than the last six inches of the sofa's seat and so sat somewhat hunched over her knees, more curved than she needed to be. She touched her glasses, of course, as she said, popping up a bit like a good student, "Neither of us." She touched her sweater. "I'm from Buffalo," she said. "Annie's from Long Island."

"Well, good," he said. He had picked up another piece of loo paper and was holding another glass up to the golden lamplight. "We've had two Americans from Binghamton here in the past two weeks and I think I've learned all there is to know about the place. State University," he said. "Three hours to New York."

"That would be Lydia," said Grace, the good student. She touched her index finger to her cheek, tapped it, raised her eyes to the shadowy ceiling, pantomiming thought. Then Grace pointed the index finger at Mr. Wallace. "And Kevin Larkin," she said.

He raised his eyebrows. "Right you are," he said. "Kevin. Rugby player, all taken up with Rupert Brooke."

Grace popped again. "That's right," she said.

"And Lydia," he went on. "Pretty girl. Mad for Wordsworth."

"Yes," Grace said, warming to the conversation. He was, after all, more or less sitting at her feet. Annie thought only of what a thing it would be to hear Mr. Wallace say of her, "Pretty girl." Lucky Lydia. She sipped her Chianti. She supposed it was the way it was meant to taste.

"But Buffalo," he said. "I'm not sure we've had anyone from Buffalo yet. What's it like?"

Grace was now clutching the stubby glass in both hands, leaning toward him. "Boring," she said and barked a short laugh, the ends of her blunt-cut hair swinging forward along her chin and then swinging back. She touched her glasses, returning to the more successful serious student guise. "No," she said. "It's nice, I guess. My parents like it. I have a lot of family there." She hunched a little more. Her head snapped to the right for just a second. It was a curious little tic Annie had seen in their tutorials; it meant that she felt her point was not yet made, that she knew her intelligence had not yet burned through the obscuring fog of her plain, chubby face. "It's where Dick Diver ends up in *Tender Is the Night*," she added. "It has that going for it."

Examining the row of glasses before him, Mr. Wallace raised his eyebrows when she said Dick Diver, and then placed his hands on his brown corduroy knees. It was likely that he was somewhat younger than his wife. He leaned toward her, rolling on his haunches. "And is it Fitzgerald you're mad for?" he asked. "You wouldn't be the first American to come to England to study Fitzgerald, or Hemingway. You're all mad for Hemingway as far as I can tell."

But Grace sat up a little straighter. It might have been in imitation of Professor Wallace—as much as a girl like Grace could aspire to imitate Professor Wallace. "I'm not, really," she said. And then added, "I love Spenser." She touched her glasses again and took another nip at her whiskey.

What a smile he had. While his wife's had been thin-lipped and wry, forgiving, insightful, his was warmly amused, reservedly delighted. He had, Annie was convinced, the best teeth in all of England. A boon, she thought, for the entire nation's dental gene pool. "Well, you'll be teacher's pet then," he said. "At least for Elizabeth," his smile grew a bit wider, a sparkle, at his wife's name. "Spenser's her man." Annie thought the smile more charming still if its source was not Grace's declaration but his pleasure at hearing his wife's man championed, or perhaps, more simply, the pleasure it gave him to say his wife's name.

Suddenly she found herself both fully enchanted and heartsick. To live, as these two did, in a comfortable, warmly lit room full of velvet chairs and old books, with cats and, yes—she was only just hearing it, or perhaps Professor Wallace had just put it on in another room—classical music playing softly somewhere, low enough for conversation, loud enough to add romance to the air. To reach over your knees at the end of a day, the book falling from your lap, to take such a man's handsome face into your hands. It was a life from a novel. It was a still life, beautifully arranged. It was a life she'd never attain. When he turned to her and said, "And who's your man?" she said, "Edith Wharton," without thinking and without an inkling of truth in it, her only impulse being that she should name a woman, since the life she wanted—their life—was all unattainable and she must begin to prepare herself to be a woman alone.

She glanced quickly at Grace to see if she would contradict her, but Grace had the glass to her lips again, her eyes on David Wallace. Annie imagined Grace felt it, too: the enchantment and the despair.

Professor Wallace swept into the room with a large, tufted footstool held high in her hands, like a farcical English maid with a tea tray. "Edith Wharton?" she said and then spun a little, her long skirt flaring, her little leather boots. "How interesting," and then, "David, my love," in that way she had of speaking in soft asides, "you'll have to move your glasses and your loo paper so I can put this down."

With a kind of salute, he stuck the roll of toilet paper under his arm. Leaning forward, he moved a few of the glasses, one at a time, as if they were chess pieces, to the side of the couch, and then gathered up the rest in his hands, the crystal clinking, and placed them and the paper on a side table. "Careful," she said. "Always," he told her. And then, so smoothly, he was on his feet again, taking the stool from her hands.

He lowered it to the ground. It was a maroon upholstered footstool with four wooden, turnip-shaped legs and on it were half a dozen small plates, black cloth napkins, a silver bowl of olives and celery, and a small black crock containing what Professor Wallace announced was pâté. She handed a napkin to each of the girls, smeared a tablespoon of pâté onto each little plate, added some olives and some thin crackers, all the while saying, "Although she married fairly young I think it's well accepted that she was a virgin until she was somewhere around forty-five." She gave Annie a little plate, and started putting together another. "She'd divorced her husband at last and fallen madly in love and taken up residence with her lover in Paris. Forty-five or so." She handed the plate to her husband, who was now in a small chair at Grace's side.

"It appears she wrote *Ethan Frome* while in the midst of a girlish middle-aged passion. Which has always struck me as curious, given the short shrift she gives poor Mrs. Frome, with all her middle-aged ailments."

Professor Wallace spun around again in her soft little boots and then took the other corner of the couch. Grace was smiling at her, ogling, Annie would have said. There was a lightness about Professor Wallace at home, a physical buoyancy she didn't have in the lecture hall. It made it seem possible that she was not older than her husband after all. "A lesson for you girls," she said, looking up, "in matters of the heart." She raised her long nose and trilled the word. "Patience," she said.

But David laughed. "Surely, Elizabeth," he told her, "you're not making a case for forty-five years of virginity." He smiled at both girls, full knowing, it seemed, that if there were sides to be on, they were on his. With his handsome face before them, forty-five years of virginity seemed worse than cruel. "I'd call that corrupting the morals of a minor," he said and his eyes flashed. They sparkled.

There was the sound of Grace's whiskey glass colliding with the bridge of her glasses.

Professor Wallace smiled her wry smile at her husband and then seemed to sip the air the way a bird sips water, her throat all exposed. "Surely I'm not," she said. And then she turned her head, regally. "But Annie must tell us," she whispered, "what it is about Wharton that she loves."

She felt all their eyes on her. Felt suddenly like a bird herself, a baby bird, helpless, wordless, her mouth opened. The truth was that she had read very little of Edith Wharton. Had thought, until a few minutes ago, that Edith Wharton was a spinster, homely and professional (she recalled a mannish jaw, a heavy pile of dark hair), with no exquisite husband waiting for her at home. It was the sole reason she had said her name. She had a vague memory of *Ethan Frome*, of laughing at it. Suicidal sled rides. Sex and death. She couldn't recall finishing *The Age of Innocence*.

"Oh, *Ethan Frome*," she said, shrugging a little. "*The Age of Innocence.*"

Mr. Wallace said, "No doubt you're a James fan as well."

And his wife said, "Being a James fan is de rigueur for Americans in England, I should think."

"*Portrait of a Lady,*" Grace chirped, not to be outdone. She held her stubby glass and her little plate to her clasped knees, hunching over them. "I read it again this summer," she said. "Before I came."

"He was a big poof, you know," David said and his wife cried, "Really, darling," and Grace ducked and giggled, and drank more whiskey, touching her fingertips to the edge of her glasses as she did. Gently, Professor Wallace leaned over and took the small plate from her lap and placed it on the cushion between them. And then, as if she were caring for a child, with her shoulder pressed languidly to the back of the couch, she lifted a cracker and spread it with pâté.

"Well, if we're going to bring up Edith Wharton's moldy virginity," he cried, charmingly, "then we might as well get it all out. Henry was a poof and William a religious fanatic and Alice was a sexual deviant, flummoxed by shyness, who figured the only way she could get professional men to come see her in her nightgown was by taking to her bed." He turned his attention to Grace, who was beet red behind the Waterford crystal, hunched and laughing into her ice cubes. "*Varieties of Religious Experience*, indeed," he said. "Have you read it?"

Professor Wallace gave her one of the spread crackers. "Never mind," she said gently, although Annie couldn't say if she was addressing her husband or the girl.

"A prototype for the modern American family," David said, smiling. The light from the lamp at his elbow only burnished his glow. "Hedonism plus Puritanism yields both deviant sex and deviant religion. What could be more American?" His eyes met his wife's. Annie thought that there was a complex intelligence even in their unspoken conversation. Only more to envy. To despair of. "But we were talking about Buffalo," he said, more gently. He turned again to Grace, who had just, obediently, bitten into the cracker, which had, in turn, broken apart in her hands. There was a tiny shower of crumbs falling from her lips to her palm to her sweater.

Graciously, he diverted his attention across the room. "And what of Long Island?" he asked Annie. "We seem to get as many from Long Island as from Binghamton."

She smiled. She did not want to appear flummoxed by shyness. "There's a lot of us," she said. She was aware of the fact that it was as close as she had come since she'd arrived to speaking a full sentence.

"And your parents are there?" he asked, more gentle still, luring her into a conversation. "Brothers? Sisters?" Implying that he recognized her shyness but knew it was his duty as her host to relieve her of it, as if it were only a heavy coat. "Big family? Small?"

"Small," she said. She would not make herself more interesting to him, more American, by mentioning Jacob. "A brother and a sister," she said. "An aunt who lives with us," she would not say "a moldering virgin," to prove herself clever. She took another sip of her wine. She saw that Professor Wallace was smiling at her, as if—it was all unaccountable—admiring her restraint. Then the buzzer rang downstairs and Professor Wallace stood, her skirt sweeping. "I'll get that," she said. They were in a play again. "If you'll refresh the girls' drinks."

Behind her when she returned were three more American students, two boys and a girl. Entering, they looked at Grace and Annie with some resentment, as if the ratio of Americans to English in the room suddenly made the occasion less interesting. Mr. Wallace stood, there was the bustle of introductions and new drinks. For a moment, the music disappeared. Monica and Nate were a couple—a bond they had formed at the same time Annie and Grace had formed theirs, in the five hours of pillow talk that was the transatlantic flight. Ben was, perhaps, Nate's version of Grace. A friend from their New York campus who held on to Nate perhaps a little too tightly now that they were abroad together, comfort in a strange land. He was a big guy, a little thick around the jaw, with dark curly hair. At his side he held a bottle in a brown paper bag, grasped by the neck as if he had just taken a swig of it and planned to take another. He greeted Mr. Wallace and said, "Beer would be great," before he seemed to remember it was there. Awkwardly, he handed it to Professor Wallace and she said, "Thank you," and "Lovely," as she slipped it out of the bag. "Drambuie," she said to her husband as she placed it on the server. "How nice," he said. Together, Ben and Nate made Professor Wallace's cozy living room seem smaller. They looked so starkly American, so comically American male that it seemed the room should have filled with the odor of gunsmoke and horse manure.

Beside them, David Wallace seemed not only the member of some more advanced, more refined civilization but a creature who must also be ranked a good deal higher on the phylogenetic scale.

"Sit, sit," David was saying once again. He had poured Chianti for Monica and opened bottles of beer for both boys. Grace caught Annie's eye and patted the empty cushion beside her, tilting her head, pleading, and against her better judgment, Annie stood and crossed over to sit with her friend. Monica took the velvet chair, Nate at her feet, his elbow in her lap. Ben went to another chair, a gold ladderback with a dark turquoise seat. It looked somewhat fragile under his thick thighs in their new jeans, although he declined, smiling, when David offered him his own chair beside the couch. "This is good," he said, the brown bottle held between his legs. Annie could see him regretting his decision to come along with Monica and Nate, and thought of her mother's injunction never to be a third wheel.

"Yes, well," David Wallace said as his wife distributed pâté and crackers, olives and celery to the new guests. Annie prayed that he wouldn't again mention Binghamton because she knew if he did she would think less of him. "Will there be more of you?" he asked the assemblage. "Tonight? Any more of you coming? That you know?"

The Americans looked at each other, frowning, shaking their heads. Grace offered, eagerly, that she didn't know.

"You don't consult?" Mr. Wallace said, smiling. "All you American students? It's rather remarkable to have five of you here all at once. I thought perhaps it was part of a plan."

They continued to look at one another, shaking their heads, "No," they said. It was clear the two boys were wary of Mr. Wallace; they suspected he was making fun of them.

"No, of course not, David," Professor Wallace said. "They hardly travel en masse. They're an independent bunch, our American students. Aren't you?" she said, looking around the room. "You're made to come together, what is it, once a month, to see how you're getting on, but that's it, isn't it?"

"Actually," Grace said, "it's every fortnight."

"Is it?" Professor Wallace asked.

"It's ridiculous," Nate said from Monica's knees. "I quit going."
Monica put her hand in his curly hair. She was loose-limbed, slim,
and large-breasted. Her face was plain but there was a luster about
her skin and her hair, a luster of sex and of good health. She shook
his head a little, playfully gripping his scalp. "You were at the last
one," she said in a tone that seemed to imply that the last one had
ended in some mad sexual transaction.

Grace had turned to Mr. Wallace, explaining. "Only a few of us
live in the same halls," she said, piling on the Britishisms (Annie,
stubbornly, still said dorms). "We're scattered about campus precisely so we don't stay to ourselves. It's sort of the point of the
whole program."

"And yet, here you all are," David Wallace said. "All on the
same evening."

Quietly, Professor Wallace slipped out of the room, through
the door to what Annie guessed was the kitchen. She wished for the
courage to join her, but felt the anchor of Grace, sitting beside her,
who was now saying, "Yes, isn't it funny?" and once more raising
her glass.

"Great minds think alike," Ben said, leaning over his lap on the
small chair. Whether he intended to or not, he sounded bitter.

Mr. Wallace then questioned the three about their hometowns.
Monica was from Long Island, too, and Nate from outside Albany.
Ben was from Staten Island, "A city boy," Mr. Wallace said, to
which Ben replied, with a tilt of his beer bottle, "I hate New York
City."

David Wallace nodded, touched his silk cravat. They could now
smell their dinner in the kitchen. "Unfortunate," he said, as if resisting his own disappointment in the boy. "Yet understandable. No
doubt you're a Wordsworth fellow as well," he added.

But Ben seemed to miss the connection. He glanced at Monica

and Nate before he spoke. "What's a Wordsworth fellow?" he asked.

Now David Wallace looked puzzled. "A fan," he said, as if the word were a colloquialism he wasn't quite sure of. "Of Wordsworth. Since you don't like the city, I assumed you'd be a devotee of someone like Wordsworth. The romantics. The pastoral poets."

Ben was looking at Mr. Wallace with what Annie had come to recognize as a particularly American look. He suspected Mr. Wallace was putting him on the spot and even before he'd demonstrated his own lack of knowledge, he was preparing his case for how useless what he didn't know really was. "Wordsworth's okay," he said, with some caution. "I guess. I don't know a lot about him." So fuck you, was only implied.

Mr. Wallace asked, pleasantly, "Well, what inspired you to study in England then?" and Ben laughed once, through his nose, and raised the bottle in his hand. "The beer," he said.

Nate dropped his head, amused at his friend. Monica leaned down over her lap to whisper something in his ear, her thick hair falling to shield them both.

Mr. Wallace turned to the two girls. "Well, that's honest at least," he said, although his face, Annie thought, also said he was sorry the conversation had taken such a boorish turn. He looked at both of their glasses. "Let me refresh those for you," he said, gently, and took the glasses out of their hands, out of their laps. Grace said, "Thank you," looking up at him, her throat and chin growing flushed. "It won't be long," he said, kindly. Annie knew he meant until dinner, but felt he might just as well have said, Till we're alone again, the way Grace's breath seemed to catch on the words. The way her fingers, reaching up to touch her frames, were trembling.

Just as he returned with their fresh drinks (over his shoulder, "Can I get you gentlemen another. Young lady?") Professor Wallace came through the door again with a tray stacked with dinner plates and silverware and a huge pot that filled the room with the woodsy odor of meat and mushrooms. In what struck the girls as marvelous choreography, one neither had ever seen in her own home, Mr. Wallace swung back into the kitchen and emerged with another large pot and then, without a single word of instruction between them, the two began to fill plates with pasta, to ladle sauce, to distribute plush throw pillows in silky Indian prints that seemed to appear miraculously from behind the couch. "You'll want these on your laps," Professor Wallace told the students. "To shorten the distance from plate to lips," she said. She shook out huge napkins to place over each pillow; she might have tucked another just under their chins, the way they all, suddenly, with pillows and napkins and plates of steaming food on their laps, felt swaddled, childish and also cared for.

Mr. Wallace took his place beside Grace again, with only a napkin, no pillow on his knee. Professor Wallace made the rounds with a small glass dish and a tiny silver spoon, sprinkling *parmigiana* like fairy dust over each plate.

Then she sat with her own next to Annie.

"This is delicious," Monica said. Nate had abandoned her knee and her lap and was hunched now over his plate. He may even have moved away from her a bit. "Oh God," he said, looking up. There was a fleck of sauce on his chin. "So good." It was a kind of moan. "The food in hall is so freaking bad."

Professor Wallace smiled. "Poor dears," she said. "I'm sure it takes some getting used to."

Beside Annie, Grace was struggling with plate and pillow and fork and the stubby glass she still held in her hand and just as Annie was about to suggest she put it down, Mr. Wallace leaned over and took it from her and put it gently on the small table at her elbow. "There," he said softly. "Easier to manage." And Grace touched her glasses and nodded and said, "Thank you." Now her skin flushed up over her chin and down, Annie noticed, the length of her plump, pale arms.

David Wallace was questioning them again. "Where are you going and where have you been?" he asked. Monica and Nate had been to Stratford and Bath and London. Annie and Grace to London and Stonehenge. Ben would be joining his parents in Dublin over Christmas. The girls wanted to get to Brontë country, of course. Ben's father wanted him to visit the village near Dover where he had been stationed during the war. Nate was hoping to get to Pamplona in the spring. (Mr. Wallace turned to Grace and said, "Hemingway, you see," as if it were an old joke they had long shared. He lifted her plate, and then her glass from the small table. Took both away and then returned with her glass once again full.)

When all the plates had been cleared, Professor Wallace brought a tray of fruit and cheese and placed it on the footstool, serving them again, this time using small plates painted with branches and birds. She recommended the Rambling Club at the university to all the American students. A lovely and inexpensive way to see the countryside. She would suggest, she said, kneeling among them, slicing a ripe pear, finding a focus for your travels. Historical, literary. Lawrence walked through the Pyrenees looking for roadside crucifixes. Read his essay. An American student once followed the route of Eleanor of Aquitaine. Another made a trip to the Hebrides, for Virginia Woolf's sake.

"Something like that," Professor Wallace said. She proffered the slices of ripe pear, the Americans reached for them, childish, Annie thought, grateful. Nate had scooted farther away from Monica, across the Turkish rug to the footstool. Closer to the food, but also to Professor Wallace's feet.

"It's nice to have a focus," Professor Wallace said, taking the couch next to Annie once again. "It's nice to see a pattern emerge out of travels that might, otherwise, seem random." She turned to Annie, looked at her down her long nose, kindly, fondly, perhaps. "You might follow in Wharton's footsteps, for instance," she said. "Find that hotel in Paris where she was so thoroughly happy."

"So thoroughly shagged," David said, and only Grace laughed with him, her blush having settled in permanently now. He looked at the other men in the room. "We were discussing it earlier," he said. "She'd been a married virgin, Edith Wharton." He turned to his wife. "Until what age, Elizabeth? Forty-five?"

Annie saw Professor Wallace put her fingertips, forefinger and thumb, to a crescent of pear on her plate and hold them there, as if, briefly, measuring something. "That's right," she said without raising her head. Then she leaned a little into Annie, there was a hint of perfume on her velvet shawl. "Poor David," she whispered and then, looking up, she said across the two girls. "My dear, I'm afraid your mind has been in that hotel room all evening."

He threw back his head and shouted a laugh. "It has!" he said. "Isn't it odd?" Now Professor Wallace was laughing, softly. If Annie hadn't been sitting beside her, feeling the laughter through the velvet shawl, she would not have known that was what she was doing. On her face, there was only that wry smile. David made a gesture that encompassed the room. "Three young beauties here for dinner and I'm a voyeur in some Parisian hotel room, wondering what it was like. I mean, at forty-five, Elizabeth. Think of it."

"It was just as it would have been at twenty-five," Professor Wallace said warmly, and now another kind of mad, sexual transaction was implied. The Americans suddenly felt they had vanished from the room. Monica had Runty in her lap and she paused with both her hands in the cat's fur. Nate on the floor, an elbow on his raised knee, held a forgotten piece of cheddar in his hand. Ben bowed his head, as if in deference to some sweet intimacy, and Grace—Annie was sure of it—raised a knuckle to her glasses to hide a tear. "She was in love, darling," Professor Wallace said softly. "I can tell you without hesitation what it was like. It was marvelous."

David Wallace smiled at his wife. It wasn't an imaginary hotel room he was thinking of now. "I'm sure," he said. "I'm sure you're right."

After the fruit and the cheese, there was a chocolate gâteau and the box of candy the girls had brought, and Ben's Drambuie. Professor Wallace ran the small glass of it under her nose and closed her eyes and then told them that when she was a child her grandmother had kept a decanter of Drambuie on the table in the front hall. During the war, she said, after they'd been down in the cellar for an air raid, she and her cousins, who had also been sent to the safer distance of their grandparents' little farm, would come up the stairs and into the hall, where their grandmother would give them each a teaspoonful of the liqueur, to reward them, or to prepare them for sleep, or only, perhaps, to steady her own nerves. Professor Wallace closed her eyes and put her lips to the glass. "It comes back," she said after she had drunk. "That time." She opened her eyes. "We would wrap ourselves in blankets and dressing gowns. In anticipation, I suppose, of shattered glass. My grandmother would divide us into groups of three, two children and an adult, my grandfather, my mother, herself, my aunt. Each adult with a child under each arm, scattered to different corners of the cellar, in case." She sighed. "In case, I suppose, some part of the ceiling came down, not, one would hope, on us all." She paused again. Annie recalled her own family, huddled in the basement, long ago. Milk that tasted like candles in their mouths. A tree had fallen. Forever after, Jacob had kept a flashlight by his bed.

"You must have been scared to death," Monica said.

Professor Wallace shrugged. "I was very young," she said, as if to acknowledge that the memory might be flawed. "I don't recall being frightened at all, only thrilled. By the adventure. Even when we could hear the bombs, the whistle and the long silence—the worst part of it, people have said, that terrible silence before the impact—I don't know that I ever cried."

"Brave girl," David said. But Professor Wallace shook her head.

"It wasn't real, to a child," she said. "The danger wasn't real. You're all sensations at that age, aren't you? The smell of the cellar and my grandfather's pipe smoke on his clothes. Oh," she said and touched her jaw, "and the satin collar of my dressing gown. That's what I remember. My cousins and I would look across the darkness at one another as if to say, Isn't this something, what do you think will happen next? The way we might have glanced at each other in the middle of a film or a play." She ran the small glass under her nose again. "And then the teaspoon of Drambuie. Like a little jewel. I'd hold it in my mouth for as long as I could." She took another sip, pursing her lips and drawing down her long nose. "It comes back," she said again.

They were all watching her, even her husband. Enchanted by her, her voice and gesture, and as if she suddenly noticed this, noticed how they were all watching her, even her husband, she raised the little glass and grimaced, freeing them from the spell she herself had cast. "What can be more tedious," she said with a laugh, "than someone else's childhood?"

"It's kind of disgusting," Nate said from the floor, and for a moment they all believed he was agreeing with her. He looked up. "How long it took the United States to notice you guys were getting the shit bombed out of you by Hitler."

"Really," Monica said, agreeing, shaking her hair. "We knocked ourselves out to save bloody Vietnam but we sat back while London got blitzed."

Beside Annie, Grace raised her own little glass, gulping the

Drambuie as if she had to catch a train. She had, Annie knew, no interest in politics or current events. In their tutorials she had announced more than once that history had meaning for her only as far as it pertained to *Henry V* or *A Tale of Two Cities*. On its own, she had said, it was all circumstance and repetition, temporal, not eternal. No more significant than the weather.

"Nixon sucks," Ben was saying.

"LBJ sucked, too," Monica added.

From across the room, Ben said, "Spiro Agnew."

Both Professor Wallace and her husband were nodding, tolerantly, as if the Americans were merely complaining about their parents.

"At least in World War II we knew what we were fighting for," Monica went on, as if, Annie thought, she and General Eisenhower were contemporaries. "At least there was Hitler."

"At least," Ben said, "we won."

Grace touched her glasses and then dug her elbow into Annie's side. She put a hand to her mouth and whispered from behind it. "Come with me." Annie stared straight ahead for a second. What an effect it would have on the assembly, she thought, were she to say, "My brother." But she felt David Wallace's eyes on them as Grace poked her again. "Please," she said and stood quickly, swaying a little as she did, in the narrow space between the couch and the big footstool. Against her will, Annie stood, too. They both sidestepped past the couch and between the small table with the lamp and Mr. Wallace's knees. Gallantly, he held a hand out to Grace as she made her way around him. She touched it briefly. Before either girl thought to ask, Professor Wallace told them, "It's just through that door there, first on the right."

Annie followed Grace into the small bathroom. She shut the door behind them both and leaned back against it. "Are you going to get sick?" she asked. Grace nodded. She was already heaving a

bit, hyperventilating, her glasses fallen down her nose and her pale
skin greenish behind the spilled red of her flush. Annie leaned forward to lift the toilet seat. She stepped back again. "I'm here,"
Annie said, imitating her mother. Grace leaned down, heaved a bit,
then knelt and vomited her dinner into the toilet. Annie turned her
head away, and then, reluctantly, stepped closer to the girl to hold
back her hair. Grace's neck at the nape was thick, her hair thin and
almost weightless in Annie's hands. "You're okay," Annie said.
This, too, was what her mother said to her sick children. "You're
okay."

When she had finished, Grace flopped back onto the tile floor,
and Annie could tell by the way her body fell that she was ready to
give up all pretense of sobriety or control, that it was not merely
drunken spinning that made her collapse, but a long-awaited giving
in to despair. She pulled off her glasses, dumped them in her lap,
gulped some air, and then, unabashedly, her legs folded in front of
her, her arms limp at her side, she began to cry.

Annie flushed the toilet and turned the water on in the sink. The
guest towels were starched linen, old-fashioned and neat. There
was a ceramic clamshell with a small cake of fragrant soap. She wet
some loo paper, making a compress of it, and handed it to Grace.
"Put this to your lips," she said. "It will make you feel better."

But Grace merely held it in her hand, the hand still in her lap.
She let her head fall back against the wall, the tears falling freely.
"Oh, God," she said. "Oh, God." Her shoulders were shaking with
her sobs. Her face was terrible, the pale, myopic eyes and the torn
mouth, the short forehead and the bloated cheeks. "I love him," she
said. "I'm so in love with him."

Annie smiled a little. "Oh, come on," she said, gently, the way
you do, the way she'd done before, to a drunken girl crying. "You
don't love him."

But Grace put her fist to her soft stomach, and then to the space between her breasts, as if the love were lodged there and so there was no denying it. "You don't understand," she said, sobbing. "I've never had a boyfriend, nothing, no one. I'm ugly and stupid and fat."

"You're not," Annie said. She crouched down beside her. "You're pretty, you're brilliant."

But Grace pressed her fist into her breast as if it were a dagger, leaning over it to bring her face to Annie's face. There were wet flecks of her dinner at the corners of her lips. "You don't understand," she said, ferociously, her eyes both furious and oddly unfocused—or focused, perhaps, on something other than what she saw. She was grimacing, showing her teeth. Annie would not have been surprised if she had punched her. "I'm lonely," she said; she seemed to extract the words from the place her fist had pierced. "I'm completely lonely." She slowly tilted her head in that gesture of hers: she wasn't making herself clear. Her eyes were a blur of tears. "I'm lonely," she said a third time, and then collapsed back again, into her tears.

After some minutes, Professor Wallace rapped at the door and asked, through it, "Is everything all right?" Annie said, "Yes, thank you," and Professor Wallace asked, gently, "May I come in?"

Annie began to stand, but Grace grabbed her wrist, looked at her through her red eyes, and then let her go. Annie opened the door and began to say, "Grace isn't feeling too well," when Professor Wallace looked beyond her to Grace on the floor and said, "My dear girl."

She was in the room, touching Grace's forehead, then helping her to stand. Grace was still crying but more gently now, as Professor Wallace said, "Silly girl," and led her out. The other Americans had left and all signs of dinner had been cleared away and the couch she and Grace had been sitting on was now made up into a bed, fresh floral sheets and a comforter and a blanket and a crisp-looking pillow.

"Well, you're not the first," Professor Wallace was saying, getting Grace to kick off her shoes. "My husband is known to be a bit liberal when he pours. Poor girl."

Annie stood by the velvet chair as Professor Wallace pulled back the sheet and fluffed the pillow for Grace, who was still crying but seemed weak with it now, not ferocious. "He's so beautiful," Grace said, a cartoon drunk. "You're both so beautiful."

"Yes, well," Professor Wallace said. "Drink will do that." She glanced at Annie, perhaps to assess how sober she was. "If I don't keep an eye on him, my husband will get everyone who enters blind drunk. He believes he alleviates suffering."

There was a satin bathrobe thrown over the back of the velvet chair, but Professor Wallace didn't mention it as she guided Grace onto the couch, between the sheets in her clothes. Grace crawling in like a weary child. "I'm so in love with him," she said as her head touched the pillow, but now she said it as if he were merely a character in a novel, as if the love were merely a source of comfort and delight. Merely a part of the delight she felt at the moment, with Professor Wallace shushing her like a child and touching her face. "Silly girl," she said again. "Is the room still spinning?" Grace, the good student once again, shook her head. "Only a little."

"There's a basin here," she said, and indicated the ceramic bowl at her feet. "If you're sick to your stomach."

Grace smiled a little, her cheek to the pillow. "Thank you," she said.

Professor Wallace looked down at her, almost fondly, and said again, "Silly girl." She turned to Annie. "I can set up a cot for you if you'd like to stay as well. You're more than welcome."

But Annie shook her head. It wasn't that late, she said. She'd get the bus.

"David will walk you down," Professor Wallace said and as if on cue, David appeared in the far doorway, creeping softly into the room. "Everything all right?" he asked. He looked over the back of the couch to Grace, who Annie knew was only pretending to sleep. "Poor child," he said, and Annie was certain Grace smiled.

David Wallace walked her to the bus stop, offering her a cigarette as he did. They stood smoking together as they waited. In the wet lamplight, with his collar turned up, he was even more handsome. He chided himself for pouring Grace too many whiskeys, and then praised Annie for handling her wine. "She leans on you a bit, does Grace," he said gently. "You're kind to be good to her." Annie shrugged. At the end of the street there was a large crescent moon, rolled over on its back. She was thousands of miles from home, across a vast ocean, out on a wet night in a strange country, and standing next to a beautiful man whom, in another life, she would have loved. He threw the cigarette into the street as the bus approached. "Or good to be kind," he said softly, "whichever you prefer." He smiled at her and she smiled back. He waited until she had taken her seat inside before he turned to walk away, back to the house and the room with the books and the cats and the music and the rugs, pâté and Chianti, and a woman whose name alone lights up his handsome face. And Grace, tonight and tomorrow morning when she woke, snug in the middle of it all. No matter who leans on whom, Annie thought, it was Grace who, tonight, had gotten what she wanted.

She put her head against the cold window. She had said Edith Wharton because she saw herself as a woman alone, square-jawed and mannish, making do, but she had been wrong. Edith Wharton had been both married and then, at a later date, madly in love. But it hardly mattered. She had seen tonight that she was a woman alone because their life was the one she wanted and she couldn't have it. She could imitate: she could adopt Professor Wallace's wry smile, she could fill her rooms with books and cats, she could find a man with ginger hair, but it would all be just that, an imitation, a diminished version of the unattainable original. Elizabeth and David Wallace themselves, precisely, was what she wanted: his eyes looking over her knees, her clever mind. Their exact lives in that exact place, not some substitute, and suddenly she found her eyes filling with childish tears, like Grace's tears, tears of utter, miserable despair.

It was a despair she already understood because she had also, once, wanted a life with both her brothers in it.

Suddenly, a boy slid into the seat beside her. He was scruffy-looking, a sparse beard over his pale cheeks, long hair, a long black coat. She had seen him as she got on, his feet up on the seat beside him, his back to the window and his eyes closed; she had instinctively avoided sitting opposite him. He leaned into her. "Are you all right?" he said. Aww right. She looked at him over her shoulder. His eyes were black with long lashes. He smelled heavily of cigarette smoke and beer.

"I'm fine," she said. There was a single tear caught on the edge of her lid and speaking made it fall. She felt it on her cheek and then her chin but didn't bother wiping it away.

He seemed to watch her for a few seconds and then shrugged. "Whatever it is," he said, "it's not worth crying over." She had begun to recognize the flat sounds of a Midlands accent. He raised his left arm to grab the handrail on the back of the seat in front of them. It became a wall over which they spoke. A safe distance. "Trust me." She was surprised to see that his fingernails were clean, everything else about him seemed so dirty.

Looking straight ahead, he asked her if she was going back to the university and she said yes. He asked her which hall she lived in and when she told him, he grimaced. "Kind of a convent," he said. She said, for lack of anything else, "I suppose." And then he turned his face toward hers, grinning, his arm still between them but their faces as close as strangers could comfortably get. His skin beneath the patchy beard was a bluish white and his face was probably childish without it. His teeth were small. "Speaking of sex," he said, "I was wondering if I could convince you," he leaned down to look out into the dark street, "in three more stops, to have a drink with me."

She turned toward the window; they were still on the residential streets that made up the wasteland between the university and the city. "Where?" she said.

"At my flat," he said. He was drunk, but she couldn't tell by how much.

She shook her head. "I don't think so."

Now he leaned his shoulder against hers, brought his lips closer to her ear. "I have books," he said and then drew back a little, raising his eyebrows. He might have said caviar or Moroccan gold. "Not just books," he said. "Fucking literature. T. S. Eliot, Pound, Byron, Coleridge," he said, as if each one made him more irresistible. "Who do you like? Christina Rossetti? Elizabeth Barrett Browning? You've got Professor Wallace, I take it. I saw her husband put you on the bus. Sir Philip Sydney, perhaps? I've got novels, too. All the big guys. Tolstoy. Or plays? Euripides, if you like. Shakespeare, of course. Fantasy? Christian allegory. I've got Tolkien and C. S. Lewis. I've got . . ." The bus stopped and he leaned across her lap to look again through the window. His long hair was tangled here and there, a little dusty-looking. "Two more stops to talk you into it," he said.

He sat up and brought his face closer to hers. "It's too early for either of us to go home," he said. "All alone." His eyes, bloodshot, looked right into hers, steadily enough, although his lids were at half-mast. He brushed a knuckle to her cheek. "And all tearful," he said.

She said, "It's almost midnight," more flatly than she had intended, sounding, she thought, like Grace. He watched her for a few more seconds. His lips were full and smooth inside the scruffy beard. Then he shrugged and dropped his arm. He slumped down in the seat beside her. She turned to look out the window. The passing, narrow houses, many of them dark, one or two with single lights burning. She recalled how Pauline had fallen off a bus one night, late, went skidding into Creedmoor. In a novel, it would have portended the fall they were all about to take.

They rode together in silence for a few minutes. He let himself be jostled against her in his dark coat. "One more," he said at the next stop.

Her eyes fell on his hands, British pale, especially under the dark sleeve of his coat, but soft-looking, faintly freckled. Edith Wharton had been a married virgin until she was forty-five, but Annie hadn't thought to ask Professor Wallace how anyone knew this. Was it something Wharton wrote about or was there some sexual autopsy performed at her death? Pauline, under her mother's care, had made her first visit to a gynecologist just last year. The doctor had said he'd broken her hymen to do the exam. Her mother couldn't understand why he hadn't kept that information to himself, and Annie had said, unkindly, "I might have asked the same about you, Mother."

She said to him, falling, skidding. "I haven't had sex with anyone since high school."

He smiled without turning to her. The bus was pulling to the curb. "High time, then," he said.

Walking into his tiny apartment, there was a moment when she stood in the dark as he paused behind her, leaning to turn on a small lamp. All the strangeness, and the danger, of what she was doing

appeared to her then, she even felt herself bracing for a blow, or—
in this land of Jack the Ripper—a cold blade to the back of her
neck. She felt a moment's pity for her parents. And then, oddly
enough, for Grace, who would be the first to come to her room tomorrow, whenever she freed herself from the Wallaces', Grace who
would be the first to know that Annie had not come home. But then
the light came on. The room was cluttered with tossed clothes and
empty teacups, papers and books (he was a doctoral student, she'd
later learn, in engineering, not literature, although the apartment
was indeed filled with hundreds of soft Penguin editions that he
would later toss on the bed where she lay, like so many pastel rose
petals). It was in its strangeness and in its familiarity an illustration
of someone else's life going on in its own way, steeped in itself, its
own business, its own dailyness, its own particular sorrow or joy, all
of it more or less predictable. It made him both less threatening and
less interesting. He was as ordinary as anyone she knew. She turned
around. He took her face in his hands.

On the five-hour flight over, she had told Grace, quite simply, a
younger sister and a brother, and felt the information trail off into
the darkness below them—the black ocean, the curved earth, the
empty space through which the plane was moving them, away from
all that and into another time as well as another place. She would
not, she knew, recalling Professor Wallace's wry smile, be the first
American student to seek to remake herself in her year abroad.

The boy was thin and pale and startlingly comfortable out of his
clothes. He remained consistently comic in response to both her reticence and her ardor. He did a funny bit, a kind of magic trick with
condom as coin, that she suspected was a well-rehearsed routine.
He pulled the books from his shelves and tossed them onto the bed
like so many pastel-colored rose petals and then climbed over them
to land in her lap. When some of the tissue-thin pages tore, he
pulled the damaged copies out from under them and set each on the

floor. He said she should take the worst of them home with her. "And when you're old and gray," he said, "and nodding by the fire, you can take down this book and say, 'What is this funny stain on this wrinkled page?' "

When the sun came up, merely a lightening at the single window, a shaded version of the gray that would mark the full day, he let his head fall back, one arm under her neck, the other stretched to the edge of the mattress. His body was white and thin and boyish, it might indeed have been carved out of marble. As if it were carved out of marble, she thought there was beauty in it as well as tremendous sorrow. Because of Jacob, she knew, she would for the rest of her life see the bodies of young men in this way—lovers, husband, her own children, if she were to have them. It was not what she wanted to do, but she had no choice in the matter, it was no longer the life she had wanted, after all.

On the mattress between them, at their feet and over their heads, were the scattered paperbacks. One was pressed uncomfortably into his side, spine up, just under his ribs, and she reached out to pull it out from under him. She held it up to the light, it was Malory's *Morte d'Arthur*. She laughed out loud, thinking of Susan: sex and death. Fucking literature. Playfully, she placed the open book on his chest. He stirred a little and then, gently, brushed it away.

With the changing light, the room seemed to grow more familiar. She was thousands of miles from home with an utter stranger at her side and yet she was falling into a pleasant, comfortable sleep, she was anticipating, with pleasure, perhaps, what the new day would bring. There was, there would always be, the snag of disappointment—it would not be the life she had wanted—but there was, at last, as well, something it would take her until the end of the year to begin to understand. At the end of the year, when she moved to London with him, quitting school, quitting home, dealing her parents (it could not be helped) another blow, she would recall the story Professor Wallace had told them that night, she would begin to see the wisdom of it—the wisdom of scattering, each to a different corner of whatever shelter they had found, so that should the worst happen, happen again, it would not take them all.

TONY PERSICHETTI got religion—or religions, his sister said. He'd spent some months on an ashram in Pennsylvania, a few more with some Krishnas in New York, then traveled across Europe with a Brooklyn girl and ended up on a kibbutz where his whole day was spent, he'd said, shoveling chicken shit. And where, inexplicably (mixing his religious metaphors, Susan said), he shaved his head.

Michael Keane laughed. "Sounds like Tony," he said.

And then home again, thin and weather-beaten, looking more like a convict than an aesthete. He came into her room and ran a hand down one of the wood panels he had helped their father to install, pressed it gently inward and withdrew a small plastic bag of brittle hash. "I've been thinking about this, waiting here for me, for months," he said.

"Did you think about Mom and Dad," Susan asked him. "You stupid fuck. They were waiting here for you, too."

Not to say that that did the trick, Susan told Michael Keane, but the next Sunday night, Tony cleaned himself up and went out and came back some hours later and called them all into the living room, his mother and father, Susan herself who was only home for the weekend because the prodigal had once again returned and her parents had begged her to help welcome him. He announced that he was an alcoholic. That he'd just gone to his first AA meeting. And that with God's help and theirs, he would get his life together at long last.

Susan couldn't help it, she told Michael, this back and forth with Tony had been going on for so long. The crazy Vietnam-vet cliché had worn pretty thin. "Do you have any particular God in mind?" she'd said.

The AA meetings were held at St. Gabriel's, in the basement cafeteria. Tony had breathed in a lungful of his old grammar-school air and found God again. Or God found him, there where he had hunkered down with his bologna sandwiches as a kid. Easier, he said, to pick up an old belief than to talk yourself into a new one. Now he began his day with 6:30 Mass, then went to the job his father had gotten him at Creedmoor, an office thing, then took classes at Queens College. He was headed for a master's in social work. He was dating a girl he'd met at school.

Her parents, she said, were holding their breaths, not yet certain, it seemed, that the troubled Vietnam-vet thing was something they could say was finally over.

"And you?" she asked. They were in a bar on the East Side, they were being jostled, backs and arms, by the after-work crowd. He told her he had a job at a Catholic school, in Brooklyn, seventh grade. He said the pay was lousy but the kids were great. "Déjà vu all over again," he said. He was sharing an apartment in the city with three friends from school. "Finally," he said, "out of the basement."

And because she knew the story, she said, "How's crazy Pauline?"

Susan was blonder than he'd remembered her, prettier, too. He added, "I'm thinking of going to law school," not sure yet if it were true.

Susan said, "The guy I live with goes to law school. NYU. It's good."

Michael nodded. His roommates were spread around the room, the familiar hunt for connections.

"He knows you," she said. "You caddied together one summer. He was in high school. You were home from college."

"This is a high-school sweetheart?" Michael said.

She slowly closed her eyes, smiled a drawn smile. "A re-acquaintance," she said. Begun when he had called her, out of the blue, to say, "There was a rumor when we were in high school and I wonder if it's true." Jill O'Meara's name was mentioned. Susan's eyes, when she opened them, were darker still. "Sometimes it's easier to pick up an old boyfriend than to talk yourself into a new one."

"A pickup, then," Michael said, and recognized his father's sense of humor.

"A serious relationship," she said coyly to disguise what a complicated thing it was, her life with this boy.

Michael raised his glass. "Good for you."

"Annie seems happy," Susan said, an apology for not being free, because she liked Michael Keane, would have loved to go out with him when, as she thought of it, she was young. "She likes it over there."

"She really does," Michael said. For the first time since they saw each other, he looked beyond her, toward the other women in the room.

"And Clare's good?" she said. "Still at dear old Mary Immaculate Academy?"

"One more year," he said. "Then college."

"Your parents will miss her."

But Michael shook his head. "They're already planning their golden years in Florida. Though God knows what they'll do with Pauline."

"Poor Pauline," Susan said.

And now their eyes met again, a prelude to separating once more.

Michael had an impulse to say—so simple—and Jacob's teaching, too, out on Long Island. Better at it than I am. Over at last, that crazy-vet thing. (Or no, he amended the tale—Sorry, Jacob): Never really did do that crazy-vet thing. Whatever was terrible over there kept to himself, the blanket pulled up over the shoulder, the head turned to the wall. The courage it took, for a kid so fearful, to keep so much to himself.

Jacob's fine, he had an impulse to say. And for just a second there would be the misapprehension on her face, for just a second, the solid past would loosen its grip. Jacob's same as always. Too nice. Married Lori Ballinger. A couple of beautiful kids yet to be born.

"It was good to see you, Michael," Susan said.

He bent down to kiss her cheek. "Good to see you, too," he said. "Say hi to Tony."

And then walked away with it written all over his face—his friends said later, kidding him—disappointment, the failure to connect, the sorrow of a lost opportunity.

CLARE KEANE returned to school that fall looking grown up. That's how some of the teachers put it. "You've grown up." Not that this was surprising to them, especially the older of them who had been witness to it for decades: the bony freshman come back as mature young woman for senior year—the time in between seeming no more, they told one another September after September, than the blink of an eye. Clare was only a little taller, and, like most of the girls, freckled and tanned, streaks of sun in her reddish brown hair. Her braces had come off—there was that difference. But there was also the way she carried herself. She had lost—one of the Sisters confided to a lay teacher and the lay teacher heartily agreed—that childish look she used to wear, wide-eyed and eager to please. She'd always been smart enough, there was no doubt about that, but there had also been about her an air of innocence that belonged, perhaps, to an earlier time, an air of innocence that in this day and age—even the Sisters said it—seemed to indicate a lack of depth.

But this fall there was a new quickness in her eye and the range of her emotions did not seem limited in its illustration to a wide smile or a solemn frown. She laughed more. She socialized with some of the more troublesome and popular girls. She had learned, apparently, over the course of what she described to everyone who

asked her as the best summer of her life, that there was a hierarchy
to her interests and her pleasures after all. Although there was still
something childish about her body, especially in the outdated shirtwaist dress that had been for too long now the school's summer uniform, there was, also, finally, an assuredness in her movements that
had not been there before. She had found a boyfriend this summer.
(Of course of course, the teachers, even the nuns told each other,
indulgent and naïve. Those who had been at the school when
Annie was a student said, with a shrug, Life goes on.) His name was
Gregory Joseph. She wore his heavy high-school ring on a gold
chain around her neck.

It had been a setup. Gregory had just finished his freshman year
at Marist College in upstate New York. His older sister, who had
been a senior at Ladycliff College, had spent most of that year
"keeping tabs" on her little brother, driving over on weekends to
surprise him in his dorm, calling him at odd hours, or sending
friends who were going that way to fetch him for Sunday brunch or
a Friday-night hamburger. From all that she could see, he had ad-
justed well to college life—he had always been to her a gentle giant,
a sweet and quiet kid whose size, from an early age, had promised
athletic prowess but whose coordination had never delivered it. Her
friends and roommates all thought him adorable, but it became
clear over the course of the year that his own social life was limited
to these visits from her and occasional weekend tagalongs to bars
and dances and rock concerts with his more sociable and hard-
drinking friends. A mere continuation, as she saw it, of his dateless
high-school days. "Never had a date," she would tell her friends
who had praised his sweetness and his shy affability. "He's going to
be *nineteen*." At the faltering Ladycliff, where the few recently enrolled male students were mostly pudgy or gaunt young men on
their way into or out of the seminary, and where nearby West Point
was the fount of romance (MPs being easier pickings than the

sometimes snotty cadets), this became a subject of many late-night studies. A blind date was in order, they concluded, but how, and with whom. Finally, sometime in second semester when a late-season snowstorm kept them all in their dorm rooms with endless bowls of buttered popcorn, Betty Kelly who lived down the hall offered up her "little cousin" Clare, who also lived on Long Island, also went to Catholic school, and had never, as far as Betty knew, had a date either.

Betty Kelly was very pretty. Even with the three feet of snow that covered the steep and winding streets of the college, and hermetically sealed the girls' dorm against the possibility of an impromptu visit from an ardent male, she resisted the day's call to slovenliness and remained impeccably well groomed. She was a senior, and engaged to a cadet. She was to be married at West Point in June, after graduation, and she would see her little cousin then, she told the girls, at her wedding.

When Betty Kelly was inclined to be kind, she thought the reconciliation with Clare's family was an indication of her mother's best nature. Betty had been fifteen at the time. At the back of the huge round church, she had watched her mother put her arms around the uncle who had lost the boy, the uncle who was only a pale stoop-shouldered version of the man in her mother's wedding photos. She had seen him close his eyes in her mother's embrace, as if it was just what he needed. There had been two other cousins that day, a boy and a girl, both older than Betty and both alternately sullen and weepy, surrounded by a changing orbit of identical friends. Only Clare was approachable, and back at the small house, Betty had sat next to her, introduced herself, and then, eventually, had taken her hand. The photographs of Jacob, the cousin she had never met, made him seem young, and, she'd told Clare, very nice. Even at fifteen, Betty believed her attractiveness came with an obligation to be good, and she had thought, that day, that both she and her mother had succeeded quite well in being beautiful and good.

But when Betty Kelly was feeling disinclined to be kind, she knew that the death of the boy in Vietnam had actually made his family more socially acceptable to her mother, more interesting at least, and that the sudden reconciliation was as motivated by her mother's desire to be an insider to the tragedy as much as it was by any pity she felt for the family's pain. Rather than expose the shallow roots of her own social history, Jacob Keane's family now provided her mother with a certain moral authority when the war was discussed with her Garden City set, few of whom knew anyone who had even served, much less died, over there. Her uncle's old car in the driveway when the family came for dinner was no longer an indication to the neighbors of a less than illustrious pedigree, but of a sympathetic noblesse oblige. This was the family, after all, who had lost a boy in Vietnam, so close to the end, and Catherine Kelly was doing what she could for them.

Betty Kelly wondered, too, from time to time, if both her mother's sympathy for the family and the satisfaction she felt at being able to display that sympathy were equally real. Preparing now to be a military wife herself, she had, on occasion, mentioned Jacob to her future in-laws, without ever adding that she and her soldier cousin had never actually met. She had seen the advantage the connection gave her; she had, to be honest with herself, savored it, without for a minute feeling any less pain for poor Clare and the gray-haired parents who were left to raise her.

The blind date, it was agreed—all the girls in the discussion warming to the possibilities—would be arranged by saying that Gregory/Clare had just broken up with his/her girlfriend/boyfriend and wanted to meet someone new. This would eliminate, it was agreed, any hint that either one of them was a loser who'd never had a date, while at the same time taking off some of the pressure to be charming that might move either one of them, shy souls both, toward total catatonia. "Just tell them it's not really a date," one of the girls offered. "They just want to have someone to talk to while they're between serious relationships."

"Just a friend," Gregory's sister said, nodding, and all the other girls in the circle of T-shirts and pajama bottoms and fuzzy slippers echoed the phrase with such wistful enthusiasm it might have been a refrain from their own prayers. "Just a friend."

Gregory's sister, who was in awe of, and a little in love with, Betty Kelly and her clean hair and pink nails and turquoise jogging suit—not to mention the diamond in its Tiffany setting—pictured Clare as a younger, shyer version of her cousin; a willowy beauty who her brother would love instantly, cherish like a delicate bird in his soft big hands: an incongruous but perfect pair.

Betty, who knew her cousin and had met Gregory in the Lady-cliff dining hall, thought more along the lines of beggars can't be choosers. At her wedding reception, with her train pinned up and her veil pushed aside, she drew Clare's arm across her beaded waist and walked her to a corner of the room. She whispered, "Would you do me a favor? Would you go out with this boy I know?" From the corner of her eye, Betty saw her new mother-in-law in her raw silk suit smiling at the two of them, making note—Betty was sure of it—that this was the cousin who had lost her brother in the war, making note of the sweet special attention Betty was giving her.

For Clare, the rapidly accumulating number of "firsts" that her blind date marked became a mantra for the entire summer: first time she talked to a boy on the phone (to set up the time and to give directions); first time she shopped for something to wear on a date; first time she showered and washed her hair and dressed for a date; first time she heard the doorbell rung by a date while she was still getting ready upstairs; first time she heard her father say, "How do you do," to a boy at the door, heard her mother's "Nice to meet you Gregory," and the self-consciously soft, mellifluous call up the stairs, "Clare"—not the usual sweetie pie or baby doll or Clare de Lune—"your date is here." First time she came down the stairs to greet a boy in the living room (first time in these new shoes, too, which were wooden-soled sandals all the girls were wearing but which she had not gotten the toe-gripping hang of yet). First time she laid eyes on him: a big guy (that was good) in neat shorts and Top-Siders (that was good) and a polo shirt and with not too long hair—all good. First time she said, "Hi," and he said, "Hi," before both of them let their eyes drop to the floor. First time her mother and father both moved forward to sweep her out the door by the side of a strange young man. First time she looked up to see Pauline at her brothers' window, giving a brief wave. First time he opened the car door for her (good) of his father's Ford Torino (okay) and got in the driver's side, and before turning the ignition leaned his head toward the steering wheel and said to her, smiling a little and from under a falling shock of his brown hair, "Hi again." First time he made her laugh.

He pulled smoothly out of the driveway and drove to the movie theater with an easy confidence. He repeated, gamely, what they both already knew ("So your cousin knows my sister from Ladycliff and my sister told your cousin all about me and your cousin told my sister all about you . . ."), leaving out, from sheer awkwardness, the part about Clare having broken up with an old boyfriend, as well as, from sheer tact, his sister's description of Clare as beautiful. He could not have been more pleased to discover that the latter, which had caused his hand to tremble when he raised it to her doorbell, was inaccurate. He could not have been this charming, he was certain, as he pulled into a parking space and opened her door for her with a bow, had it been true.

First time to find herself among the denizens of date night—

a newly discovered time of day lit by streetlight and movie mar-
quee and scented with aftershave and patchouli and popcorn and
spearmint gum. First time to sit beside a boy at a movie, to make
small talk before it begins ("So, do you want to go to Ladycliff?"),
sharing a tub of popcorn, elbows touching on the single armrest
which she had always, until now, thought unnecessarily stingy. First
time to laugh, in this new society of her dating peers, when someone cried out, "Start the fucking movie already," and the whole of
the theater erupted in applause.

They went to the diner after. He ordered a cheeseburger platter
and she, demurely, a grilled cheese on whole wheat. In his car in
front of her house, he put his arm across the back of the seat as they
talked more about the difference between college and high school.
Her first kiss was soft and gentle and lasted long enough to make
her wonder how to breathe. His tongue tasted of dill pickle. Hypo-
thetically, her plans about how far to go with a boy when the opportunity came involved the coy catching of a hand or the playful but
firm whisper of "No, no, no." But the reality was that this was the
first time she had been held in anyone's arms and there was no certainty whatsoever that it would happen again, so rather than the co-
quettish straightening of the spine and the flirtatious reprimand, she
found herself simply giving in, falling into him, letting his tongue
fill her mouth and his hand brush her arm, her thigh, and gently
make its way under her shirt to her bare skin. His fingers covered
her breast and he stirred and sighed and moved his legs out from
under the steering wheel. His fingertips hooked themselves over the
cup of her bra and tugged a little and were it not for the fact that
Betty Kelly had told her he had just broken up with a longtime girlfriend, she might have seen this as an indication of his inexperience.
He moved his hand to her back, brushed the hooks of her bra, and
then, as if he had been barred from the door, moved his hand out of
her shirt and onto her arm. He lifted her own hand and placed it on

his thigh and were it not for his sister's lie, he, too, would have seen the way she simply kept it there, unmoving, as proof of her inexperience as well. As it was, they both believed the other's awkward hesitation was due to a painful remnant of affection for someone else and they broke apart, a little breathless and shy once more.

Each of them wondering if they could ever replace the phantom ex in the other's loyal heart.

At her door he said, his eyes on the welcome mat, "Do you want to go out again tomorrow?" and she said, softly, "Okay. That'd be good."

In only a few weeks' time, the refrain of first—first party together, first walk on the beach, first dinner in a restaurant—exhausted itself in the social realm and came to refer exclusively to the physical milestones they marked during their hours together in the dark: first love bite, first success with those hooks, first glimpse of her bare breasts in the shadowy streetlights, first obedient touch of her hand, first nakedness against the plush cloth seat, first astonished completion of what they had begun, the silver shimmer of their success spread across her bare belly.

That summer, Barb Luce, who had been Clare's best friend since fifth grade, accused her of abandoning their friendship because of a boy—an error they had marked in other girls at their school and had always condemned—and Clare denied it, but without conviction. She would not return to those suffocating Saturday nights of TV movies and cake mixes and playing with each other's hair for all the best girlfriends in the world. "Maybe we can double date sometime," she told Barb. "You know, when you meet someone." And that was the end of that.

It was the girls who already had boyfriends, or who already had a string of them, who noticed his ring around her neck the first morning back at school. Clare was part of their sorority now.

In the second week of the term, a priest visited, as was tradition, to hear confessions and to say Mass, but he was a young guy—a new assistant at a nearby parish—with thinning hair and an effeminate voice, and in an effort to keep the sacrament relevant to the girls he asked that they first meet with him in small groups so they could all have a conversation about life, about their accomplishments (he said) as well as their transgressions, before he met with them individually to offer absolution. He was pale and earnest, gay, they were pretty sure.

In Clare's group discussion, held in the small room that usually served as the PE teacher's office, she and Christine Dodd and Cynthia Pechulis talked about being nasty behind their friends' backs and lying to their parents about stupid things and using fake IDs to buy beer, but no one said anything about sex. In her individual meeting, Clare shyly bent her head when the young priest asked her if she had anything more she wanted to discuss. He suggested that they both take a minute to "open our hearts to God" before they said an Act of Contrition together, and although she bowed her head again, it was not as easy, at that moment, to keep a silent conscience. For surely if she had ever sinned it was when she had first let him, helped him, to slip her sweater up over her head, to slide her jeans off over her hips.

Without opening his eyes, the young priest suddenly began to say an Act of Contrition and softly, Clare followed along. He then blessed her, and absolved her, and as he did, she noticed that his fingernails were bitten to the core. It was the kind of thing Pauline would have pointed out. It was the kind of thing that indicated, Clare already knew, that the man wasn't as sure of himself as he seemed.

That Saturday afternoon she walked down to St. Gabriel's and slipped through the eight-paneled door of one of the confessionals. This, too, in the way of contemporary churches, was just a room, not terribly different from the PE teacher's office at school, but empty except for a freestanding kneeler before a folded screen. Early on (Clare had memories of her first confessions here), when everything still smelled of wood and paint, there had been just two chairs, but her parents, and others, it seemed, had claimed Father McShane had taken the modernization thing too far and the kneeling bench and the screen had been added. Father McShane, now Monsignor McShane, was seated behind the screen, she could see his profile clearly, his cheek in his hand. There had been rumors, when she was in grammar school, that he slept through most confessions, sometimes even snored if you went on too long. She repeated the list of sins she had been confessing since those days— adding only "I let my boyfriend take some liberties," which she placed between, "I lied to my mother three times" and "I took the Lord's name in vain twice." The priest prescribed for her penance four Our Father's and four Hail Mary's and the avoidance of the "occasion of sin."

Kneeling in the pew to say her prayers, she recalled how she once had thought an occasion of sin meant a social occasion dedicated to wrongdoing—St. Patrick's Day or Mardi Gras most likely. She smiled into her hands. Of course, what it meant now was the backseat of Greg's father's car, the couch in her basement when her parents weren't home, the friend's apartment near Marist where, he had assured her, he and she would have a room to themselves, undisturbed, when she came up to visit him this weekend, getting a ride from his sister, who would stay with friends at Ladycliff and assure both sets of parents that Clare too was staying there. She had bought new pajamas. He said he was buying new sheets. She would brush her teeth and wash her face, tie up her hair in a ribbon and then kiss him. They would sleep together in the same bed for the first time and in the morning they'd go out to breakfast together— he'd said the diners upstate were pretty lousy but he had a favorite spot for waffles and fresh juice. After breakfast, they would take a long walk—he had the trail all planned. The leaves were just changing and he knew a farm where they sold hot cider. There was a rugby game to watch Saturday afternoon and a keg party that night. His friends would treat her with that delicious graciousness otherwise wild and sometimes gross boys reserved for the girls who were loved by their buddies. And then a second night in bed together, like a married couple.

She could feel her own heart under the softness of her breast, beating against her folded hands as she knelt, anticipating it, the best weekend of her life, losing count of what prayer she was on, or how it was, here in St. Gabriel's, that her thoughts had wandered so pleasurably and so far. She raised her eyes. In the past few months, statues had been added to the altar, a recognizable Joseph and Mary, a formidable Saint Gabriel, blond and fine-featured, kneeling on one knee. It was what the parishioners had wanted, realistic statues, easily identifiable. She blessed herself and rose and slipped out of the pew, suddenly struck by the conviction that she was going to have the happiest life. And then she paused and knelt again to say a prayer to Jacob, who had once sat beside her, here in this place, to thank him for it.

Her baby began, as she reckoned it, sometime during the first cold days of that autumn. She pictured it forming like the far-off swirl of some distant galaxy in the darkness of her womb, more blood than flesh, and then, perhaps by Christmas, more flesh than blood. Because she had always been so thin, no one was surprised to find she had begun to fill out, and because the winter uniform meant wool skirt and soft blouse and V-neck sweater, if you wished, under the blue blazer, because Pauline had shown her years ago how to adjust a hem and open a seam, she had no worry all through the winter that she would have to tell anyone yet. Not Gregory or her parents or the teachers at school. Gregory had midterms just after the first of the year and then the weather turned bad, so he was spending fewer weekends home. With only a vague idea of what next year would be like, she told her parents she'd decided she'd rather go to college nearby and applied only to Malloy and St. John's. On Saturdays she drove herself to the library and spent long hours in the overheated rooms studying biology books and medical texts, Dr. Spock and *Our Bodies, Ourselves*, but mostly the lovely full-color photos from an old *Life* magazine that showed a fetus floating like a spacewalker in the limitless universe of a uterus, a thin and otherworldly baby crooking an arm, sucking a thumb, lifting a snub nose and a dark, an ancient, eye to the top of the page. Breathing slowly, with a sleeper's rhythm, she placed one hand on her waist and touched Gregory's ring with the other, leaning over these pictures. The best afternoons were the ones when a cold rain, or a sleet, or a bit of snow fell from a colorless sky and hit the library windows, making her believe this deep winter would never end.

In her prayers she sometimes said, "What you could do for me, what you could do for me, is let this winter never end."

It was only the birth itself that frightened her. In health class that fall, they'd been shown a film: a hospital birth, the woman red-faced and panting, her pale, raised knees, more blood and less privacy than any of them had imagined. A scalpel moving in for what they called the episiotomy ("It won't appease me," was the joke later). Girls with their hands over their mouths stumbled from the room. All week long, as the film was shown to each class, green-faced students could be found lined up on the floor in the hallways, slumped against the walls like wounded soldiers in trenches. Later, there was talk of a conspiracy: moral injunctions having failed, the powers that be at Mary Immaculate Academy were merely trying to terrify them into chastity. "Too late," the more troublesome and popular girls had said, laughing, Clare now among them. "Try not to think about it."

In the library, bent over the amber-tinted photographs of a baby coming into life, she could manage not to think about it: the pain she was headed for in eight, then seven, then six months' time, the humiliation of bare knees raised, body convulsed, nothing appeased. In the warmth and quiet of the library—the smell of books, the rustle of newspapers, the occasional voice of a child—she thought instead of the life that was forming, not just the baby's life but the life of nights in bed beside him and the mornings she would wake with him at her side.

She set the weekend of daylight savings, the beginning of spring, for the time to shake herself out of her lovely stupor and face the world. She told Gregory on the phone on Saturday, and he cursed softly, the way he did when he made a wrong turn while driving or left his wallet in his other pants, cursing himself and his own stupidity. "What do you want to do?" he said, finally. "What is there?" she said, not really a question, and he cursed again.

She made her way into Pauline's room that night, touched her gently on the hip and then sat on the edge of Michael's bed. With her sister gone, she no longer troubled to give the excuse that she had to sleep here because Annie was reading. She was certain Pauline never bought it anyway. She came in here because it was where Jacob had slept all the years he was home, even in the years before she was born, and there was comfort in looking into the same darkness he had known, guessing at the shapes beneath the same shadows. She sat on Michael's bed. This was the hour, she guessed, that they were meant to spring forward. The hour erased out of time from this night until the one in the fall, when it would be restored again. As good a time as any, she thought, to plan with a bit more precision just what she wanted to do.

She told her mother the next night, the first Sunday evening when there was still light left after dinner. They had finished eating, her father and Pauline had left the table, and she watched her mother's mouth draw down crookedly, searing a line through her chin.

Her mother slapped her and then burst into tears and Clare's pain and astonishment were so great she could barely catch her breath. She put her face in her hands, awoken, at last, from the winter's spell. She said, through her own tears, "A grandchild for you," but even she heard how ridiculous this was, something spoken out of the illogic of a long dream.

Her mother's tears brought her father in from the living room and he stood in the doorway with his hand to his bald head as Mary Keane told him, crying, "She's pregnant." Looking at neither her husband nor her child, she said, to the air, it seemed, "How much more can I take?"

Her father limped to the phone on the wall. "What's the number?" he said and Clare had a silly impulse to say 911. "The Josephs," her father said. "Greg's parents. What's their phone number?"

Weakly, she said, "No, Daddy," but her mother was up already, rummaging through a drawer for her phone book. She read the number out loud as her father dialed. In his business voice he asked to speak to Gregory's father. But he had only begun the conversation ("It seems your boy," he said) when his face twisted into a terrible mask and her mother had to take the phone.

Clare bowed her head and put her arms over her widening waist. There was nothing to be done, she knew, because the future was already here, inside her—she had already begun to feel the baby stir—and the thought seemed to trump everything else, her mother's now steady voice, her father's muffled tears, which were not for her, she knew even then, but for Jacob, at long last. The sun had begun to set and the kitchen was darkening, an hour later than it would have just yesterday. Her cheek still stung from where her mother had slapped her. The baby moved, as if waving a thin arm at her from that once-distant galaxy, now a single star, a sun (a son, she thought) well within her sight, warm. When she looked up, Pauline was standing in the kitchen doorway, her hand on the frame and something in her mouth, perhaps a butterscotch or a hard candy pushed behind her teeth. Clare got up and stood beside her, and, as she had been doing all her life, lifted and held the old woman's hand as if Pauline herself had offered it.

That evening, Gregory's parents came to the house and sat with Clare's in the small living room. Her mother had straightened the slipcover on the couch and drawn the thick curtains and set out coffee and cookies on her wedding china. Clare listened from the top of the stairs. His parents had called Gregory at school. They said he was very sorry, full of remorse. They added as well that it takes, of course, two to tango. Mary Keane drew a sharp breath and said Gregory was a large boy, and older. Coercion was not out of the question. Mrs. Joseph said her boy was certainly not like that. John Keane said nor was their daughter. Mr. Joseph said either way, there wasn't going to be any shotgun wedding. Mr. Keane said there weren't going to be any bastard children either. Watch your goddamn language, Mr. Joseph said. Watch yours, Mr. Keane said. The two women made a soothing sound. They were both good kids, it was agreed. Neither one of them a moment's trouble for their parents. Neither one of them had ever even dated before. It was the future that had to be considered now, Mary Keane said. What was past, was past. Clare had high school to finish, they both needed to get through college. Adoption was mentioned. A Catholic agency. A good Catholic family.

Gregory came home from school the next weekend and stood his full height and full, soft girth in the small living room and said he and Clare would get married before the baby was born and then he'd finish the semester, come home, get a job, and get a degree at night. He had spoken to a priest at school. It was the right thing to do. John Keane gazed at him sullenly while he spoke, feeling himself begin to relent only when the boy added, with a shrug and a crooked smile, that his grades at Marist weren't all that hot anyway. Something of Jacob, of course, in the sweet, hapless, self-deprecation; the shudder of fate contained in something as simple as not-so-hot grades.

He looked beyond the boy to his father—both parents as well as Gregory's remorseful sister had been brought along for the announcement. John Keane thought he saw in the man's eye a kind of admiration, even pride, as Gregory spoke. Nothing he would feel if the tables were turned and it was his daughter who faced the ordeal, the risk, of childbirth at only seventeen. Both mothers wept again and Gregory's sister hung her head. But Greg had the priest on his side and the startling power of his own conviction. Her conviction, really. It was what Clare wanted, he said, glancing at her. And whatever Clare wanted it was now his obligation to provide.

"And where will you live?" Gregory's mother asked. "How will you pay rent?"

"We thought we'd live here," Clare said, and looked to her mother. It was the plan she had devised in that lost hour, in Jacob's room. "We thought we'd make an apartment, out of the basement. Until we can afford something more." She smiled, as if it had all been arranged already, as if it were all working out quite well already. "You and Pauline will be here to help me with the baby, especially if I want to take some classes at Malloy. And if you guys want to move to Florida, well, maybe by then"—it was all part of what she and Pauline had planned, whispering in that lost hour—"we can rent this house from you, or even buy it, if we have jobs. You won't have to sell it to strangers, anyway." She looked at Pauline. "We can keep the house, and, if Pauline wants to, she can stay."

Sister Marie Ignatius, the school principal, met with Clare's parents in her office early the next evening when the school was empty. Outside her office window the green lawn and the dark hedge, now edged with daffodils, were lovely in the restored light of the new spring. Although the air was still cool, she'd pushed open one of the small panes to freshen the room. She had to say, of course, that she could not have been more surprised. Clare, of all girls. She would never have imagined it. She did not say, as she had told the other Sisters in the convent, still waters run deep, but she did point out that even the best of girls can, after all, be led astray these days. The pressure is tremendous: the music, the movies, the feminists, the hippies. In the past, and Sister Marie Ignatius had run the school for twelve years, such girls would simply go away. There was, in fact, an unwed mother's home in upstate New York that Sister Marie had once contacted almost annually. But the stigma, these days, was perhaps not as great as it used to be and with abortion now a legal option, it was up to the school to help its students in trouble in the kindest and most positive way possible. And the fact that Clare had not given any teacher in the school a single moment of worry or concern certainly worked to her advantage now.

Kindly, her hands folded in front of her on her desk, Sister

agreed that Clare could stay in school for the next month or so—
she would request only that as little as possible be said about her
condition and her marriage (she did not want Clare's situation to
set either a precedent or an appealing example)—and that she eventually leave school (mononucleosis might be a good excuse) once
the situation became apparent. It would be both a humiliation for
Clare and a mockery of all the school stood for to have her appear
in uniform in her eighth or ninth month. Academic matters could
easily be arranged. She could take her finals at home. She would
miss graduation, of course, the ceremony itself, but she would still
graduate.

Sister Marie walked the parents to the door. She would tell the
Sisters later that both of them looked like they'd "been through the
mill." Her heart went out to them, and to their daughter, but there
was also the school to run, an enrollment rate to maintain, funds
to raise from alumnae, many of whom were mothers of the daughters enrolled today. There were—as much for her as for Clare's
parents—the neighbors to consider. There was also an extremely
generous alum who had married well being honored at this year's
graduation. It was not the time for a senior with a huge belly under
her robes to be climbing the stage to accept her diploma. Married
or not.

The parents smiled weakly, inclined to linger although all that
needed to be said had been said. Sister sometimes joked that these
were the "Climb Every Mountain" moments when she wished she
could sing. She opened the door for them.

"Let's remember," she told them, "that there's a new life on the
way." The corridor outside her office was brightly lit, eerily empty,
harsh splashes of light against the linoleum and the painted fronts
of the girls' lockers. "And life," she said, turning back, "is always a
cause for celebration." And then could have bitten her tongue be-

cause these were the Keanes she was talking to—she recalled Annie on that terrible morning, in this same hallway, she recalled seeing through the glass door of her own office the great shadow of Sister Maureen Crosby rising from her seat behind the reception desk, catching the two weeping girls in her arms. These were the Keanes she was spouting clichés at, the Keanes who had lost a son in that useless war.

Father McShane, Monsignor McShane, pouted a bit, his hands folded over his belly, but quickly relented, telling John Keane he would open the church himself for the family, for the wedding, eight o'clock on the following Sunday night. He'd do the honors, too, he said, the path of least resistance having always been his preference in matters such as unwed mothers, mixed marriages, annulments, and birth control. He could see the humiliation on the poor man's face—one of these old-fashioned Irishmen who in his near seventy years could hardly bring himself to mention sex in the confessional now sitting here in the rectory saying his little daughter was already six months gone. A man whose biggest concern, at this age, should be his golf swing.

Pity's fool, Monsignor even offered to call the choir director to see if he couldn't come down and play a tune for the ceremony, but John Keane said his wife had already made arrangements with one of their neighbors, the MacLeods, Presbyterians whose nephew played the piano at Juilliard. She had heard the music coming from their house just yesterday, when the boy was visiting. She'd knocked on the door to ask the name of the tune. One thing led to another—she'd been looking for an opportunity to break the news about Clare to the neighbors—and the boy had agreed to come in from the city to play. If that was all right with the Monsignor.

Monsignor McShane held out his hands. "I don't think the

church will collapse," he said, "if a Protestant plays." Or if, for that matter (he thought), a girl six months pregnant walks down the aisle in a white dress to marry a boy with a priest, instead of a shotgun, at his back. "We built her pretty strong, John. With your help, as I recall. I don't think she'll fall."

The only bother was letting the piano player in half an hour early so he could "get a feel" for the instrument. Because he liked to linger over his Sunday supper, usually with *60 Minutes* on, the Monsignor asked old Mrs. Arnold to hold his dinner until after the ceremony and told the other two priests to go ahead and eat without him. He watched the first half of the show with only a glass of sherry and some cheese and crackers to tide him over, and then left the rectory at 7:25. It was a lovely night. The sky was that polished blue it sometimes got after a storm, or a long winter. Even the traffic along the boulevard, which had become intolerable of late, seemed subdued by the color. He climbed the steps to one of the side doors, let himself in with the key. Over at the school, there were lights on only in the old section, the cafeteria where the AA meetings were held on Sundays. He turned on the lights above the altar and then in the choir where the piano was. Someone had already put a vase of flowers on the altar, a simple blue vase with only a handful of white roses, and he seemed to recall some connection between white roses and unborn babies—was it the Mothers Club that sold white roses on Mother's Day to help save the unborn babies, or was it the Fathers Club that sold white roses on Mother's Day to help save the men who had forgotten a present? It was poppies on Veterans Day in any case—Flanders Fields—and the thought reminded him that it was the Keanes, of course, who had lost a boy in Vietnam.

Trouble piled on trouble, Monsignor thought, as he walked down the center aisle (grateful that this would be a quick and simple ceremony, no messing with candles lit at the end of every pew, as was so much in vogue these days, wax dripping everywhere). It struck him, not for the first time, that his modern church, such a miracle to him just a decade ago, would grow dated in the coming years—an old man's mistaken enthusiasm for the wrong kind of future. He'd already weathered the fight over the return of the old statues, the confessional screens. They'd be asking for Latin again next.

The piano player was just coming up the steps as Monsignor McShane opened the front doors. He was a young guy, small and dark-haired. A young man's beard under the fair skin. He wore a suit and carried a briefcase and introduced himself with a Scots Irish name that Monsignor didn't bother to retain. The two walked up the aisle together. "This is some church," the kid said, craning his neck to take in the Danish modern stained glass, the circus-tent ceiling. He then mentioned that he occasionally played at another Catholic church, an old-fashioned one, St. Paul's, near his school. "I went to St. Paul's," Monsignor said, "as a boy." And knew immediately, as if he had never understood it before, what his parishioners were lonesome for, in this monstrosity of his. It was not the future they'd been objecting to, but the loss of the past. As if it was his fault that you could not have one without the other.

He went into the vestry while the boy ran his fingers over the keys. You did not have to be a musician to hear the difference, once he got started, between what this kid could do and what the ordinary Sunday musicians played. Monsignor put on his vestments, prepared the altar, walked down the central aisle again to see that there'd been nothing left behind in the pews this morning, checked that he'd left the front doors unlocked, and then walked back up again, still with twenty minutes to spare. He swallowed a little indigestion, a little impatience, thinking of his dinner. He walked across the altar, touching gaudy, literal Saint Gabriel on the knee, and then stood by the boy. You would have to be a musician to explain the difference, but the priest knew it was there. There were the ordinary pianists who played, no doubt, as they had been taught to play, earnest, obedient, faithful to each note (don't even mention, Monsignor would have said, those awful folk-mass singers with their guitars), and then there was a kid like this, who played in a trance, eyes closed, transformed, transported, inspired (that was the word)—not the engine for the instrument but a conduit for some music that was already there, that had always been there, in the air, some music, some pattern, sacred, profound, barely apprehensible, inscrutable, really, something just beyond the shell of earth and sky that had always been there and that needed only this boy, a boy like this, to bring it, briefly, briefly, to his untrained ear.

Something he hadn't even known he'd been straining to hear.

The boy finished the piece and in the fading of the last notes came the voices at the front door of the church, the Keanes and (he had their names on a slip of paper in his pocket) the other parents, the groom, and the young, expectant bride.

"Have you taken a lot of lessons?" the priest asked, before he walked down the aisle to greet them (because it would be an informal wedding, the best kind, really, softly spoken, unrehearsed). "Or have you always known how to play?"

The boy was arranging the pages of his music. He looked over his shoulder at the priest. The lights from the altar cast the shadow of his long lashes across his cheeks. A young man, beautiful in his way. "Both," he said, politely. "A lot of lessons, but it seems I've always known how to play."

Monsignor nodded. John Keane in his gray suit was coming toward them from one of the side aisles, favoring that bad leg, his son, his other son, just behind him, and then what had to be the bridegroom looking like the oversize boy he was in his first suit, well-scrubbed, determined, afraid. The women in their pale wedding clothes were gathered at the door.

"It's a gift, then," the priest said.